Important: Do not remove this date due reminder.

DATE DUE

WITHDRAWN

THE LIBRARY STORE   #47-0201

FROM THE HEARTLANDS

photos and essays from the midwest

Introduction & Editing by Larry Smith

Photo Editor, Zita Sodeika

MIDWEST WRITERS SERIES #1

BOTTOM DOG PRESS
HURON, OHIO

© Copyright by Bottom Dog Press, Inc., 1988
ISBN 0-933087-13-6 $8.95

MIDWEST WRITERS SERIES #1

Cover Design by Larry Smith & Zita Sodeika

Cover Photos: Front, Indiana Farmhouse, Roger Pfingston; back, Ohio Barn, Tom Koba.

**Acknowledgements & Photo Credits
listed in the back.**

PS
563
.F76
1988

Funded Through
Ohio Arts Council
---
727 East Main Street
Columbus, Ohio 43205-1796
(614) 466-2613

CONTENTS

INTRODUCTION	1	Larry Smith
OUR MIDWESTS	10	Mark Vinz
THE BLACKSMITH SHOP	16	Jim Barnes
BLOOD FOR THE SUN	22	Conger Beasley, Jr.
SALT CREEK, TRULY TOOTHACHER, AND STRINGTOWN LANE	30	Martha Bergland
HIGHER EDUCATION AND HOME DEFENSE	38	Wendell Berry
EULOGY IN A CHURCHYARD	46	John Calderazzo
HOW TO BUILD A HOUSE	56	Christian Davis
WINDMILLS		Susan Strayer Deal
CHASING THE RIVER GODS: A FISHING TRILOGY	66	Michael Delp
FROM AN AMERCIAN CHILDHOOD	74	Annie Dillard
THE SENSE OF A PLACE	86	Nancy Dunham
DOG HOLLER	94	Robert Fox
INQUIRY INTO THE "NEAREST OF THE ENERGIES OF THE UNIVERSE AND THE GREATEST WITHIN THE RANGE OF MAN'S NEEDS"	106	Jeff Gundy

BUT BABY IT'S COLD OUTSIDE: MEMORIES OF MINNESOTA WINTERS	112	Craig Hergert
ON HOMESICKNESS AND HERE-SICKNESS AND THE LONGING FOR BUCKEYES	118	Diane Kendig
THE CHAIR-SIDE HISTORY OF A MASTER CRAFTSMAN	124	Mark Masse
THE LATHS OF MEMORY	130	Kay Murphy
POETRY IN THE MID(DLE) (ST) (DEN), AND...	140	Joe Napora
LAND LESSONS	148	Robert Richter
UNDER THE SIGN OF WONDER BREAD AND BELMONT CASKETS	154	Michael J. Rosen
STONE TOWNS AND THE COUNTRY BETWEEN	178	Scott Russell Sanders
WELLS	192	David Shields
DUCK SPRING	200	Tony Tommasi
SWIMMING POOLS	206	Susan Allen Toth

Jim Galbraith (HARTLAND)

INTRODUCTION

A SENSE OF PLACE

The landscape artists have always had it, that sense of personal and universal *location* engendered from a particular time and place. Milieu, locus, atmosphere—the best films are immersed in it. Still photographers are perhaps our most natural zen artists, 'stilling' themselves into a sense of identification or interpenetration with the immediate concrete world. Music often communicates the inexpressible 'atmosphere' around a place. Yet, declares French writer Max Jacob, "All writing must be *situated,"*—which I interpret as *located*—grounded in a concrete world of images, a direct human voice, a heightened sense of time and place conveying a direct *thusness* of existence. You'll find it here.

We're talking about more here than a regionalism or local color, where place details are merely called up to suggest a quick atmosphere (much like the backdrop of a television sit-com). In fact, Wendell Berry warns against the dangers of seeing our earth, even our home, as simply our "surroundings," the "scenery" of our lives:

Once we see our place, our part of the world, as *surrounding* us, we have already made a profound division between it and ourselves. We have given up the understanding...that we and our country create one another, depend on one another, are literally part of one another, that our land passes in and out of our bodies just as our bodies pass in and out of our land; that as we and our land are part of one another; so all who are living as neighbors here, human and plant and animal, are part of one another, and so cannot possibly flourish alone; that, therefore, our culture must be our response to our place, our culture and our place are images of each other and inseparable from each other, and so neither can be better than the other. *(The Unsettling of America, 22)*

So what we are describing is a geographic self-identity (not one defined by artificial borders but by land and culture), our rooted link with the world, our native ground, our community. We soon realize that we are pointing to an emotional and primal sense of connection—earth to self to others—that keeps us grounded or centered in our lives. The jazzmen often speak of it in mystic-real terms as "where it's at"—"really there." Young people talk of "being there," of "being who you are where you are," in that felt oneness with your world and life.

Midwesterners seem particularly blessed with it—though in truth its blessing is sometimes mixed and brings its own ambivalence, as in Quentin Compson's frantic response to his feelings for the South, *"I don't hate it* he thought, panting in the cold air, the iron New England dark; *I don't. I don't! I don't hate it! I don't hate it!" (Absolom, Absolom,* 378). I once lectured at the American Studies Center in Rome on the American sense of place, and after my talk a young Italian woman told me bluntly, "Yes, but here we are weighted down with this sense of the past in our place—just look around you—ruins everywhere." What we each learned that day was that an ambivalence toward place is not only natural but can be healthy, even a strength, once it is recognized. And that a place sense itself is essential.

We all know the alternative—an uprooted, transcient estrangement from life that can leave us non-engaged, caught in a vague nostalgia for something we can't define—a place and a peace denied. British psychologist Paul Tournier quotes the Book of Matthew in this context: "He who has once had the experience of belonging in a place, always finds a place for himself afterwards; whereas he who has been deprived of it, searches everywhere in vain." One woman lacking a place sense declared, "It seems that all my life I have been standing in a train station ready to leave." Wendell Berry's warning above makes us realize that such alienation is not only unhealthy for the person but for the place, for the world that we share. One classic folk song presents a person lamenting, "I'm leaving on a jet plane,/ Don't know when I'll be back again." Those lines from singer-song writer John Denver confirm the estrangement; his life, however, leads us to another aspect of place—despite Matthew's warning, it can be found or re-established. Denver, an army child, moved from base to base throughout his childhood never finding roots anywhere until at twenty-five, standing on the rocky Colorado ground he could declare "I've found my place." Contemporary song writers have found this place sense a common theme, whether that place is Billy

Joel's "Allentown,", John Cougar Mellencamp's "Smalltown," or Bruce Springsteen's "My Hometown." Happily the feeling and theme are both universal and contemporary.

What Denver probably discovered were the beginnings of roots that with cultivation could be grown into something strong. What so many of us do is to reject our very place sense (along with our blood or ethnic ties) because it is being *forced* upon us. We tear away at our roots, the very things that can ground us for really creative lives. The natural vegetal analogy is a good one. The growth and sustenance only comes when we recognize, accept, embrace, essentially *realize* our existence in time and space for ourselves. Just as novelist Thomas Wolfe aptly warned *You Can't Go Home Again,* so poet Gary Snyder speaks rightly when he declares, "I can be at home anywhere." You can transplant your place sense—take your ability to relate to places with you anywhere. It is not only possible, but healthy. We can spot a *tourist* anywhere—they don't respect our place. A traveller is something else.

Again, it is Tournier who declares the place sense as basic to our very personality and so practices developing a sense of place as a way of helping the subconscious integrate. Along with Carl Jung, he reminds us of the primacy of place images in our memory and dreams (houses, doors, attics, stairs, and in the deep archetypal images of people gathered around a fireplace, that lamp glowing in a window). It's seen too in the symbolic resonance we feel for our birth and death places, as we journey from womb to tomb. Further, we come to recognize our physical bodies as a central place of our existence. "We bury our youth in our body," declares William Carlos Williams, and we know how essential Whitman found the human body to the spirit. Let our bodies change rapidly (weight, hair, pregnancy, amputation) and we know fully the displacement it causes. One woman reminded me of the very intimacy of childbirth when one shares her body place with another. This helps us understand the post-partum blues of mothers, and perhaps gives insight to the real intimacy of sex. And certainly our minds are a place we carry inside of us and sometimes share with others, asking a simple respect for our place, our space in the world. Tournier suggests, and I think rightly, that as we venture further into outer space our need for a sense of inner space grows.

As our place sense deepens through practice and realization, it becomes more timeless and eternal, as in the American Indians who kept their earth-wisdom in their rites and in their simple acts—their refusal to separate self from earth, in their walking and sitting directly on the ground. Their songs most often praise a living earth:

WHITE FEATHERS
Downy white feathers
are moving beneath
the sunset
and along the edge of the earth.

THE BUSH
The bush
is sitting
under a tree
and singing.

They bring a sense of acceptance and connection in their deep respect, revealed in the very transparency of their writing:

> I am walking
> toward calm and shady places.
> I am walking
> on the earth.

Gary Snyder speaks often and well of the nature and importance of this place sense in his essays, and it is embodied in his poetry. One Amerindian rite he practices is 'singing the landscape,' standing at a distance and singing notes and rhythms to correspond to the heights and widths of the hills on the horizon. What is important here is how essential it is to *internalize* the place sense. In fact, the writers of place speak from it, rarely to or about it, as in this segment from an early Snyder poem "A Walk":

> Sunday the only day we don't work:
> Mules farting around the meadow,
>   Murphy fishing,
> The tent flaps in the warm
> Early sun: I've eaten breakfast and I'll
>   take a walk
> To Benson Lake. Packed a lunch,
> Goodbye. Hopping on creekbed boulders
> Up the rock throat three miles
>   Piute Creek—
> In steep gorge glacier-slick rattlesnake country
> Jump, land by a pool, trout skitter,
> The clear sky. Deer tracks.
> Bad place by a falls, boulders big as houses,
> Lunch tied to belt,
> I stemmed a crack and almost fell

But rolled out safe on a ledge
And ambled on.
Quail chicks freeze underfoot, color of stone...
(THE BACK COUNTRY)

We realize immediately how organic is the process of place sense, both in the person and the writing. We are immediately there, located in a timeless present, inside a larger self that is not only attentive but interdependent with all the details as he moves among them. The theme is in the stance and in the location it emparts, as it is with all the writings here.

We know that in Snyder's case, his place sense is deepened by his Zen Buddhist practice, his earth grounded wisdom is enlightened by his sense of universal oneness. He calls for a realization of "the eternity of the present...bringing us back to our original, true natures from whatever habit-molds that our perceptions, that our thinking and feeling get formed into. And bringing us back to original true mind, seeing the universe freshly in eternity yet any moment." Snyder quotes this lesson on interdependence, "The Buddha once said, bhikshus, if you can understand this blade of rice, you can understand the laws of interdependence and origination. If you can understand the laws of interdependence and origination, you can understand the Dharma...." For Snyder the writers of place perceive these networks and laws of interdependence and are able "to transmit to others...a certain quality of truth about the world" *(The Real Work,* 35). A place sense is integral to Zen just as it is to any outlook that finds life's significance immersed in this world, in the daily significance of ordinary life. All of these writings sing of it.

Another American, Henry David Thoreau advised us to "love your life" however mean we find it, and he advocated the local, "I have travelled much in Concord." Further in the line of American Romanticism, Walt Whitman attempted to tie all of America together, its native land and people with its immigrant dreams, in his "Song of Self." Critic Ben Bellit declares that most American writers have been listening intently ever after to what it was Whitman heard when he "heard America singing." Much of the writing of place is a response to an individual sense of America and its opportunity—an affective and intuitive demonstration of how to approach the fundamental question of one's geographical identity. Subject and theme are as interdependent here as is self to place as each writer seeks an organic response to his/her growth of this basic life consciousness. The self becomes the Self, my life becomes our life.

Each of these writers seems to imply the practical analogy of the trapeze artist who first must learn to hold the bar well before letting go. The writer's sense of location is embodied in the stance, one that unites content and form. It is at once inevitable and essential, what we are born into and keep moving towards. Wendell Berry's call is clearly for a life and writing that will give us "access to the wilderness of Creation where we must go to be reborn—to receive the awareness, at once humbling and exhilarating, grievous and joyful, that we are a part of Creation, one with all that we live from and all that, in turn, lives from us" *(The Unsettling Of America,* 104).

PHOTOS AND WRITINGS OF PLACE

Editing this book of Midwestern photos and prose has taught us many things. Confirming our belief that the Midwest remains a fertile and challenging place in which to live and work, we were nevertheless surprised by the quantity, quality, and diversity of the writing and photography that materialized. We have writing here from and about Pennsylvania, Ohio, Kentucky, Indiana, Illinois, Michigan, Wisconsin, Minnesota, Iowa, Missouri, Kansas, Nebraska, and the Dakotas. This diversity is a part of the heartlands, as is the great myth of a Midwest. As any midwesterner knows, there is no Midwest, but thousands of Midwests, products of place and time and personality. Geographers cannot agree on what it includes (nor can midwesterners)— from the Appalachians to the Rockies, above the Mason-Dixon line says one, another includes the central provinces of Canada, etc.

Though we don't readily draw its borders, we do recognize it as a central state of mind. Because much of it is so flat or plain, it requires a special sensitivity and persistence of vision to know its beauty. Our chief vantage point is our closeness—we stand in the midst of a corn field breathing and touching it with our senses. We meet our neighbors at the service station, the grocery store, or the town meeting. A midwestern directness and bluntness thus evolves. The artists here all tended to hold an historic eye, the past and future caught up in the present. More than nostalgic, these writers and photographers have a way of connecting, rooting the present sensory moments in an emotional sense of past, an intuitive forecast of future—we expect change to be slow and to last in the character of the place. A new collection from the University of Iowa Press bears the title *A Place Of Sense,* and that title implies a basis in the sensory as well as in the human and earth logic of a place. One reads the intention of the people and places in the way life goes on... in the midst of forests and plains, lakes and fields, industries and farms, in the good sense of connections, in the closeness they impart..

If there is diversity, there is also sameness, a universality that runs through these pieces like wood grain, like the earth toned background for the bright threads of personality and particularity woven here. The basketball hoops may be on a city lot or the fronts of barns, but they are there throughout as part of the mythic fabric of place. It may be a little colder in Minnesota, a little flatter in Iowa, a little quieter in Nebraska, a little more suburban in Columbus, a little more urban in Pittsburgh, but it is a coldness, a flatness, a quietness, a surburan or urban quality that any midwesterner can relate to. They all speak of and for the country's middle, its heartland.

From the countless writers who evolve out of the Midwest (and we seem to grow them a plenty, whether they stay here or not) there is a sense of universality, a writing from the core if you will that helps them relate to all others. These essays and photos send out vibrations that are felt in the whole body as well as the heart and mind. There is a truth and a 'knowing' in the vision they impart. The place speaks through the person, the person through the place. The vision is extremely human and humane.

I confess here that we had intended some type of grouping of the essays—some sort of wrong-headedness that all books must be divided into three parts, perhaps derived from a Western outlook of coming at things by breaking them apart, the drive to separate. We found instead that synthesis and union are basic thrusts of these works—the writings bind person and place just as they combine modes of persuasion with description, characterization with narration, emotional truth with humor. Many of them extend the art of the personal essay by enhancing prose with poetry, by blending reporting with opinion, by incorporating cinematic techniques to narration. By example they each celebrate the art of the essay. Mark Vinz provided us with an ideal opening onto "Our Midwests"; after that, in a wiser deference, we fall back upon an alphabetical ordering by author inviting you to experience the random diversity one finds when driving across this country's heartlands. Each essay is an arrival, and the journey is a part of the place we carry inside us. Find your own route.

Many of these writers and photographers also work as feature writers, but more often they are fiction writers and poets. In fact poets seem to be one of the chief produce of the Midwest—James Wright, Wendell Berry, Philip Levine, Robert Bly, Kenneth

Rexroth, John Berryman, Theodore Roethke, Gwendolyn Brooks, Nikki Giovanni, Mona Van Duyn, Mary Oliver...the list is thankfully endless. And in the essayists here we see a need to touch that life with a relaxed yet pointed prose, one that captures a midwestern informality and directness, the voices of our neighbors of the Midwest.

We especially want to thank the senior writers in this book who generously shared not only their work but their advice. We trust that readers will find not only connections but confirmations for their lives. Whether in essay or photo, in our art or our talk, in the work and joy of our lives, our deep place sense makes poets of us all.

Larry Smith (August 1988)
Huron, Ohio

HEARTLANDS—9

Farm with Silos, Route 177. Edith Lehman

MARK VINZ

OUR MIDWESTS

"I'm a life-long Midwesterner—grew up in Minneapolis and the Kansas City area." Mark Vinz is also a poet *(Climbing the Stair,* 1983, and *The Weird Kid,* 1985) and short story writer. Like many small press writers, he also serves as an editor of midwestern poetry through the *Dacotah Territory* journal and press—which has recently published the midwestern anthology *Common Ground.* He also teaches English and American Studies at Moorhead State University in Northwestern Minnesota.

In "Our Midwests" Vinz moves through our historical and literary background toward a contemporary assessment of the elusive midwestern character. What he finds is not a simple definition but a multiplicity of characteristics broad enough to contain contradictions. Ultimately he arrives at an approach—open to the subtleties beneath the flatness, "probing the tensions between extremes such as harsh and beautiful." The writing here combines a personal directness with an authoritative comprehensiveness. His questioning becomes a way of knowing. "Our Midwests" provides an excellent introduction to our sense of place subject.

OUR MIDWESTS

A few years ago, a colleague asked me to take over an American Studies course called The Midwest, assuring me I could teach pretty much whatever I wanted. After all, there was plenty of material from which I could choose—from literary chestnuts such as *Giants in the Earth, Main Street,* and *Winesburg, Ohio* to the paintings of Thomas Hart Benton and Grant Wood, from films such as *Northern Lights* to just about any Garrison Keillor broadcast tape. Indeed, Midwestern *material* has never been the problem—like the landscape itself, it's quietly there, usually taken for granted, waiting patiently to be discovered. More than anything else, what I and my students have become preoccupied with is something far less tangible. It is a set of attitudes, often extremely diverse and contradictory ones, often stereotypical, and frequently misunderstood. In short, a course that sounded quite manageable at the outset quickly became difficult to pin down—and worse, all-consuming. It still is, after four attempts at teaching it.

One of the first things I do in the course is conduct a survey, asking the students what might be seen as two very simple questions: where is the Midwest, and what characterizes Midwesterners? It's hard to tell which question has confused them more or produced a greater variety of responses.

To the first question, *where is the Midwest?* answers ranged from Montana and Wyoming in the west to Pennsylvania in the east and Oklahoma in the south (nobody, at least, included Texas, though a few have argued for inclusion of Manitoba and Sasketchewan). Since most of the students in the class come from western Minnesota and eastern North Dakota, the typical response has been to include those two states, South Dakota, Iowa, Kansas (because of Dorothy, of course), and perhaps Illinois (a few have visited Chicago). Surprisingly, many seem to forget Nebraska and Wisconsin, and almost no one includes Michigan, Ohio, Indiana, or Missouri. To these students, Midwest means *Upper* Midwest—"God's Country" as some of them like to call it (and others argue it's because no one else but God would have it). "Forty below," they say. "Keeps the riff-raff out."

To my students, as to many of us, the Midwest also remains rural—farm and small town—not urban. They feel a far greater kinship with the remotest regions of Kansas or Indiana than with Chicago or Detroit. Indeed, they are probably right in one sense. The greatest diversity in the Midwest is not between the far flung extremities of the 12-state region (as it's traditionally defined), but between its large cities and the "outstate."

The real divisions begin with the second question, *what characterizes Midwesterners?* What we seem to agree upon, at least at the outset, is the mainstream stereotype: Midwesterners are generally hardworking and industrious, polite and reticent, orderly, moral, honest, family-oriented, and (outside the cities, at least) preoccupied with weather. What begins to split us is a series of familiar dualities: friendly vs. clannish (even xenophobic), conservative vs. liberal, laconic vs. garrulous, independent vs. dependent, isolated vs. mainstream, to name a few. It's very hard, for instance, for most of my North Dakota students to make sense of their state's visibly conservative Republicanism as opposed to its tradition of mavericks and radicals, going back to the Non-Partisan League. It's hard, too, for them to deal with notions of being isolated and "behind the times," since many will not stay in the region for those very reasons, yet they are at the same time fiercely defensive of the region's moral superiority (to the point of smugness), marshalling evidence from crime and divorce rate statistics. At the same time, while they are delighted in recent surveys that say this is the "least stressful" place in the U.S., they can see daily the media reports on trials and disasters in the farm economy.

What begins to emerge as we move along is the pattern of contradictions that are themselves the essential fact of the Midwest—a region that is simple only to the outsider passing through quickly. Stereotypes—their sources and applications—become a heated issue, and nowhere do they appear more clearly than in the PBS "Salute to North Dakota" program (part of the "Portrait of America" series hosted by Hal Holbrook). As a Midwesterner might expect, the 60 minutes are full of images of remoteness, barrenness, extremes of harsh weather, and "down home" (if not backward) people (and sometimes underscored with hilariously inappropriate Appalachian banjo music). Watching the tape, an outsider would have to conclude that North Dakota was devoid of anything resembling culture, cities, or even up-to-date farm equipment. In short, if Eric Sevareid many years ago noted that to the rest of the U.S. North Dakota was a "blank spot," there's much to perpetuate that image today.

If, indeed, we in the Midwest tend to be better known from stereotypes than from realities, the stereotypes themselves are often at odds with each other. At one extreme, for example, the Norman Rockwell images persist, locating the Midwest in a distantly romantic past of fishin' holes and cracker barrels, as the seat of all those good ole American virtues and still the best place to bring up kids. At the other extreme, of course, the ghost of Sinclair Lewis and all the naysayers before and after him still evokes the "Main Street virus" of smug provincialism, suffocating conformity, and rampant knownothingness. The truth, of course, is what lies between those extremes, partaking of each yet depending on neither. That's the trouble with studying the Midwest, my students say. Everything is a contradiction. Nothing gets resolved!

That, I tell them, is the only healthy attitude one can take toward this—or any other—region, and they must examine those contradictions in their own lives and attitudes as well. Most, for instance, are vitally interested in being "hip," yet they have never confronted some of the basic questions about themselves. "You have a very interesting family name," I've said to several of them. "Tell me where it comes from." Even in this post-*Roots* era, few of them have ever really thought about it, so, as we read and talk about the history of the region, I ask them to investigate their own ancestry. The following scene is also quite typical.

"How's your family history project going?" I ask one of my students returning from Christmas vacation. "I just don't know," she says, and I can sense a tinge of resentment in her voice. "But my mother loves it! She spent most of vacation dragging stuff down from the attic to show me."

Never again will that particular student see the Midwest in quite the same way—not a textbook sense, and certainly not a more personal one.

What I try to tell my students, finally, is what Midwestern writers and artists have been doing for decades: it's all a matter of learning how to *see*. The first thing we see is all of the contradictory images I've been mentioning. Then, perhaps, it's a set of discoveries about the past—the pioneer past, the Indian past, the personal past. All of it leads to a probing further, too. Just as the Midwestern landscape has less picture-postcard scenery than one might find in another region, one has to *learn* to appreciate its subtleties. What's flat and boring to some is diverse and exciting to others. One will never know if one doesn't stop the car and get out, so to speak. As William Least Heat Moon so aptly put it in *Blue Highways:* "Boredom lies only with the traveler's limited perception and his failure to explore deeply enough."

Just so, William Inge has noted the difference between the tourist's sense of *flat* and the native's sense of *level,* and John R. Milton emphasizes that the truest sense of the Midwest comes from probing the tensions between extremes such as harsh and beautiful. If my students have done their homework, they indeed discover those tensions that unite the Midwest's many extremes, none of which is more important than loving vs. hating. Without the loving, one simply becomes a cynic, blind to possibilities. Without some measure of hate—or at least a healthy skepticism—one is simply a sentimentalist, or worse, a booster.

All of us who are Midwesterners have been marked by those extremes, and that process of *marking* is what I ask my students to consider finally, for many of them will indeed be expatriates. As for countless others before them, the Midwest will *finally* be only what they look back on from an increasing distance. So, I have to remind them of what one of the most famous expatriates from this region, Bob Dylan, said a number of years ago in an interview—and which, I would guess, he'd say again today: "I'm not a New Yorker. I'm North Dakota-Minnesota—Midwestern. I'm that color. I speak that way....My brains and feelings come from there."

I remind my students, too—indeed, we remind each other—to think in terms of plurals, for there is no such thing as *the* Midwest. It's something closer to *our Midwests,* which suggests, I hope, a continuing dialogue. Even Sinclair Lewis and Norman Rockwell might agree with *that.*

Dennis Horan

JIM BARNES

THE BLACKSMITH SHOP

Jim Barnes was born in the hill country of eastern Oklahoma at the end of the Great Depression. After ten years as a lumberjack in Oregon he returned to the Midwest to study at the University of Arkansas. He now teaches comparative literature at Northeast Missouri State University, where he also edits the international journal *The Chariton Review*.

Barnes's books of poetry include *American Book of the Dead* (1982), *Season of Loss* (1985), and *The La Plata Contata* (due out in 1989). He summarizes his view of writing in the Midwest this way, "Life is short; good writing anywhere, including the mythic Midwest, is hard."

In "The Blacksmith Shop" he welds the past, present, and future in a telling portrait of a time and place. Like the myth of the Midwest, his early place sense becomes a part of his being and perception of the world. His images are nostalgic but real and capture his ambivalence about change.

THE BLACKSMITH SHOP

The earliest memory of the blacksmith shop I have is one of darkness. Not blackness, but darkness, as in a cave. Even the pile of coal taking up the whole south side of the shop gave the effect of a dark, crumbling cave wall. The atmosphere was close and smelling always of the thick, sweet, sulphurous odor of burning coal. Although the large double doors to the front of the shop were usually open, there was a heavy sense of confinement, even when you were allowed to stand by the forge and turn the crank that made the bellows make the fire glow to an intense red, then almost white, heat. But it felt good to be there. You were always sure of that.

Perhaps it had something to do with the smith himself. His skill with the hammer and anvil was something any child could see. The way he could weld metal on metal by heating and pounding was a mystery to me as deep as night itself. He was the blacksmith, and we knew him in no other way. That—now that I think of it—is the way we knew anyone in those days, by what one did day by day. Who the smith was did not matter then; what mattered was what he was.

The shop was no larger than twelve by sixteen, its floor hardpan almost ceramic to the touch except where the water bin sloshed over during the periodic dunking of hot iron. It seemed larger to a six-year-old. I can remember being very frightened the first time my father took me inside the shop. A dark winter's day it was at that, the smudges on the arms and face of the smith not helping matters at all. But my fears were short-lived. I was allowed to turn the crank while my father's plow points were reddening in the mass of glowing coal. I watched as the smith then hammered away the dullness of the iron points, reshaping them into the tools that would slice through the earth of our small farm in early spring.

From that day on, I was a regular visitor to the shop. Nearly every afternoon after school, I would stop by, before walking the mile and a half home, to watch the smith at work. Once, over the course of several days, I got to see the construction of a wagon wheel. From white oak lumber, mostly two by fours and two by sixes, all the sections of the wheel except the tire were made—the hub, which was then bound by two strips of iron heat-and-hammer welded, the spokes, the rim. To have seen the final step of the construction, the shaping of the flat iron tire to a perfect welded circle which was then fitted miraculously, perfectly, over the bracing rim that held the spokes in place, was almost like having seen the invention of the wheel; for in truth everything made in the shop was made from no plan except that which lay in the mind of the smith.

Years later I would read about the shield of Achilleus and recall the wagon wheel I saw take shape in that dim place. I would tell myself the smithy of the gods had little on the smith I knew, for he was the creator of things through and beyond the ordinary—the magical plow points and wheels that would never break—and his world was a world of fire and water and darkness. Not air, not light, not beauty. But the solid world of things that would outlast all the childish dreams I knew.

In later years when the smith had hung up his tongs and hammer, the shop was silent most days of the week. But on Saturdays this one and that would, with the permission of the present owner, the proprietor of Curtis' Grocery, open the shop in order to shape shoes for his horse or mule. The art of horseshoeing was a vanishing art as far back as the early forties. The only way anyone learned how to shoe horses in our neck of the woods was to be at the blacksmith shop on Saturday, the only day of the week that the smith would consent to shoe horses and mules. When the smith retired and moved away from our small community, the romance of the blacksmith shop was gone for me. The novice cyclopes now at the forge were poor images of a way of life that seemed to have passed with the smith's going. The mystery was no longer there; the shop was little more than a small dirty hovel that had lost its dark luster with the passing of an era.

By the end of World War II the blacksmith shop was closed even on Saturdays. Only rarely would you find the doors propped open and the bellows whirling, for the few farmers or ranchers who survived the Great Depression and World War II were trucking their horses to Wister, twelve miles to the northeast, for shoeing. In time the shop became little more than another outdoor privy and shelter for stray dogs. But somewhere in the interval, about the time I started high school, it became a kind of clubhouse par excellence for me and several of the boys I ran around with. We could always hang out there without fear of our parents' intrusion. After all, there was a massive chain and lock holding the doors securely together, and no one but we knew of the secret entrance, two loose boards on the blind side of the building. We could roll our own Bull Durham cigarettes there without fear of discovery.

The amazing thing I learned about the blacksmith shop was that it was not first a blacksmith shop at all—amazing to me as a child because I could not visualize anything beyond the glowing forge, the coal, the massive forearms of the smith. For a long while, after my first few visits to the shop, I had been aware that adjacent to the one room of the forge was another, longer, room. I found that both rooms of the building had been used as a repair shop and garage before World War I, when my own uncle, Jack Adams, had a service station and repair shop where he serviced an occasional Model T Ford. The smith used the larger room as a scrap heap for junk iron, which he was constantly sorting through for useable materials. After the shop had closed for good, my buddies and I discovered there was much more to it than what we had assumed in the past.

Partially hidden among all the junk of decades were several tin cases of movie reels that, presumably, had been stored in the room before the smith had started his great junk pile. We had heard that Audie Sisk, whose ancient parents still lived directly behind the blacksmith shop, once operated a movie house in Summerfield, way back in the early years of the Depression, before he migrated to California along with half the population of eastern Oklahoma. Why he had left the films there remained a mystery we could not fathom. We could see they were silent films from the captions on some of the frames we squinted to read. To our infinite delight we would spend long Saturdays rolling and unrolling each reel, looking at each sequence of frames on every film. It was as if we held the lives of characters in our hands, as if they were our own secret lives. We discovered that we could rig a flashlight so that it would be used to project a dim semblance of picture upon the wall of the room. This was better than a real movie, this was our secret thing, and we reveled in it. We were willing captives in the blacksmith's cave. It was a reality that we preferred over the mundane outside world.

Then we discovered our reality was flammable. And to my infinite sorrow, we mutilated the films by cutting long strips from them and setting fire to the strips on the darkest nights in the middle of the one street of our town for the sole purpose of watching the rapid burning of silver nitrate. I am sure some of the neighbors must have seen something amazing, fire zipping along the street for a long moment then vanishing, before tracking the flame to its source, our pocketed matches. Our parents were told; then we were told. The remainder of the films simply disappeared, and secretly I think we were glad to have them gone. Modern technology (matches) had tempted us, and we had sacrificed (burned) that which was giving us lasting pleasure for that which gave us only a momentary high.

I drank my first wine in the recesses of that dark place. I brewed it there from sheep-showers, a kind of purplish clover which you ferment by adding sugar and water and letting it lie in shadows for two weeks. All that was forbidden I contemplated there—city lights, circus, sex. Whatever I wanted I could imagine freely there, discuss the finer points in livid debate with my friends, and occasionally blueprint the execution of some great plan.

Then as we began to forget, the blacksmith shop burned; and in its ashes lay my childhood and adolescence. I was finishing high school, swearing on the flysheets of annuals never to return to this jerkwater town where the only sound of life was the Sunday Baptist bell banging out of tone. But I have not left, not in mind; for the blacksmith shop remains a retreat, a sanctuary of the mind, where I can, through images of the past, dwell in safe refuge from the threatening forces of the millennium.

Two Horses. Roger Pfingston

CONGER BEASLEY, JR.

BLOOD FOR THE SUN

Conger Beasley, Jr. was born in St. Joseph, Missouri, and educated on the East Coast, only to return in 1965. "By temperament and instinct I did not belong there. I tried, but the yearning for space, for inland valleys and sweeping rivers, overcame whatever desire I may have had to transform myself into a cosmopolitan urban dandy." He has brought his Midwestern sense of place to his writing—novels, *Hidalgo's Beard* and *The Ptomaine Kid,* short stories, *My Manhattan,* and poetry, *Canyon De Chelley: The Timeless Fold* (1988).

In "Blood for the Sun" he creates a forceful confrontive style that brings his writer's respect for detail to his deeper respect for the rituals of our native American Indians. In particular, it is the Oglala Sioux of Pine Ridge Reservation of South Dakota who share their rite of the Sun Dance with us here. Beasley gives us the full sense of tradition behind the blood rite that includes the act of piercing, and relates it to our own traditions. He spares no details in bringing us up close, and records another story in revealing the effects of this land rite upon the writer-witness.

BLOOD FOR THE SUN

We had eaten lunch—discretely out of sight behind our car—and had just stepped back under the brush arbor when we saw something that neither of us had ever seen before. Two men, suspended by ropes pinned to the flesh above their shoulder blades, were hanging six feet over the ground. Dark blood trickled down their backs; their long, glossy hair gleamed like a raven's wing. Each man clutched an eagle feather, which he flapped urgently up and down.

A hot August sun boiled overhead. Under the shade of the arbor, other men, clad in T-shirts and ballcaps, beat drums and wailed in high-pitched voices. A throbbing sound mixed with ululating cries floated out over the tall cottonwood trunk in the center of the circle. From the topmost branches dangled taut ropes with their grisly human cargo. A stiff breeze whirled across the arbor kicking up curlicues of dust.

The contents of the cheese sandwich I had just devoured rumbled ominously in my stomach. For most of the morning we had watched other types of piercing, mainly involving young men and boys. With pegs protruding from their chests, they had pulled back with all their strength against ropes tied to the sacred tree until...the pegs popped free. That was absorbing enough. But the two men hanging limply from the branches was a sight we could not comprehend. We could acknowledge what was happening, though the reasons seemed mysterious and arcane. We were confronted by a spectacle that plumbed the very heart of aboriginal America.

An ancient ritual known as the Sun Dance is performed every summer out on the Great Plains at the Sioux, Cheyenne, and Crow Indian Reservations. It is one of the most extraordinary Native American rituals, rivaling anything else on the continent in power and mysticism, including the Hopi Snake Dance and the Yaqui Deer Dance. The one we witnessed took place on the Pine Ridge Reservation of South Dakota, home of the Oglala Sioux.

The Olglala have an interesting history. The largest branch of the Teton or Western Sioux, anthropologists trace their ancestry all the way back to Tennessee and North Carolina. External pressures in the 16th century forced them to embark upon a long migration through the Ohio River Valley to Minnesota, where, in the late 17th century, they first encountered French traders and trappers. Driven from Minnesota by the Chippewa, they ventured out onto the northern plains, reaching the Black Hills around 1775. During the long struggle against European encroachment onto their hunting grounds, they were led by such legendary figures as Red Cloud and Crazy Horse. In battles along the Bozeman Trail (1866-68) and at the Rosebud (1876) and Little Big Horn Rivers (1876), they either defeated federal troops or fought them to a standstill. In December 1890, at a place called Wounded Knee, they fought the last major engagement between Indians and U.S. Army troops on North American soil.

The 1880s were a grim time for the Oglala. With the buffalo ruthlessly decimated by white hunters, they were forced to live on reservations where rations could be doled out to them. The Sun Dance was outlawed in 1884, and for good reason. Anyone willing to subject themselves to such an ordeal would most likely find campaigning against the U.S. Cavalry an invigorating sport. And so, like many practices censored by the federal government, the Sun Dance went underground and for nearly half a century was performed away from disapproving eyes in remote pockets of the Pine Ridge Reservation. In 1934, as a result of the Indian Reorganization Act which established the legality (in white parlance) of many religious activities, the Sun Dance resurfaced, albeit in a bowdlerized version that did not include piercing. In the 1960s—with the advent of the Red Power movement and the corresponding heightening of Indian consciousness—piercing recommenced in earnest.

It is an unsettling spectacle for a *wasicu* (white person) to witness. Our Judaeo-Christian tradition sanctions martyrdom, but only when it holds out the promise of transfiguration. Christ suffered fearsome torments on the Cross, but he was finally relieved of his agony by death and the ascension of his spirit into Heaven. But to suffer physical agony for *life* —so that one's people may benefit—is not as comprehensible. And yet that is why today, as in the past, young Oglala men and old subject themselves to the rigors of piercing.

Participation in the ritual is voluntary. Not every man feels compelled to undertake it; certainly not everyone wants to. A sign or signal in the form of a dream or vision usually indicates a person's willingness. Others, primarily older, participate to give thanks for having survived a crisis. The intensity of suffering forms a deep bond, not only between the dancers but with the oldest and most sacred tribal traditions. Personal motives aside, the ultimate aim of the ordeal is to bring one into contact with *Wakan Tanka,* the supreme embodiment of spiritual power in the Sioux cosmology. The circle formed by the brush arbor, of which the tree is the center, is a holy and mysterious place. Many astounding events occur within it during the four-day ceremony. Frank Fools Crow, a venerable Oglala shaman, has said, "Sometimes we see eagles flying among the branches, or even an airplane in there. Everyone sees these things, and we see different things each day."

The ordeal is vitally important to Oglala traditionalists. Above all, it is *theirs,* uncorrupted by white or Christian influences. It is the most compelling antidote they can offer to the negative impact that *wasicu* culture has had on their own; it offers a viable alternative to alcoholism, immorality, and spiritual lassitude. The ordeal is inimitably *Indian,* intensely physical and sublimely visionary, a commitment of body and soul to the preservation of the profoundest ideals of the people.

This type of offering has no equivalent in our culture. It can't be satisfied by signing a fat check or turning over old clothes to a welfare agency or doing volunteer work in a soup kitchen; the offering can be made only in blood suffering. "The Indian religion is a hard one," an old man told me afterwards. "It has to be. We have faced the threat of extinction for so long that in order to survive we must be as hard as the granite core of our beloved Black Hills." Flesh and blood, then, palpable human stuff that spills and oozes. The sort of thing that the two Lawrences, D.H. and T.E.—one from the perspective of a voyeur, the other as a participant—rhapsodized about in their prose. During a Sun Dance, friends and family often will have little pieces of flesh gouged out of their arms. The offerings are then deposited on a buffalo skull to dry in the sun to help the dancer endure the misery of hanging by a rope attached to his body by sharp skewers jabbed through the skin. Blood for blood . . . your blood for mine . . . our blood for the people.

As we watched, one of the young men suspended from the ropes passed out, and like a bag of grain attached to a pulley, twisted slowly in the breeze. A shaman elbowed him in the ribs, whereupon the young man began to beat, feebly at first and then with growing ardor, the eagle feathers clutched in each hand. The weight of his body pulled the pegs away from his shoulder blades in wads of frightfully puckered flesh. Over the dusty, trampled ground he drifted like a curious bird, bound not by any coil to the earth but rather by an implacable tether to the sky. The chanting and drum beats uptempoed from under the brush arbor. Waving his arms wildly, he tried to break free but couldn't. Finally, in a stupendous act of courage, he pulled himself up higher on the rope, and letting go, spread out his legs and arms like a sky diver. The shock ripped the pegs out of his back with a sound like ripe pears striking a concrete floor.

Two shamans rushed forward, one to rub an herbal compound into the deep puncture wounds in his back. A few minutes later the man was up and dancing around the brush corral, his face shining with a mixture of agony and exaltation.

We were witnessing the climax of a complicated four-day ceremony, and for the participants the culmination of a long period of instruction and fasting that ends in an apotheosis of blood and pain. Most men subject themselves to the ordeal only once. The wounds inflicted by the skewers are by no means crippling, though they do leave indelible scars. Those men marked on both the chest and back have usually performed the ceremony at least twice. The scars are a special talisman of bravery and fortitude which does not go unnoticed in the Oglala community.

Traditionally, young men performed the dance to test their courage and endurance for the trials of warfare at which they hoped to make their mark; today, there are other inducements. One man in his 60s, recently recovered from cancer, had his back pierced in two places just below the shoulder blades. Accompanied by the frantic pounding of drums, he dragged an unwieldy bobble of eight buffalo skulls several times around the brush circle until the weight of the skulls finally tore the pegs out of his back. A woman whispered to me that he was undergoing the ordeal to give thanks to the Great Spirit for curing him of the white man's disease.

Before the dance, each participant undergoes lengthy religious instruction. Piercing does not usually commence until the third or fourth day; the first two days are spent in fasting and prayer, with the participants facing into the sun and mouthing incantations. Friends and relatives come and go; Indians or family members who wish to show their support can remove their shoes and join the dancers in the circle. These dancers are vividly clad in tribal costume and form a kind of supporting chorus to the men undergoing piercing. For hours in the grueling sun they shuffle back and forth to the din of drums, tooting shrilly on eagle-bone whistles.

One ceremony we witnessed that morning involved a boy of about twelve. Two circles painted over his nipples indicated that he was to perform. A skirt, beaded around the hem, covered his legs; his wrists and head were banded with wreaths of silver sage. Two shamans placed him on his back at the foot of the cottonwood. One bit the flesh on his chest and quickly inserted the skewers. Then the boy stood up and backpeddled away from the tree until the rope went taut. The weight of his body caused the flesh over his nipples to bulge alarmingly; then he dashed forward and placed both hands against the cottonwood. Again and again he repeated this action, each time hurling himself harder against the stiff rope, trying to wrench the pegs out of his chest.

Finally a shaman escorted him back to the tree where they prayed together. Then, hooking him around the waist with one arm, the shaman (facing the opposite direction) ran with the boy and, as the rope grew tight, pulled with all his might. The pegs blew out of the boy's chest with an audible pop, triggering a spray of fresh blood. Relieved of his burden, eyes gaping, the boy staggered back into the arms of his family, who swarmed over him with tenderness and concern.

A few minutes later other shamans paraded the boy around the brush corral. There was no cheering or applause, only silence, though most of the spectators rose gravely to their feet. A sort of victory lap like at the Olympics, with no cameras to record the event and only Wakan Tanka and the people as witnesses. The shamans stutter-stepped grimly at his side. The boy's round face was stained with tears. After finishing the lap, he rejoined his family.

To the cloistered eye, the land seems boundless, devoid of meaningful features. It isn't flat—there are other parts of the Great Plains, notably the *Llano Estacado* of Texas, that are much flatter; rather, it's like a succession of broken slabs, cracked and tilted by erosion into a variety of surface planes. At intervals these slabs warp up into tree-covered buttes and tables, with truncated tops like platforms. Myriad creeks snake down through the draws and gullies. Though bone dry in summer, they conceal a water table that nourishes dense stands of elm and ash and cottonwood, along with plum and chokecherry thickets.

On hot afternoons cottonwood leaves make soft fluttery sounds that delicately overlap one another and meld into a thick, latery hum. In the morning cumulus clouds stack up over the Black Hills, 50 miles to the west; by midafternoon, propelled by westerly winds, they douse the parched grass of the Pine Ridge Reservations with intense rainsqualls. Lightning forks down from the thunderheads, striking the slopes and occasionally igniting fires.

Scorching in summer, ravaged by Arctic winds in winter, it is a land of extremes, with temperate periods of short duration in between. The Teton Sioux—of whom the Oglala are the most numerous—arrived out here (so anthropologists say) in the mid-18th century. The Oglala think they've been here a lot longer, almost as long as the buffalo, which first emerged from a hole in the Black

Hills. In the centuries since, against both Indian and white enemies, the Oglala have fought for this land.

The soaring arch of the sky pulls the gaze up naturally to the clouds. The emptiness cries out for a vision to personify it, a sign or portent that man, insignificant in comparison to all this space, has a purpose and a function. And so for generations Oglala warriors have fasted on top of flat-topped buttes or hung from ropes in an effort to focus the vagaries of their uncertain existence into the radiance of a visionary experience that will unite earth with sky, themselves with *Wakan Tanka*. At the pitch of their suffering, with the metaphoric grace of poets, they fuse the elements of their harsh lives into luminous wholes. This is powerful country, ageless and unspoiled, redolent with magic, strong as a buffalo heart.

Dress Up, Sweet Springs, Missouri 1930's. Courtesy of Carolyn Berry

MARTHA BERGLAND

SALT CREEK, TRULY TOOTHACHER, AND STRINGTOWN LANE

Martha Bergland is a prize winning essayist and short story writer living in Glendale, Wisconsin. Like most of the writers assembled here, her midwestern voice has been heard regionally and nationally in her poetry, fiction, and essays.

In our essay she presents a personal portrait of her rural childhood in eastern-central Illinois. Through an informal narrative she compiles specific and concrete details into a sharpened sense of place as it weathers the change of time and man. "The regularly spaced expansion joints on those roads set up a railroad click-clack that put babies to sleep in the car before either Salt Creek bridge. The State Aid was a gravel, sometimes oiled, crowned road with no lines down the middle."

A sense of location is paramount here as we contemplate the lines of geography and memory in the mind of a ten year old girl. The essay blends people and places—the vibrations around names—in a music of memory, rising to a rhapsody of awareness. "As I look at a map of where I grew up, I am amazed to realize how much of 'where I grew up' was what I had to imagine."

Bergland's voice is at once lyrical and persuasive—compelling in its brevity and its sensitivity. From a misty gentleness it mounts fully and clearly, with all the inevitability of a rain.

SALT CREEK, TRULY TOOTHACHER, AND STRINGTOWN LANE

My mother knows a woman named Truly Toothacher; I never met Truly Toothacher (my mother met her at a Woman's Club "whingding"—would be my dad's word), so I don't know if she was born a Toothacher or if she married one, but she was related to this other woman named Bertha Turnipseed, and both Truly and Bertha were remotely related to Ulavon Walters who, with her husband Oliver, lived and farmed across the road from us for more than twenty years.

I wish I could tell you that we Berglands and the Walters lived on Stringtown Lane because in rural east-central Illinois that was the only road with a name, though not one you would find on a road sign or on any map of Illinois. We and the Walters lived on "the road past Berglands" or "the road past Walters" or "the Seals' road," depending on who asked and who they knew and where they wanted to go. But you could take our road a mile past Mike and Elsie Seal's (my brother and I thought her name was just letters: LCCL), turn right or left, and that road which looked just like ours was Stringtown Lane. It was called Stringtown Lane because it strung little towns together clear across the state of Illinois. You could go east on that country road—between corn fields and bean fields, and in the Fifties, oats and wheat—for eighty miles and end up in Indiana. Or you could turn left past LCCL's, drive two hundred miles straight west on that same little road (there were some jogs, but few curves), and get to the Mississippi River just north of Quincy and south of an island in the river called Long Island.

I can clearly picture all seven of us in the salmon-colored station wagon we had in the Fifties driving along Stringtown Lane. I see my three blond little brothers in the back looking behind at where we've been; I am (about ten years old) in the middle seat beside my year-old sister; Mom and Dad are in front looking at where we're going. One of us asks: Are we on Stringtown Lane? Then we are all riding along picturing the same thing, the same eastern or western vanishing point of Stringtown Lane. The pictures are hazy but alike—small, green landscapes inside of cartoon balloons floating just over our heads and beneath the perforated headliner of the old Ford. I see this, broadside. Our silhouettes go down the road. It is the pictures that are facing me here and now.

However, the places that Stringtown Lane strung together were not places that we or anybody else needed to get to very often, so I am sure we didn't drive on it enough for this memory to be so strong in my mind. Stringtown Lane always did figure more in the imagination than it did in the day-to-day getting from here to there. And the memory itself is an impossibility. My youngest brother was not yet born when I was ten, and that salmon-colored Ford (western motif inside—brown simulated-leather upholstery stamped with brands and horseshoes) was traded in long before he was born. Like many memories, this one is vivid, somehow anchored in space, but floating loose in time.

On the Legend of my 1975 Illinois Highway Map, there are three categories of highway: Principal Through Highways (nine kinds of these), Other Through Highways (five of these), and Other Highways. In the last category, there are Paved, Dustless, and Other All Weather. The road past our house and the Walters' and LCCL's is not on the map at all. It must be in some category not included in the Legend: Dusty or Some Weather or Goes Nowhere, even though the road wasn't all that dusty and we could and did drive on it in all weather—almost all weather.

Stretches of Stringtown Lane are on the map; they are blue dashed lines (Dustless) which make the road seem to go underground in places, surfacing now and then for ten miles or so. One stretch heads west out of Maroa, then goes back under right at a Dustless north-south road which would take you from Hallsville west of Clinton over to Harristown west of Decatur, if you wanted it to. Another piece of it shows up at Westville, right on the eastern edge of the state, where it may cross Grape Creek (I can't tell from the map), but it does cross the Vermillion River which is almost the last thing it does before it gets to Indiana, where, by definition, it has to stop being Stringtown Lane.

As I look at a map of where I grew up, I am amazed to realize how much of "where I grew up" was what I had to imagine. Not ten miles from our farm, there are towns I've never been to and roads on which I've never gone.

Almost everyone I knew in Illinois in the Fifties called all roads besides "our road" and Stringtown Lane by a number, or a source of funding, or a type of surface, e.g. "48," "the State Aid," or "the hard road." Both 48 and 10 were "hard roads," that is, two-lane concrete roads with dotted lines down the middle. The regularly spaced expansion joints on those straight roads set up a railroad click-clack that put babies to sleep in the car before either Salt Creek bridge. The State Aid was a gravel, sometimes oiled, crowned road with no lines down the middle. Our road was narrower than the State Aid and frequently full of pot holes and not frequently oiled, except during the years that the road commissioner lived on the same mile.

Retired farmers who lived in the little towns and wore hats with brims drove on the hard roads in big cars. Teenagers driving with one hand, young farmers in a hurry to pick up parts, aesthetes, and wide machinery took the State Aid. No one ever saw the sheriff or the state police on the State Aid, so you could go eighty or you could slow down and look at the scenery, when you got to the scenery.

Scenery was about seven miles from our place by the State Aid. In those days our whole family was starved for scenery, that is, hills, trees, water, curves. On trips we stopped at all the views. At home we had to use sky for scenery and there was plenty of that. Sometimes clouds would pile up all around the horizon, which out there was in every direction, and, if the light was right, we could imagine the clouds as mountain ranges and momentarily feel *enclosed* is I guess the word for it. Now we all live among hills or in cities and what we try to imagine is all that sky; what we try to clear out of our eyes is scenery so we can see the fronts coming through. Sometimes fronts out there were so black and straight-edged that seeing one was like watching a plowed field come your way through the air.

Though the two hard roads and the State Aid go off in different directions, they all cross Salt Creek. Stringtown Lane does not, though Salt Creek dips south at one point and almost touches it. I would like to drive sometime on that stretch of road east of Broadwell and see what you can see from there of Salt Creek.

Salt Creek seemed to us the source of the gentle hills around it, therefore the source of our only near, earthly scenery. Salt Creek was the only thing around not squared off; the straight lines of the surveyors and speculators had to stop at Salt Creek and make some consideration of something other than their purposes which were to mark and to own, then use.

Salt Creek was unpredictable. The weather was, of course, unpredictable, but everything that we could see that was not weather or sky (which wasn't all that much, as I think about it—fields, roads, buildings, power lines) was something you could count on to stay the same, not necessarily the same color, but at least the same size. Salt Creek was in some seasons a narrow, slow, green creek; in others, a ripe, brown river; and in the winter—frozen and covered with snow—indistinguishable from the low land it passed through. Salt Creek's floods were the lakes for us land-locked. Salt Creek gave us, every few years, shores and—odd under all that sky and set in all that black earth—a wide, dazzling reflection of sky. The floods were, I suppose, economic disasters for some, but when we were all in the car going to look, we were as excited as if we had overflowed our banks.

I don't know why it's called Salt Creek; it didn't taste salty; anyway, once in about 1955 it didn't taste salty. It tasted like a field diluted, which is what it was. Though usually shallow, Salt Creek was never something you could see to the bottom of. Salt Creek meandered all around that flat land with exactly the opposite intentions of Stringtown Lane.

There's a house on 48 near Salt Creek which my mother used to point out to us: "Truly Toothacher lives there," and she'd laugh, and so would the rest of us. Then we'd all think of Bertha Turnipseed and we'd say the names out loud and wonder what it would be like going through life with a name like Turnipseed.

Truly Toothacher's house was a white farmhouse with narrow clapboards, some lacy trim around the porch, and old cedar trees in a side yard. Her place did not seem as businesslike as the farms near us where there was no gingerbread and the clapboards were wider and all the trees were box elder. Though Truly Toothacher's house was on the side of 48 where the fields were spare, it overlooked an oval of pasture which sloped down to the creek; oaks grew at the edges and willows in the lowest places.

Not far down the road from Truly Toothacher's, my mother would point off to the right down toward Salt Creek, down into a half-moon pasture enclosed on the far side by a bend in the creek: Centered alone in that pasture as a fountain in a park was the prettiest tree any of us had ever seen. It was an old but delicate-looking native crabapple—various colors in various seasons. Its placement and its shape were formal and somehow exotic; the tree seemed feminine and we all thought of Africa and acacias.

I write this to point, as my mother still does, to the little crabapple tree that is now under a man-made lake. I write this because Bertha Turnipseed and Truly Toothacher might not have been exactly related, though they did or do exist. I write to get to curve the stories that are too short and straight. I write to say the names over and over: Bertha Turnipseed, Truly Toothacher, Stringtown Lane. I write to both save and make up the vanishing points a family imagined as the ends of a road. I write because dredging and damming to make a nuclear power plant's cooling lake have made Salt Creek into a permanent, ugly lake almost as straight as the hard road. I write because a diagonal interstate highway cut across that part of the country, so now no one can even imagine driving across Illinois from the Vermillion River to the Mississippi on a country road some called Stringtown Lane.

Tom Koba

WENDELL BERRY

HIGHER EDUCATION AND HOME DEFENSE

Wendell Berry is described by Edward Abbey as "a good novelist, a fine poet, and the best essayist now working in America." Berry is also a practical farmer and diligent conservationist of thirty years on his farm in Henry County, Kentucky, where he was born in 1934. His voice of conscience and vision calls the reader to pause, take stalk, and begin again cleanly and wholly. He finds common ground in personal and universal values of respect. Berry has elsewhere been described as "the closest we have to a modern Thoreau, and in a prose as transparent and healing as a clear mountain lake he emerges as a prophetic conscience of the nation"*(Publisher's Weekly)*, a tribute he would, no doubt, share with Annie Dillard.

Berry's conservationist stance includes a consistent vision of our interdependence and wholeness—in the life of man, animals, plants, the land. His clear strong voice also draws us homeward in its deep respect for language as man's most trusted tool for truth. Like Thoreau, he is a most mindful craftsman and confidant.

Our essay "Higher Education and Our Home Defense" is as pointed as it is persuasive, as challenging as it is direct. It attacks a rootless institution of education that forces a self-alienation that compels us "to leave home," with all that implies in a loss of character and culture to ourselves and our community.

Starting with an incident and using definition as its basic motive, the essay moves smoothly and clearly from a fundamental questioning to a fuller, human understanding.

Wendell Berry's chief writings include these books of essays: *Recollected Essays* 1969-1988 (1988), *Standing by Words* (1983), *The Unsettling of America* (1977, rev. 1986), *Home Economics* (1987)*The Gift of Good Land* (1981), *A Continuous Harmony* (1972). His poetry from seven books has appeared in 1984 as the *Collected Poems:* 1957-1982. His rural fiction exists in the novels *Nathan Coulter* (1960), *A Place on Earth* (1967), *The Memory of Old Jack* (1974), and in the story collection *The Wildbirds* (1986).

HIGHER EDUCATION AND HOME DEFENSE

Several years ago, I attended a meeting in Madison, Indiana, that I have been unable to forget, it seems so emblematic of the fate of our country in our time. In the audience at that meeting were many citizens of local communities, my own among them, who were distrustful of the nuclear power plant then being built (but now discontinued) at Marble Hill. Seated on the stage were representatives of Public Service Indiana, the company that was building the power plant, and members of the Nuclear Regulatory Commission, whose job it presumably was to protect us from the acknowledged dangers of the use of nuclear power, as well as from the already recognized deceits and ineptitudes of Publice Service Indiana.

The meeting proceeded as such meetings typically proceed. The fears, objections, questions, and complaints of the local people were met with technical jargon and with bland assurances that the chance of catastrophe was small. In such a confrontation, the official assumption apparently is that those who speak most incomprehensibly and dispassionately are right and that those who speak plainly and with feeling are wrong. Local allegiances, personal loyalties, and private fears are not scientifically respectable; they do not weigh at all against "objective consideration of the facts"—even though some of the "facts" may be highly speculative or even false. Indeed, in the history of such confrontations, the victories have mainly gone to the objective considerers of the so-called facts.

Those considerers were then still winning at Marble Hill, even though the fraud and incompetence of Public Service Indiana was a matter of public record. But that meeting produced one question and one answer that tell us all we need to know about the nature of such an enterprise, and about the role of education in it. A lady rose in the audience and asked the fifteen or twenty personages on the stage to tell us how many of them lived within the fifty-mile danger zone around Marble Hill. The question proved tactically brilliant, apparently shocking the personages on the stage, who were forced to give it the shortest, plainest answer of the evening: *Not one.* Not a single one of those well-paid, well-educated, successful, important men would need to worry about his family or his property in the event of a catastrophic mistake at Marble Hill.

This story would be less interesting if it were unusual. My point, of course, is that it is *not* unusual. Some version of it is now happening in this country virtually everywhere, virtually every day. Everywhere, every day, local life is being discomforted, disrupted, endangered, or destroyed by powerful people who live, or who are privileged to think that they live, beyond the bad effects of their bad work.

A powerful class of itinerant professional vandals is now pillaging the country and laying it waste. Their vandalism is not called by that name because of its enormous profitability (to some) and the grandeur of its scale. If one wrecks a private home, that is vandalism, but if, to build a nuclear power plant, one destroys good farmland, disrupts a local community, and jeopardizes lives, homes, and properties within an area of several thousand square miles, *that* is industrial progress.

The members of this prestigious class of rampaging professionals must meet two requirements. The first is that they must be the purest sort of careerists—"upwardly mobile" transients who will permit no stay or place to interrupt their personal advance. They must have no local allegiances; they must not have a local point of view. In order to be able to desecrate, endanger, or destroy a *place,* after all, one must be able to leave it and to forget it. One must never think of any place as one's home; one must never think of any place as anyone else's home. One must believe that no place is as valuable as what it might be changed into or as what might be taken out of it. Unlike a life at home, which makes ever more particular and precious the places and creatures of this world, the careerist's life generalizes the world, reducing its abundant and comely diversity to "raw material."

I do not mean to say that people with local allegiances and local points of view can have no legitimate interest in energy. I do mean to say that their interest is different in both quality and kind from the present *professional* interest. Local people would not willingly use energy that destroyed its natural or human source or that endangered the user or the place of use. They would not believe that they could improve their neighborhoods by making them unhealthy or dangerous. They would not believe that it could be necessary to destroy their community in order to save it.

The second requirement for entrance into the class of professional vandals is "higher education." One's eligibility must be certified by a college, for, whatever the real condition or quality of the minds in it, this class is both intellectual and elitist. It proposes to do its vandalism by thinking; insofar as its purposes will require dirty hands, *other* hands will be employed.

Many of these professionals have been educated, at considerable public expense, in colleges or universities that had originally a clear mandate to serve localities or regions—to receive the daughters and sons of their regions, educate them, and send them home again to serve and strengthen their communities. The outcome shows, I think, that they have generally betrayed this mandate, having worked instead to uproot the best brains and talents, to direct them away from home into exploitative careers in one or another of the professions, and so to make them predators of communities and homelands, their own as well as other people's.

Education in the true sense, of course, is an enablement to *serve*—both the living human community in its natural household or neighborhood and the precious cultural possessions that the living community inherits or should inherit. To educate is, literally, to "bring up," to bring young people to a responsible maturity, to help them to be good caretakers of what they have been given, to help them to be charitable toward fellow creatures. Such an education is obviously pleasant and useful to have; that a sizable number of humans should have it is probably also one of the necessities of human life in this world. And if this education is to be used well, it is obvious that it must be used some *where;* it must be used where one lives, where one intends to continue to live; it must be brought home.

When educational institutions educate people to *leave* home, then they have redefined education as "career preparation." In doing so, they have made it a commodity—something to be *bought* in order to make money. The great wrong in this is that it obscures the fact that education—real education—is free. I am necessarily well aware that schools and books have a cost that must be paid, but I am sure nevertheless that what is taught and learned is free. None of us would be so foolish as to suppose that the worth of a good book is the same as the money value of its paper and ink or that the worth of good teaching could be computed in salaries. What is taught and learned is free—priceless, but free. To make a commodity of it is to work its ruin, for, when we put a price on it, we both reduce its value and blind the recipient to the obligations that always accompany good gifts: namely, to use them well and to hand them on unimpaired. To make a commodity of education, then, is inevitably to make a kind of weapon of it because, when it is dissociated from the sense of obligation, it can be put directly at the service of greed.

The people on the stage at the Marble Hill meeting may have thought of themselves as "public servants." But they were servants, at best, of the *general* public, which means, in practice, that they might be enemies at any time to any particular segment of the general public. As servants of the "general good," they stood ready to sacrifice the good of any particular community or place—which, of course, is a way of saying that they had no reliable way to distinguish between the public interest and their own. When they appeared before us, they were serving their own professional commitment and their own ambition. They had not come to reassure us so far as they honestly could do so or to redress our just grievances. They had not come even to determine if our grievances were just. They had come to mislead us, to bewilder us with the jargon of their expertise, to imply that our fears were ignorant and selfish. Their manner of paying attention to us was simply a way of ignoring us.

That meeting, then, was not really a meeting at all but one of the enactments of a division that is rapidly deepening in our country: a division between people who are trying to defend the health, the integrity, even the existence of places whose values they sum up in the words "home" and "community," and people for whom those words signify no value at all.

Elephant Keeper & Tent Circus, Bloomington, Indiana. Roger Pfingston

JOHN CALDERAZZO

EULOGY IN A CHURCHYARD

John Calderazzo came from Long Island, New York, to Bowling Green, Ohio in 1978, and now lives and teaches at Colorado State University at Fort Collins. From 1983-1984 he taught English at Xian Foreign Languages Institute of China. "I'd spent significant chunks of my life living all over the map, but when I first came to rural northwest Ohio, I was flabbergasted. I just couldn't understand the place, the small towns, the way people thought and felt crawling across all those flat farmlands and living under that cardboard grey sky, from which rain seeps more than it falls. The longer I stayed, though, the more I began to listen to people's stories, and to learn how to listen. And so I started to write nonfiction. Eventually, Ohio became the only place that I was able to write about while I was still living there. Now, teaching on the edge of the Rocky Mountains, I occasionally miss Ohio's lushness, the vegetables bursting out of the black earth."

Calderazzo's fiction has won him the Young Writers' fiction prize from *North American Review*. His essays are marked by a sense of location—a careful reportage, an intuitive sense of people and places, and a creative yet direct style. His essays and articles have appeared nationally and often reveal his deep sense of humanity and the environment.

In "Eulogy in a Churchyard," the author, like a good filmmaker, draws his characters out through their vivid talk and simple gestures against a strong setting. The universal truths he reveals are colored by a strong sense of personality. He listens.

EULOGY IN A CHURCHYARD

a gravemaker:
the houses that he makes
last till doomsday

Hamlet, Act V, Scene i

They were a boisterous bunch, the Bridinger kids, one girl and four large boys who would grow to the size of pro football tackles. They lived with their parents, Chalmor and Madeline, in an old clapboard farmhouse, courtesy of Tiffin, Ohio's Greenlawn Cemetery, whose gentle slopes started just across the street from their front porch. And now and then, on the days when the boys were being boys and their nonsense had exhausted their parents' patience and imprecations, their father—all 6'4" and 170 lbs. of him—might have to deliver the Ultimate Threat.

"You damn kids don't behave, you ain't gonna ride in any more funerals!"

That would do it, especially for young Tom. Tom *lived* for funerals. They were the most important and exciting events he could imagine, and once, twice, three times a week, rain or shine or blizzard, they took place literally right under his nose.

Out from town along the country road they would come—long lines of shiny cars filled with adults in their Sunday best, even on weekdays. And at the head of it all, lights flashing impressively like the Indy 500 pacer, was the lead car that had stopped traffic for miles and drawn the stares of downtown shoppers and even, if he was lucky, Tom's schoolmates. In that car sat Tom's father, Chalmor—cemetery superintendent, chief groundskeeper, gravedigger *nonpareil*—the man one of his employees called "The Mayor of Marble City."

And if Tom was very lucky indeed, he would get to ride along and lead the parade, help his dad help all those people who had come to bury their dead. More important, he would be helping the dead themselves.

"After all," says Tom, "digging a grave is the last special thing you can do for someone."

Saturday morning. Hollywood could not have created more perfect weather for grave digging: bone-chilly, a wet sheen covering the roads like sealskin, ragged clots of fog standing in the fields, blurring the point where a herd of sheep ends and the fog begins. You wouldn't be surprised to see a druid standing behind a tree, or a hunchback limping along the shoulder of the road.

"God, Dad loved it out here," says Tom, loading three shovels, a pick, an ax, and assorted metal rods into the bed of a battered dump truck. "He knew every tree in the place and said there were as many kinds as there were counties in Ohio—88. He tried factory work in town once. After a year he said, 'That's history' and never worked indoors again." Tom wrenches open the truck door and cranks up the engine with an unmuffled roar.

"Funerals were family affairs for us. For years my granddad was foreman of the cemetery. He taught the business to Dad, and after Dad died, Ma took over as superintendent. Over the years Dad had all us kids out here, mowing, trimming around the monuments with a sickle, watering flowers, laying foundations for the headstones. Of course, as we got older, he taught us to dig."

Tom pulls out of the driveway of the house that he still lives in with his mother and one brother, Mike, who sells tombstones across town and coaches football at Tiffin University. In a few seconds he's rumbled through Greenlawn's tall front gates and is curving past tombstone-covered slopes. Even on a grey morning it's obvious that it's a pretty place, 100 rolling acres sitting among thick woods, a park, and corn fields—a few of them owned by the cemetery, Tom says, "for future development."

Today he'll be digging the long-postponed second half of a double grave. After years of widowhood in the warm south, an elderly Tiffin woman has returned to lie beside her husband—a typical story in Marble Cities all over the north. In the end, no matter how far they've strayed, native sons and daughters often move back to the serene, silent suburbs of the livelier towns they grew up in.

"Sometimes I need a map to find where to dig," says Tom, as the cemetery road winds between glistening, rain-black buckeyes and maples. "But Dad, he'd take you right to 'em. He knew everybody in the place, and became friends with a lot of their families, too, as they'd drop by to visit. You'd be surprised how many old ladies around town left him things in their wills, a favorite chair, whatever." At age 61, when Chalmor was himself buried at Greenlawn, he had worked here more than half a century. Tom, who's now 34, apprenticed as a grave-digger to his father when he was 13.

Tom finds his spot, backs up the truck, and jumps out. He's wearing his grave-digging regs—work boots, orange sweat pants, a red sweat shirt with a towel curled around his neck. At 6'2" and 200 lbs—down 30 from just a few months back—Tom could pass for a heavyweight boxer, or the honorable mention all-Ohio quarterback he once was at Tiffin's Calvert Catholic High School. Football earned him a scholarship to Temple University, where he toiled unhappily as an interior lineman and fantasized for a while about becoming "a fancy Philadelphia lawyer." But that was before he caught the teaching bug. Now he teaches English at Calvert and PE at the junior high, plus coaches JV basketball at Tiffin University. Sometimes, on the day after he's been up late digging a grave, his high school students notice his red eyes and say, "Didja get another one last night? Didja?"

He teaches at the cemetery, too. "A grave should be 7'10" by 3'2". I used to have to measure, but Dad taught me to eyeball it, and now I can pretty much step it off. You hear all that stuff about six feet under, but graves actually aren't much more than four feet deep. Hell, if I went down much farther, I couldn't get out. I'd be digging my own grave."

But before he stakes out the corners, he pushes a thin metal rod into the earth. A couple of feet down it stops with a thud—the sound of metal against concrete. He tries again a few inches over and presses the rod smoothly in. Here's where he'll dig.

Normally he slices the sod into strips with a special shovel and rolls them cleanly back, like carpets, to be unrolled and tamped back down after the burial. But today, because of the muck and the sparseness of the grass, he just digs right in with a spade. "Hey, not too bad! No frost, not even next to the headstone, where you always get it first. This won't take more than three, three-and-a-half hours. The drainage is bad in this part of the cemetery, though. Once I hit water at the bottom of a grave at five below zero."

Since death does not keep banker's hours, Tom has worked under every condition imaginable: by car headlights or lanterns in the middle of the night, a stereo headset clamped to his head; swinging the pick for nine hours at clay baked hard as stone; filling a hole with water, like a private swimming pool, so he wouldn't pass out from the heat; digging and bailing in downpours; chipping at frost three feet deep—ground so tough he finally called in an old crony of his dad's, 74-year-old Leonard Graham, who went at it with an air hammer.

Tom has seen one graveside mourner punch another who said that, frankly, he'd never much cared for the deceased. He's seen a motorcycle gang serenade a fallen comrade by revving up their Harleys and lifting their front wheels as the coffin was being lowered. One time a man leaned over an open coffin and slipped a hundred-dollar bill into the suit pocket of the dead man. "A hundred bucks!" says Tom. "I felt like exchanging it later for a blank check."

Tom peels down to a Kansas City Chiefs sweat shirt and drapes his old one over the headstone. He switches to a sixteen-inch spade and starts tearing through roots, prying out long smooth sections of soil and tossing them into the truck bed.

"Dad was from the old school. He'd have a fit if he saw the dump truck out here. It had to be a *wheelbarrow*. And he dug entirely by hand because he thought that was the only way to do it right—no fancy backhoe for him. He could read the grain in the wood handle of this shovel like you and I read a baseball bat.

"The cemetery was his whole life, but it's only part of mine. About a month ago I met a gal from Texas. Boy, does she love to dance! But after a couple of dates, she said, 'Hon, you don't *really* dig graves, do you? That's not what you wanna do the rest of your life, is it?' I don't know . . . sometimes I think about moving away—Texas might be nice. Sometimes I think I'd like to stay here and dig forever, at least part-time."

A breeze comes up and riffles the faded American flags that the Legion has put on the graves of veterans. "I mean, I can't think of anything negative about it. It's great exercise, plus it relaxes me, helps me straighten out my thoughts. I can hear Dad talking to me when I dig, saying, 'Do it right, Dummy!' or telling me to suck it up or whatever and keep going. I'm also practicing an art that's been passed down through my family—carving something out of the earth for somebody who needs it. When I'm about to take that last shovelful of dirt, I always think of a sculptor getting ready to take the final chip off a statue—you know, the hammer poised over the tip of the nose or the chin."

Tom leans forward on his shovel. "Not that it's all serious business. Once, a doctor who was treating Dad's heart condition asked him what he did for a living. He said, 'Well, Doc, I cover up your mistakes.' They didn't get on too well after that."

Tom always digs a grave in three layers, like a cake, carefully removing all the "crumbs," or loose soil, before moving down a level. Halfway through layer two on this dark Saturday morning, the gloom thickens.

"A lot of people think a cemetery is dead and cold, Edgar Allen Poe stuff. But to me, it's alive and warm. It's a transitional place.

The only time I saw Dad cry was when I was a small child. Look around, this place is full of people; every headstone is a book about somebody's life. Death *is* life—or the next life, anyway."

Far off in town, the bells of a church begin to chime. "Lunch!" says Tom. He carefully gathers his tools. "You'd be surprised what people'll steal out here. They'll even switch around the plastic flowers."

"I didn't lose thirty pounds eating like this." Tom looks happily at his mother's kitchen table with its steaming bowls of bratwurst, mashed potatoes, and home-made sauerkraut, plus huge servings of fruit salad, cheese, ice cream and bread. Then he attacks. "When we were kids," he says between mouthfuls, "Dad told folks, 'The little bastards sit at one end of the table with their mouths open and I just *tip* it.' "

Madeline Bridinger, leaning against the stove, puffs a cigarette and watches the food disappear. "You know, it's amazing, Tommy gets more for digging one grave these days than Chal used to make for a whole week, and we brung up five kids. Why Denny, he's the oldest and a high school principal, he could polish off a loaf of bread, a head of lettuce, and a gallon of milk at a sitting. He got up to 295 and once made the final cut with the Cleveland Browns."

She gazes over Tom's head at the refrigerator, where a sticker on the door says KEEP SMILING. "How'd we make do on so little money? We stuck together as a *family*. And this was a great place to raise one—plenty of work for the kids in the cemetery, them woods to play in, and the park for sports.

"You know that old barn down the hill? There were horses boarded there, and in the winter we'd hook 'em to one of those old-fashioned sleighs and all of us ride through the cemetery and then down the back roads. Every year Chal would shinny up a pine and chop the top off for a Christmas tree. Shoot, you didn't need money to have fun." She plunks a tin of coffee cake on the table. "Full yet!"

Driving back through the cemetery, Tom says, "Ma's a real peach, huh? And *tough*. One day during a football game I got absolutely crunched near the sideline, and when I looked up she was leaning right over me, hissing, 'You PUSS, get back in there!' Neither she nor Dad ever had new clothes when we were growing up, but they always made sure we had the best football, the best baseball glove.

"But for a long time now the cemetery business has been changing, it's much more a money game, and that makes her sad. She's been kind of eased out as superintendent by new ownership. It's a good thing Mike and I bought the house from the cemetery a few years back.

"And of course she misses Dad terribly. He had a spot picked out near the house, but when he died she said, 'Get him out of there. I don't want to look out the window every day and see him.' "

Tom drives a few hundred yards past the half-finished grave, then stops the truck and gets out. He saunters up a slight rise, moving from tombstone to tombstone in a way that suggests a nature guide pointing out flowers. Or books.

"Now, this is my best friend when I was a kid. He died in a cycle accident. I dug his grave. This one, she's a former teacher of mine. Here's an old man who said he didn't want to go on living without his wife. He was gone in a couple of months. Here's a girl who was a dancer, blonde--God, she was beautiful. She died of cancer at 22." Her epitaph reads: "And when the earth shall claim your limbs, then shall you truly dance."

Near the top of the rise, Tom stops. He slowly folds his arms. "And here's Dad. He picked the stone himself, naturally."

It's an ordinary-looking stone with one exception—no dates. "Dad always said, 'It's nobody's business, plus I'll never really die, anyway. I'll always be with you.' And he didn't want an open coffin. He said, 'If the sons of bitches didn't wanna see me when I was alive, I don't want 'em looking at me now.'

Of course, hard as it was, I carved his grave. My sister came and helped—she was real close to him, too—and some friends. It was snowing. The ground was hard and there were lots of roots to tear through, and I could hear him laughing at how long it was taking. Laughing and saying things like "Get the hell off the crumbs!" or "Get out of that hole and pay attention to the way I do it!"

Tom stares at the ground as though the grave were still open. "Yeah, this one's my masterpiece. My Picasso, my Pieta."

Tom works on the third and final layer, sparks shooting up as he grazes a rock while squaring a corner. He's got his rhythm now and digs hard, sensing the end. "I'd like to get my jogs in before nightfall," he says. The mist has lifted, but the air still feels as wet as the clay that squishes around his feet.

"These people that buy $12,000 copper valuts while there are kids starving all over the world—I can't see it. We're gonna go back to dust anyway. Me, I'll be cremated. I'll have them put my ashes right next to Dad. Or right on top."

He's near the bottom now. A few worms wriggle out of the walls and drop to the heavy clay that makes sucking noises whenever he tries to lift a boot. Tom looks down for a moment, then reaches for a cup of water he's propped in the vase-holder of the headstone. It's a long way from dancing in Texas.

He measures the depth of the grave with his shovel, then scoops out a little more mud and says, "That's it." He places an arm firmly on the edge of the hole. "Here's how you get out—Dad could do it one-handed even in his late fifties." He kicks up his inside leg and jumps, but the muck at the bottom clings hard to his other leg.

At this moment, Hollywood might well freeze this frame, leaving you with the image of a man—tall and muscular and bristling with energy—caught midway between earth and air, a man frozen between worlds. But this isn't the movies, it's reality; and as the clay lets go with a loud suck, Tom Bridinger, son of the mayor of Marble City, rises up, up, and *out*.

Ohio Farmhouse. Joel Rudinger

CHRISTIAN DAVIS

HOW TO BUILD A HOUSE

"I have lived in the Midwest for ten years, most of that time in the woods and rolling farm country of West Central Wisconsin. I have taught creative writing and poetry workshops and given readings of my work at university campuses and on Twin Cities radio. I am a journeyman carpenter, though for the last three years I have made my living as a bartender, in St. Paul, working at night, writing in the daytime."

Christian Davis has also won awards for his writing which is as refreshing as a fall breeze across the Great Plains. In "How To Build a House" he delivers wit and charm along with an earth bound wisdom, proving himself a good neighbor to us all.

HOW TO BUILD A HOUSE

Step 1: Fall asleep in your chair, shoes off, feet up, cat in your lap with its motor running. Drift back over the years to a time when you were little and needed comforting, just as you do now. Try and find that room where your uncle or grandma smoothed away your pain; your favorite room in all the world, the secret place you went to be alone until the hurting stopped and the dreams began. Remember the feeling. Remember the sunny window and the way the curtain billowed in the breeze. That's it. You're getting it. Start from there.

All right, wake up. Put on a pot of strong coffee. Decide who you are. Make some sketches on the back of an envelope. That's good enough—you don't want to overdo it. Leave yourself some elbow room for when you change your mind.

Now, take a walk around the property, find the nicest spot on the place—and stay the hell away from it. The reason it's so nice is because no one has built anything on it. If you don't either, it will remain that way, and you'll have it to look out on when you're finished.

Don't expect to reach a point where everything's all ready to go. If you wait until you're ready, you're sunk. Just start. It's better to do something wrong than to wait for things to be perfect. It's OK to be a little afraid, too. In fact, if you aren't, watch out. That could mean you're using the wrong part of your brain. Building a house is serious business, and it needs the exhilaration of risk. Take a shovel out there and dig a hole. You may have to fill it up again when you change your mind, but that's perfectly alright. Dirt's cheap, and besides, you're exploring. There'll be plenty of time later on to take a compass and line the walls up with the sun.

It is amazing the ideas that come to you while you're digging. Even a hole in the wrong place has some value; it acquaints you with the temperament of the ground you'll be living on.

Things will come to you in the wrong order, but don't worry about it. It's that way in life all the time. If you hit a big rock, go over and bother a neighbor for a while. Introduce yourself. Maybe he'll give you some coffee and turn out to be a nice man. Besides, he might ask you questions about your house you hadn't thought of yet, which is another good way to get your mind working. Also, it will give you a chance to size him up. If you're lucky, he will be a gold mine of lore and information, and that will inspire you to get busy. A good neighbor is a wonderful thing. He can show you how to fit a new axe handle, or help you curse government agencies. Either way, he's a resource you'll do well to cultivate. There may not be many like him left.

Try to avoid buying anything new. Any fool with money can spend it. But you're not only building yourself a house, here; you're discovering and developing your own inner resources and ingenuity. That old pile of boards you bid on may be five different widths, but in the long run, after you've thoroughly cussed them up one side and down the other, you're going to feel mighty pleased with yourself for figuring ways to use them. Unless you're building under duress, the time you lose will be made up with the rush of pride you'll feel at having done a difficult thing with cleverness and economy. Besides, with the money you save you can take your sweetie on a date. Go someplace fancy. Buy a canoe. Smile when you paddle past the bank.

Do not be intimidated by practical considerations—practicality has far too much influence on our lives. It has all gotten way out of hand. This is *your* house, and it doesn't have to make logical sense to anyone but you. Just remember: castles are not built by the rational mind and logic never freed a frog with its kiss. Not all by itself, it didn't. So, if you're standing there around the hay wagon, in a crowd of practical people, and the auctioneer comes up with a barn cupola from the year 1928, and it strikes your fancy, hang the practicality and buy it. It may turn out to be one of the most inspired things you will ever do.

Now, please be aware that I'm not suggesting you by-pass those coffee cans filled with all sorts of useful nuts and bolts, only that you do not rule out the cupola just because it may seem impractical. Leave room for surprises. (Naturally, there will be times when you find yourself dragging home things, like a steamer trunk full of cotter pins, but don't worry about that. Those things will happen, and you should figure on making a few mistakes, anyway.)

If you build your house so that all four walls face south, you have gone too far. You will have created a two-dimensional space, a plane—which, when you think about it, is what any theory becomes when it is allowed to become dogma. You're going to need a third dimension. Take that sudden leap of eccentric humanness; without it each day falls heavily into its gray place, one upon the next, without distinction, or humor, or urgency.

Now a word about scheduling. Don't. Don't even try. The simplist task takes forever; the most complex often just falls into place. If you plan something that must be done by Thanksgiving, but aren't ready for it, that will only discourage you and leach away the fragile confidence you have managed to accumulate. Expect everything to take triple the time you set for it. Then, if things work out sooner, you can always celebrate and do a little dance on the ridgepole. The thing is, don't let it get you down when work is going slowly. It's unhealthy to get too much done without taking the time to understand and appreciate what it is you're doing. Economists and politicians like to measure progress in terms of the Gross National Product. Well, I'm thinking maybe they ought to start measuring the Gross National Pleasure, or the Gross National Pride, and see what happens.

Finally, if you follow these instructions with reasonable faith, it's quite possible you will never completely finish your house, and your wife will want to leave you and your dog will walk away in disgust. But, if you can keep mind and body together, holding on with your strength of vision and wit and your whimsical heart—despite the struggle and pain and financial uncertainty and every other possible calamity that will unerringly find its way to your door—you will have done something that most people never do. You will have cut from the wild hills an earthly house where the song you sing is your own.

Oxford Township Landscape. Edith Lehman

SUSAN STRAYER DEAL

WINDMILLS

Susan Strayer Deal grew up in Nebraska where she knew a landscape of windmills intimately. Most of her fiction, poetry, and essays deal with her youth in Nebraska and with its landscape and people.

Her books of poetry include *No Moving Parts* (1980) and *The Dark is a Door* (1984). She works at the library and teaches English at the University of Nebraska in Lincoln.

"Windmills" is a good example of the type of impressionistic writing—blending prose rhythms with poetic imagery—that sense of place writing calls from us. Its movement is quiet and sure, and the images deep and real.

WINDMILLS

Grow up with windmills and you look for windmills as landmarks forever. Grow up with skies and you look for skies. Deep skies and black with a million ice cold stars blinking down reminding you of how small you are. Not scary but just a fact. In the middle of the middle of the plains on a dark September night or a December night, or a July night the stars remind. You look up and dissolve in the hugeness. The plains always sweep you away.

And if not the skies, the wind or the vagaires of the weather remind. Nature is everywhere and barns and silos and windmills or fence posts are the only anchors for the eye and the mind.

You grow up loving the trees because they are rare and special here. You could name each one; the cottonwoods, the elms, the oaks, the Russian olives all dressed in their own greens and doing their particular dance in the wind. You look for them when you travel through the landscape and when they are gone. The landscape reminds of how transitory and small our signposts are. And the windmills too are a sort of tree without leaves, without branches, but with one long tap root sinking down to the water table. I love the look of windmills, old ones, new ones, small or large ones. Clearly not as beautiful as trees and in some instances quite ugly. But symbolically windmills are life givers, sustainers. Their metal parts in tune to a soft rhythmic dance with the wind, providing sometimes the only outpost for miles where living things can come for water. Water from deep in the womb of the flat earth. Water precious and cold and essential. Windmills connecting the earth to the sky just as trees do.

The dance of the windmills is not particularly pretty or graceful. Their huge metal heads heavily rotate to the strokes of the wind and it is the wind that decides the dance they do. But something in the sound of their pumping can he hypnotic on a hot summer's day. The long shaft of the windmill working with the wind. The earth surrendering to the strokes. The water spilling up into the tank and standing cold under the fierce sun. It is a sort of man made mechanical dance that synchronizes to its open environment. The wooden towers often blend into the color of the brown hills. The large horse tanks often soften their metal and corrode to the same color as the water that they catch and hold. Over the course of time many windmills seem to/ belong where they stand. Seem to have grown there. They are not presumptious or gaudy or foreign to the eye. They take on the seasonal rhythms of their work, and their seasonal colors.

Beyond their metallic music, cacophonous sometimes, fluid and/swift at others, when the wind dies at sunset, their shapes can be starkly pleasing, a sort of black half tree, half pyramid outlined against a red sun. Or they soften in the morning to a gray, a gray as gray as the ground fog rising around them, soft as old wood aged by years of hot dry wind. Far away, blending or standing starkly against the landscape the eye falls on them pleasingly. The windmills belong, like a weathered sculpture.

And close up to the windmill, on a hot day, riding a horse up through the pastures or walking up to it there may occur a rare strange, mystical moment. A moment when a sharing takes place. When the hand dips in and takes the water waiting. When overhead the blades sing their particular chant. Where one partakes, not only of water, but of everything elemental; earth wind and sky. The windmill becomes a sacred place for an instant, high on a hill in the middle of nowhere. You take what the earth gives simply and are satisfied. You belong. Or the windmill may remain simply and efficiently a place of water, a watering hole for those who are thirsty. A place made comfortable by hoof prints and footsteps.

Grow up with windmills and you look for windmills for the eye and the mind. They stay deep like a brand in the memory. You can close your eyes and see them centered there, blended into the landscape, pumping water, doing their work, making music, pumping water, connecting. Half tree, half pyramid, simple and simply working in remote places or out in the open in sync to the wind and landscape, pumping water, making music, doing their work.

Hubcaps, Queensville, Indiana. Roger Pfingston

MICHAEL DELP

CHASING THE RIVER GODS:
A FISHING TRILOGY

"I am haunted by Northern Michigan," confesses Michael Delp, who was born (1948) and raised in Greenville, Michigan. He admits another obsession, "Raised summers on Bass Lake, I acquired an addiction to fishing. Moved to Northern Michigan in 1971 where I began trout fishing with a vengeance."
   He is also the director of the creative writing program at Interlochen Arts Academy. His fiction and nonfiction have appeared regionally and nationally. His book of poems *Over the Graves of Horses* is being published by Wayne State University. He is the co-editor of *Contemporary Michigan Poetry: The Third Coast,* also by Wayne State University.
   Delp's writings on nature are unflinching in their directness, full of rich surfaces and deep images that reflect a subsconcious connection between detail and ritual. The voice, as demonstrated in these three related pieces, can be relaxed—exacting—even haunting in its search for meaning in the acts and facts of reality. His writing cuts deep into the American grain of experience, yet, like his grandfather's fishing tools, it is "blessed by the blood of fish, blessed by the way his hands used these simple artifacts, blessed by his patience and blessed by the knowledge that he knew the very fundamental necessities of fishing."

CHASING THE RIVER GODS: A FISHING TRILOGY

I. RIVER GODS

You may have heard this story. Maybe a long time ago. Maybe it was in a little cafe with a few old calendars askew on the walls, some gut busting eggs, frying on the back griddle. But when you heard it, you knew it was legend:

It was a story about going to the river every spring. He was almost sixty the last time he did it, he said. He had fished the same water for five decades with his grandfather and his father. They called it "their water". The rituals were carried out meticulously each season: opening day breakfast, checking the gear, exchanging small presents, then the walk to the river. And after both of them had died, he kept a secret, he said, something he always did in private, always at the same spot where the creek fed into the mainstream.

He had borrowed this, he was saying. Borrowed this part of his own private ritual from an Aborigine tribe in Australia. It was something about respect, about giving yourself over. He always used the same knife, he said, and pulled an old Boy Scout jack-knife out of his front pocket.

Then he showed the motion he used. Not a quick slice over his wrist, but a slow, delicate draw over his forearm. Then he pulled up his sleeve and the scars laced his arm. Each one small, distinct, his left forearm covered with inch-long memories.

The bleeding never lasted long, he said. Just long enough to let a little blood fall into the river. He'd mix it slowly with his hand, then wave it along. He never said anything, only watched the way the blood swirled into the clear water, then dissolved, disappeared, became the river. Twenty seasons. Twenty cuts.

After he left, I looked at my own smooth forearm, thought of the rivers I knew, the dream rivers I fished in my sleep, rivers full of mermaids, phantoms. And that day, after I heard his story I found an old Barlow knife my father had given me at Hartwick Pines and cleaned it up.

It was there in the basement, halfway into early morning, that I felt the edge, honed perfectly. And I thought about the small gods who bless rivers, the ones who bless our fishing lives, the ones who bless our hands, the ones who bless each drop of water. I thought of my life somehow transported into each one of their favors. I thought of heading out in April, through early mist, perhaps the apparitions of ghost relatives, or the visions of waking dreams lining the path to the river. I knew the exact spot near the AuSable over a pure spring where I would kneel down, roll up my sleeve and make the cut, and begin the process of giving myself over.

II. THE LEGACY OF WORMS

To a fly fisherman who has an inflated opinion of himself and his fraternity, nothing is quite as loathsome as a worm fisherman.

Perhaps, because of the media attention over the years about the "purity" of fly fishing, worming has gotten some bad ink. I must confess to a certain snobbishness at times. After all, who am I kidding when I step into the AuSable with a thousand dollars worth of Orvis gear. I'm fishing. I'm worthy of practicing deception. I've got the stuff to prove it: fly boxes, graphite rods, tiny gadgets with the right logo. But this is all fakery. We all know when we drool over equipment that, somehow, beyond this world of high-tech, boron-graphite fibers, underneath all this foppery, there is instinct.

Maybe it was instinct that told me to get up early with my father to go looking for worms. He knew the best places: under leaves, cool and moist. Or we went out late at night on the summer lawn, feeling the dark for crawlers, remembering later how they slipped like greased sausages through our fingers. Even now, from a distance of thirty years, I can still hear the sound they made when they plunked into the wet leaves and dirt at the bottom of a rusty Hills Brothers worm can.

If fishing is about anything for me, it is about recollection, the way my mind has of letting itself unravel and hook around the sensation that the dead are surely watching us from the banks or are standing on shore measuring each cast.

Inevitably, when I think of ancestors and fishing I remember Bass Lake and my grandfather's cottage. I go back to fishing with live bait, almost always worms, any kind of worm we find. It was back then, in the '50's, I learned the secret techniques from my father and grandfather about how to think of the hook as a kind of needle, the worm as fabric, the whole rig set up to keep the worm alive as long as possible, moving, imagining its slow dance underwater.

And the ghosts are always there when I fish now. I can see my grandfather baiting up for perch using tiny red worms, or my father and me anchored just off a deserted island, how we sifted through the can of crawlers for the patriarch of all worms, the one that felt lucky. Then he'd break one in half and spit on it, and I'd make that long cast toward the lily pads, waiting for the bass to explode up out of the weeds.

There are other visions, some taken from father's stories, and always they are visions of ritualistic, nearly sacred value: men hunched over hooks in the rain, mumbling old fishing prayers, invocations carried on the souls of countless worms.

But the one image I hold most stunning is one passed on about one of my father's old fishing buddies from the '40's, Fred Lewis, and how he must have looked when he turned toward a question just after baiting up, the hook in his teeth and a gob of nightcrawlers dribbling down the side of his mouth.

Now, each year, maybe out of respect for the dead, maybe out of superstition, before I set my gear up, before I get out my hundred and fifty dollar fly reels, the flashy graphite rods, the Wheatley Fly boxes, I go into my study and take out the bandana where I have wrapped the talismans of my life which keep me going. A power stone from Lake Superior is hidden in there and a lovely hand-made Chinese fish given as a gift from an equally lovely student. Perhaps, most powerful of all, there are bits and pieces of what's left of my grandfather's tackle: misshapen sinkers, rusted books, used crawler harnesses, the stuff of fishing a lifetime with worms.

What was handed down from his gear as legacy has all been blessed: blessed by the blood of fish, blessed by the way his hands used these simple fishing artifacts, blessed by his patience and blessed by the knowledge that he knew the very fundamental necessities of fishing.

III. STEEL HEAD DREAMS

Tonight, just before I fall asleep, I hear the wind kick up in the red pines outside the house. I begin to go under, begin to submerge myself in a dream I know is waiting for me. "The steelhead run with the wind", I remember someone saying. And I think of thousands of fish gathering at the mouths of rivers up and down Lake Michigan. I begin to think of my bed and how I lay on top of it as some kind of way I am able to hover just over the dream. As if the dream itself were made of water and I could lower myself down into a river choked with March ice. Holding. Just off a river mouth.

I listen. Underwater the wind sounds like thousands of waterfalls. A dull roar. A roar coming from far off and seeping gradually into my head. There are hundreds of fish waiting. They fan slowly, move up and down, some sideways in the current coming out of the river.

If I listen clearly enough to the inside of my head, I can hear the sound of some old command, some old memory let loose far upstream calling me in.

The water turns chemical. Chemicals loose in the tiny brains of these fishing washing through their bodies, urging them upriver.

They surge through deadfall, upstream, rounding bends deep underwater, the sound of the river mixing with the sound of the wind. All chemical. Something drifting now in their bodies. Bodies that look like pure aluminum muscles loose in the water.

First light. The fish stop just below the dam. The water moves past their eyes, churning with ice. In the steelhand dream I drift just off bottom. The bed, mattress, the room gone icy. I think I hear echoes in my head. The sound of rocks moving underwater. Fish moving against each other. The spawning run ends here at the dam, ten miles upstream. Each fish noses into the current, settling toward bottom. My arms and wrists go limp in the dream, only a few hours left to rest here. Hold close to bottom. Pretend I know the way back. Pretend I can somehow rise back into my body, barely able to lift myself toward sunrise.

The fishermen move out of their houses hours before dawn. Maybe the river is twenty, thirty miles away. Or maybe they come from the cities, drive all night, migrating north.

In their cars, their heads begin to turn to steel. They imagine their arms and legs slowly churning to the color of slate blue. Their eyesight narrows. Their cars begin to swim through the darkness and when they stop to rest and step out into the night they believe the stars are the tiny points of hooks. They move further north, not by watching the constellations, but by following the magnetic pull of steel forming in their heads. In their brains the cells are vibrating in close time with the river. So close they hardly notice their bodies turning silver, their muscles taut, eyes running against the current of darkness flowing up over their hoods.

I send the line out 30 feet. "Steelhead run with the wind", Driscoll tells me. It drifts down the chute formed by the dam. I feel the lead weight bounce over gravel for 20, perhaps 30 yards. Three minutes in the water and my feet go numb. Ice forms on my rod tip. I pull back slowly, hoping for a slight resistance, the mouth of a steelhead nosing my fly. Nothing.

Driscoll casts into the current. In four years, he has landed over 300 steelhead. He tells me he fishes steelhead because it gives him some balance. Fishing he tells me, particularly steelhead fishing, has nothing to do with thinking. It is the balance between the cerebral, meditative and physical. The biggest thing, he says is the directness with which you catch a steelhead.

I have fished for trout for years. Never for steelhead. Mostly alone. Mostly in the early morning. Streamers laid out then retrieved slowly. Meditative. Now, there are men upstream and down. Close. Packed in like fish. I cast perhaps forty times. Nothing.

Downstream men bunch together over the holes. They cast into the growing light. Suddenly, back near the dam a steelhead plunges upstream.

Someone's rod bends toward the water, the fish surges back downstream, then turns sideways against the current. The man holds. We pull our lines in. Everyone watches as he walks past us, holding the rod in close, bent almost double.

In the current the fish looks live a silver missile ripping upstream. Twenty minutes later he walks by, holding 30 inches of pure silver muscle, his fingers hooked under the gills.

We head home empty. I remember what Driscoll says about this sport. It's all in the drift, the length of your lead, the test line you use and the weight and placement of spit shot, he says. He tells me to walk the rivers, find out, he says where the fish are and aren't and then figure out why they aren't.

We go out another night. Fish the "rope hole" on the Platte River out of an old duck hunting canoe. 40 degrees and raining/snowing, the wind ripping into my parka. "Steelhead run with the wind", he says again. We break several lines, casting again and again under the influence of mercury vapor lights from nearby cabins. Nothing.

I begin to think about this kind of fishing. Begin to think of the sheer numbers of fishermen standing next to each other at the Homestead Dam and the sport turns narcotic. I begin to realize that the steelhead is in the brain. It runs deep, cuts down through the medulla, cerebellum, runs like a vein directly down the spinal column.

We leave again with nothing. On the way home I imagine the road to be a kind of river. I am guiding the truck directly into driving rain and snow. Both of us sit encased in steel. Steelhead fishermen. Driving home. Empty. Behind us the steelhead surge and circle at the river-mouth. The truck fishtails through slush. A truck made of steel. Heads of steel. And on the hood: ice clinging to steel.

License Branch, Elletsville, Indiana. Roger Pfingston

ANNIE DILLARD

FROM

AN AMERICAN CHILDHOOD

Born in 1945 in Pittsburgh, with its backdoor open to the Midwest, Annie Dillard describes the horizons of her native grounds in her autobiographical *An American Childhood* (1987): "Pittsburgh's summer skies are pale, as they are in many river valleys. The blinding haze spread overhead and glittered up from the river. It was the biggest sky in town" (201). Dillard's acute sense of observation, so well documented in her *Pilgrim at Tinker Creek* (1974), is given further expansion through her equally vivid inner imagination. She describes her industrial-urban birthplace thusly, "I will see the city poured rolling down the mountain valleys like slag, and see the city lights sprinkled and curved around the hills' curves, rows of bonfires winding. At sunset a red light like housefires shines from the narrow hillside windows; the houses' bricks burn like glowing coals"(3).

Writing in a kind of memory collage—"I woke in bits, like all children, piecemeal over the years. I discovered myself and the world, and forgot them, and discovered them again" (11)—Dillard is that rare meditative observer—a "stalker" and "explorer"—who shocks us with her piercing insights. Seeing from both the outside and the inside, she presents a landscape both sensual in detail and spiritual in suggestion. Also a poet *(Tickets for A Prayer Wheel,* 1974), Dillard creates a prose style equally rich in its vivid texture and its rhythmic intensification. Her literary studies *Living by Fiction* (1979) and *Encounters with Chinese Writers* (1987) reveal a further side of her background.

HEARTLANDS— 75

Robert DiYanni describes Dillard's homeland as an essential part of the midwestern heartlands: "To go with Dillard to Tinker Creek or to any of her other haunts is to go on a journey into the heartland. But it is also to go beyond the heartland into uncharted regions of the mind and spirit."

In these two pieces from the opening and closing of her acclaimed *An American Childhood,* we witness her poetic and impressionistic weaving of the threads of experience.

AN AMERICAN CHILDHOOD

When everything else has gone from my brain—the President's name, the state capitals, the neighborhoods where I lived, and then my own name and what it was on earth I sought, and then at length the faces of my friends, and finally the faces of my family—when all this has dissolved, what will be left, I believe, is topology: the dreaming memory of land as it lay this way and that.

I will see the city poured rolling down the mountain valleys like slag, and see the city lights sprinkled and curved around the hills' curves, rows of bonfires winding. At sunset a red light like housefires shines from the narrow hillside windows; the houses' bricks burn like glowing coals.

The three wide rivers divide and cool the mountains. Calm old bridges span the banks and link the hills. The Allegheny River flows in brawling from the north, from near the shore of Lake Erie, and from Lake Chautauqua in New York and eastward. The Monongahela River flows in shallow and slow from the south, from West Virginia. The Allegheny and the Monongahela meet and form the westward-wending Ohio.

Where the two rivers join lies an acute point of flat land from which rises the city. The tall buildings rise lighted to their tips. Their lights illumine other buildings' clean sides, and illumine the narrow city canyons below, where people move, and shine reflected red and white at night from the black waters.

When the shining city, too, fades, I will see only those forested mountains and hills, and the way the rivers lie flat and moving among them, and the way the low land lies wooded among them, and the blunt mountains rise in darkness from the rivers' banks, steep from the rugged south and rolling from the north, and from farther, from the inclined eastward plateau where the high ridges begin to run so long north and south unbroken that to get around them you practically have to navigate Cape Horn....

* * *

In 1955, when I was ten, my father's reading went to his head

My father's reading during that time, and for many years before and after, consisted for the most part of *Life on the Mississippi*. He was a young executive in the old family firm, American Standard;

sometimes he traveled alone on business. Traveling, he checked into a hotel, found a bookstore, and chose for the night's reading, after what I fancy to have been long deliberation, yet another copy of *Life on the Mississippi*. He brought all these books home. There were dozens of copies of *Life on the Mississippi* on the living-room shelves. From time to time, I read one.

Down the Mississippi hazarded the cub riverboat pilot, down the Mississippi from St. Louis to New Orleans. His chief, the pilot Mr. Bixby, taught him how to lay the boat in her marks and dart between points; he learned to pick a way fastidiously inside a certain snag and outside a shifting shoal in the black dark; he learned to clamber down a memorized channel in his head. On tricky crossings the leadsmen sang out the soundings, so familiar I seemed to have heard them the length of my life: "Mark four!... Quarter-less-four!... Half three!... Mark three!... Quarter-less ..." It was an old story.

When all this reading went to my father's head, he took action. From Pittsburgh he went down the river. Although no one else that our family knew kept a boat on the Allegheny River, our father did, and now he was going all the way with it. He quit the firm his great-grandfather had founded a hundred years earlier down the river at his family's seat in Louisville, Kentucky; he sold his own holdings in the firm. He was taking off for New Orleans.

New Orleans was the source of the music he loved: Dixieland jazz, O Dixieland. In New Orleans men would blow it in the air and beat it underfoot, the music that hustled and snapped, the music whose zip matched his when he was a man-about-town at home in Pittsburgh, working for the family firm; the music he tapped his foot to when he was a man-about-town in New York for a few years after college working for the family firm by day and by night hanging out at Jimmy Ryan's on Fifty-second Street with Zutty Singleton, the black drummer who befriended him, and the rest of the house band. A certain kind of Dixieland suited him best. They played it at Jimmy Ryan's, and Pee Wee Russell and Eddie Condon played it too—New Orleans Dixieland chilled a bit by its journey up the river, and smoothed by its sojourns in Chicago and New York.

Back in New Orleans where he was headed they would play the old stuff, the hot, rough stuff—bastardized for tourists maybe, but still the big and muddy source of it all. Back in New Orleans where he was headed the music would smell like the river itself, maybe, like a thicker, older version of the Allegheny River at Pittsburgh, where he heard the music beat in the roar of his boat's inboard motor; like a thicker, older version of the wide Ohio River at Louisville, Kentucky, where at his family's summer house he'd spent his boyhood summers mucking about in boats.

Getting ready for the trip one Saturday, he roamed around our big brick house snapping his fingers. He had put a record on: Sharkey Bonano, "Li'l Liza Jane." I was reading Robert Louis Stevenson on the sunporch: *Kidnapped*. I looked up from my book and saw him outside; he had wandered out to the lawn and was standing in the wind between the buckeye trees and looking up at what must have been a small patch of wild sky. Old Low-Pockets. He was six feet four, all lanky and leggy; he had thick brown hair and shaggy brows, and a mild and dreamy expression in his blue eyes.

When our mother met Frank Doak, he was twenty-seven: witty, boyish, bookish, unsnobbish, a good dancer. He had grown up an only child in Pittsburgh, attended Shady Side Academy, and Washington and Jefferson College in Pennsylvania, where he studied history. He was a lapsed Presbyterian and a believing Republican. "Books make the man," read the blue bookplate in all his books. "Frank Doak." The bookplate's woodcut showed a square-rigged ship under way in a steep following sea. Father had hung around jazz in New York, and halfheartedly played the drums; he had smoked marijuana, written poems, begun a novel, painted in oils, imagined a career as a riverboat pilot, and acted for more than ten seasons in amateur and small-time professional theater. At American Standard, Amstan Division, he was the personnel manager.

But not for long, and never again; Mother told us he was quitting to go down the river. I was sorry he'd be leaving the Manufacturers' Building downtown. From his office on the fourteenth floor, he often saw suicides, which he reported at dinner. The suicides grieved him, but they thrilled us kids. My sister Amy was seven.

People jumped from the Sixth Street bridge into the Allegheny River. Because the bridge was low, they shinnied all the way up the steel suspension cables to the bridge towers before they jumped. Father saw them from his desk in silhouette, far away. A man vigorously climbed a slanting cable. He slowed near the top, where the cables hung almost vertically; he paused on the stone tower, seeming to sway against the sky, high over the bridge and the river below. Priests, firemen, and others—presumably family members or passersby—gathered on the bridge. In about half the cases, Father said, these people talked the suicide down. The ones who jumped kicked off from the tower so they'd miss the bridge, and fell tumbling a long way down.

Pittsburgh was a cheerful town, and had far fewer suicides than most other cities its size. Yet people jumped so often that Father and his colleagues on the fourteenth floor had a betting pool going. They guessed the date and time of day the next jumper would appear. If a man got talked down before he jumped, he still counted for the betting pool, thank God; no manager of American Standard ever wanted to hope, even in the smallest part of himself, that the fellow would go ahead and jump. Father said he and the other men used to gather at the biggest window and holler, "No! Don't do it, buddy, don't!" Now he was leaving American Standard to go down the river, and he was a couple of bucks in the hole.

While I was reading *Kidnapped* on this Saturday morning, I heard him come inside and roam from the kitchen to the pantry to the bar, to the dining room, the living room, and the sunporch, snapping his fingers. He was snapping the fingers of both hands, and shaking his head, to the record—"Li'l Liza Jane"—the sound that was beating, big and jivey, all over the house. He walked lightly, long-legged, like a soft-shoe hoofer barely in touch with the floor. When he played the drums, he played lightly, coming down soft with the steel brushes that sounded like a Slinky falling, not making the beat but just sizzling along with it. He wandered into the sunporch, unseeing; he was snapping his fingers lightly, too, as if he were feeling between them a fine layer of the Mississippi silt. The big buckeyes outside the glass sunporch walls were waving.

A week later, he bade a cheerful farewell to us—to Mother, who had encouraged him, to us oblivious daughters, ten and seven, and to the new baby girl, six months old. He loaded his twenty-four-foot cabin cruiser with canned food, pushed off from the dock of the wretched boat club that Mother hated, and pointed his bow downstream, down the Allegheny River. From there it was only a few miles to the Ohio River at Pittsburgh's point, where the Monongahela came in. He wore on westward down the Ohio; he watched West Virginia float past his port bow and Ohio past his starboard. It was 138 river miles to New Martinsville, West Virginia, where he lingered for some races. Back on the move, he tied up nights at club docks he'd seen on the charts; he poured himself water for drinks from dockside hoses. By day he rode through locks, twenty of them in all. He conversed with the lockmasters, those lone men who paced silhouetted in overalls on the concrete lock-chamber walls and threw the big switches that flooded or drained the locks: "Hello, up there!" "So long, down there!"

He continued down the river along the Kentucky border with Ohio, bumping down the locks. He passed through Cincinnati. He moved along down the Kentucky border with Indiana. After 640 miles of river travel, he reached Louisville, Kentucky. There he visited relatives at their summer house on the river.

It was a long way to New Orleans, at this rate another couple of months. He was finding the river lonesome. It got dark too early. It was September; people had abandoned their pleasure boats for the season; their children were back in school. There were no old salts on the docks talking river talk. People weren't so friendly as they were in Pittsburgh. There was no music except the dreary yacht-club jukeboxes playing "How Much Is That Doggie in the Window?" Jazz had come up the river once and for all; it wasn't still coming, he couldn't hear it across the water at night rambling and blowing and banging along high and tuneful, sneaking upstream to Chicago to get educated. He wasn't free so much as loose. He was living alone on beans in a boat and having witless conversations with lockmasters. He mailed out sad postcards.

From phone booths all down the Ohio River he talked to Mother. She told him that she was lonesome, too, and that three children—maid and nanny or no—were a handful. She said, further, that people were starting to talk. She knew Father couldn't bear people's talking. For all his dreaminess, he prized respectability above all; it was our young mother, whose circumstances bespoke such dignity, who loved to shock the world. After only six weeks, then—on the Ohio River at Louisville—he sold the boat and flew home.

I was just waking up then, just barely. Other things were changing. The highly entertaining new baby, Molly, had taken up residence in a former guest room. The great outer world hove into view and began to fill with things that had apparently been there all along: mineralogy, detective work, lepidopterology, ponds and streams, flying, society. My younger sister Amy and I were to start at private school that year: the Ellis School, on Fifth Avenue. I would start dancing school.

Children ten years old wake up and find themselves here, discover themselves to have been here all along; is this sad? They wake like sleepwalkers, in full stride; they wake like people brought back from cardiac arrest or from drowning: *in medias res,* surrounded by familiar people and objects, equipped with a hundred skills. They know the neighborhood, they can read and write English, they are old hands at the commonplace mysteries, and yet they feel themselves to have just stepped off the boat, just converged with their bodies, just flown down from a trance, to lodge in an eerily familiar life already well under way.

I woke in bits, like all children, piecemeal over the years. I discovered myself and the world, and forgot them, and discovered them again. I woke at intervals until, by that September when Father went down the river, the intervals of waking tipped the scales, and I was more often awake than not. I noticed this process of waking, and predicted with terrifying logic that one of these years not far away I would be awake continuously and never slip back, and never be free of myself again.

Consciousness converges with the child as a landing tern touches the outspread feet of its shadow on the sand: precisely, toe hits toe. The tern folds its wings to sit; its shadow dips and spreads over the sand to meet and cup its breast.

Like any child, I slid into myself perfectly fitted, as a diver meets her reflection in a pool. Her fingertips enter the fingertips on the water, her wrists slide up her arms. The diver wraps herself in her reflection wholly, sealing it at the toes, and wears it as she climbs rising from the pool, and ever after.

I never woke, at first, without recalling, chilled, all those other waking times, those similar stark views from similarly lighted precipices: dizzying precipices from which the distant, glittering world revealed itself as a brooding and separated scene—and so let slip a queer implication, that I myself was both observer and observable, and so a possible object of my own humming awareness. Whenever I stepped into the porcelain bathtub, the bath's hot water sent a shock traveling up my bones. The skin on my arms pricked up, and the hair rose on the back of my skull. I saw my own firm foot press the tub, and the pale shadows waver over it, as if I were looking down from the sky and remembering this scene forever. The skin on my face tightened, as it had always done whenever I stepped into the tub, and remembering it all drew a swinging line, loops connecting the dots, all the way back. You again.

* * *

A dream consists of little more than its setting, as anyone knows who tells a dream or hears a dream told:

We were squeezing up the stone street of an Old West village.

We were climbing down the gangway of an oceangoing ship, carrying a baby.

We broke through the woods on the crest of a ridge and saw water; we grounded our blunt raft on a charred point of land.

We were lying on boughs of a tree in an alley.

We were dancing in a darkened ballroom, and the curtains were blowing.

The setting of our urgent lives is an intricate maze whose blind corridors we learn one by one—village street, ocean vessel, forested slope—without remembering how or where they connect in space.

You travel, settle, move on, stay put, go. You point your car down the riveside road to the blurred foot of the mountain. The mountain rolls back from the floodplain and hides its own height in its trees. You get out, stand on gravel, and cool your eyes watching the river move south. You lean on the car's hot hood and look up at the old mountain, up the slope of its green western flank. It is September; the golden-rod is out, and the asters. The tattered hardwood leaves darken before they die. The mountain occupies most of the sky. You can see where the route ahead through the woods will cross a fire scar, will vanish behind a slide of shale, and perhaps reemerge there on that piny ridge now visible across the hanging valley—that ridge apparently inaccessible, but with a faint track that fingers its greenish spine. You don't notice starting to walk; the sight of the trail has impelled you along it, as the sight of the earth moves the sun.

Before you the mountain's body curves away backward like a gymnast; the mountain's peak is somewhere south, rolled backward, too, and out of sight. Below you lies the pale and widening river; its far bank is forest now, and hills, and more blue hills behind them, hiding the yellow plain. Overhead and on the mountain's side, clouds collect and part. The clouds soak the ridges; the wayside plants tap water on your legs.

Now: if here while you are walking, or there when you've attained the far ridge and can see the yellow plain and the river shining through it—if you notice unbidden that you are afoot on this particular mountain on this particular day in the company of these particular changing fragments of clouds,—if you pause in your daze to connect your own skull-locked and interior mumble with the skin of your senses and sense, and notice you are living,—then will you not conjure up in imagination a map or a globe and locate this low mountain ridge on it, and find on one western slope the dot which represents you walking here astonished?

You may then wonder where they have gone, those other dim dots that were you: you in the flesh swimming in a swift river, swinging a bat on the first pitch, opening a footlocker with a screwdriver, inking and painting clowns on celluloid, stepping out of a revolving door into the swift crowd on a sidewalk, being kissed and kissing till your brain grew smooth, stepping out of the cold woods into a warm field full of crows, or lying awake in bed aware of your legs and suddenly aware of all of it, that the ceiling above you was under the sky—in what country, what town?

You may wonder, that is, as I sometimes wonder privately, but it doesn't matter. For it is not you or I that is important, neither what sort we might be or how we came to be each where we are. What is important is anyone's coming awake and discovering a place, finding in full orbit a spinning globe one can lean over, catch, and jump on. What is important is the moment of opening a life and feeling it touch—with an electric hiss and cry—this speckled mineral sphere, our present world.

On your mountain slope now you must take on faith that those apparently discrete dots of you were contiguous: that little earnest dot, so easily amused; that alien, angry adolescent; and this woman with loosening skin on bony hands, hands now fifteen years older than your mother's hands when you pinched their knuckle skin into mountain ridges on an end table. You must take on faith that those severed places cohered, too—the dozens of desks, bedrooms, kitchens, yards, landscapes—if only through the motion and shed molecules of the traveler. You take it on faith that the multiform and variously lighted latitudes and longitudes were part of one world, that you didn't drop chopped from house to house, coast to coast, life to life, but in some once comprehensible way moved there, a city block at a time, a highway mile at a time, a degree of latitude and longitude at a time, carrying a fielder's mitt and the Penguin *Rimbaud* for old time's sake, and a sealed envelope, like a fetish, of untouchable stock certificates someone one hundred years ago gave your grandmother, and a comb. You take it on faith, for the connections are down now, the trail grown over, the highway moved; you can't remember despite all your vowing and memorization, and the way back is lost.

Your very cells have been replaced, and so have most of your feelings—except for two, two that connect back as far as you can remember. One is the chilling sensation of lowering one foot into a hot bath. The other, which can and does occur at any time, never fails to occur when you lower one foot into a hot bath, and when you feel the chill spread inside your shoulders, shoot down your arms and rise to your lips, and when you remember having felt this sensation from always, from when your mother lifted you down toward the bath and you curled up your legs: it is the dizzying overreal sensation of noticing that you are here. You feel life wipe your face like a big brush.

You may read this in your summer bed while the stars roll westward over your roof as they always do, while the constellation Crazy Swan nosedives over your steaming roof and into the tilled prairie once again. You may read this in your winter chair while Orion vaults over your snowy roof and over the hard continent to dive behind a California wave. "O'Ryan," Father called Orion, "that Irishman." Any two points in time, however distant, meet through the points in between; any two points in our atmosphere touch through the air. So we meet.

I write this at a wide desk in a pine shed as I always do these recent years, in this life I pray will last, while the summer sun closes the sky to Orion and to all the other winter stars over my roof. The young oaks growing just outside my windows wave in the light, so that concentrating, lost in the past, I see the pale leaves wag and think as my blood leaps: Is someone coming?

Is it Mother coming for me, to carry me home? Could it be my own young, glorious Mother, coming across the grass for me, the morning light on her skin, to get me and bring me back? Back to where I last knew all I needed, the way to her two strong arms?

And I wake a little more and reason, No, it is the oak leaves in the sun, pale as a face. I am here now, with this my own dear family, up here at this high latitude, out here at the farthest exploratory tip of this my present bewildering age. And still I break up through the skin of awareness a thousand times a day, as dolphins burst through seas, and dive again, and rise, and dive.

Sandusky Bay Bridge near Port Clinton. Charles F. Corbeil, Sr.

NANCY DUNHAM

THE SENSE OF A PLACE

A Toledo native, Nancy Dunham has made the small Lake Erie town of Port Clinton, Ohio, her home. This piece gauges the growth of a twenty-five year friendship with the area. It reveals how people and places unite over time. We witness her arrival, the growth of her three children, her years of teaching in the public schools, her continuous struggle to know a place, exist in it, measure its change, and find her own peace there. It is an essay of ideas and feelings, of exact details and close images. Its questions are universal, its truths earned over time.

Dunham is also a poet, fiction writer, and visual artist who actively works to preserve and enhance the literacy of her place.

THE SENSE OF A PLACE

The other day I heard someone talking about Sherwood Anderson. "He dramatized the isolation of people in small towns," the speaker said. "He changed the direction of American literature." Anderson wrote at least three generations ago. I wish I could know what he would write today about this region, this current small town generation.

Sherwood Anderson's fictional hometown, Winesburg (Clyde, Ohio) lies about 20 miles southeast of here. It creates part of the ambience that pushes from Ohio's wheated, railroad centered, inland towns west to the edge of Lake Erie. This is not to imply that many of us who dwell along this plush, green-foilaged shore know much about the famous author.

I have lived on the shores of Lake Erie for over thirty years, long enough that when I look from my window at the water, I can see more than the what is there; more than the opposite shoreline, the Davis-Besse nuclear tower, ruthless and serene on the horizon, or my neighbor's breakwall, boulders from a quarry on one of the islands, all even-sized and briny white.

I came to this community right out of college and have taught English at the high school ever since. In those early days, my strength was still untested. I brought with me a confident past: classrooms, seminars, the intense talks that take place late at night in campus bars. I still belonged to the larger world of ideas.

After the first year, my husband Nick and I bought a little cottage by the lake. I remember transplanting iris bulbs into the heavy clay soil, trying to civilize our yard. Our neighbor, two houses away, dead now, gave them to me, saying "They'll grow anywhere." In true Emersonian style, I felt like that. We carry our worlds within us, and we can survive anywhere.

I didn't understand the limits of human nature or how the physical body adjusts to new environments.

Not just the shoreline defined this community. Its richness came from the old families whose appendages can still be seen occasionally at a crossing on the street ("Why that's Phoebe Parker!"); or a former student (Tommy Jamieson) discovered at a party returned to see his family from a new life somewhere (San Francisco, Boston).

Most of those early acquaintances represented descendents of fishermen, boat manufacturers, orchard keepers, or owners of the small businesses like that supported the town. I joined a study club at the library and even attended a Sunday morning class at the Methodist Church. I went to meetings in Victorian mansions facing water or cottages built stone by stone, hand carried from the lake. I wanted to know the people.

To the newcomer, the culture of the region slowly emerged. A few weather strafed fishing shacks remained to suggest the area's history. Stories told by natives in the old hotel reinforced the lore of the lake insinuated by the paintings in the room. Almost every house, regardless of the owner's social standing, held skeletons. In the 20's and 30's the short water route to Canada espoused many midnight crossings and linked the town with syndicates of Chicago, Toledo, Cleveland.

The push and pull of whitecaps, sucked under and over, under and over, created rhythms. That first year I looked out over the expanse of water, moving and restless and exclaimed, like a tourist, I don't ever want to leave.

I've come a way since that first response to the lake, which, like first love, has proven both curse and blessing. I've watched my children tossed in fiber sailboats drift across the seaweed toward a lonely beach; or, sand-coated and choked with lake water, watched Nick and I pull ourselves across mossy rocks and up the grassy bank.

After teaching a few years, I began to wonder where I was headed. I loved the broad sweep of consciousness which literature represented. I looked at Mr. Phetzer and Mrs. Clark, two teachers who exemplified authority and community respect. They appeared daily in the teacher's lounge, grade books in hand, preoccupied with details of the day—filmstrips, attendance, deadlines. Their outlooks appeared contained, structured, limited. Was I also bound in this direction?

In those days, the edge of the town was the edge of the lake: crevices, rotted openings, weedbeds, boulders, misty fish-air, docks bleached and lapped against. Beyond, lay the open lake, and for those shorebound, the memory of docks out on the islands where the ferries bumped, rugged and trailing with gulls, out where the gambling casinos were.

There's no doubt about it. In those days, the lake was a soul to the town, mystic, musty-cornered, with dim lights, low by the water at night and the sound of motors. Insects, fish, remnants of life's cycles washed up, deposited everywhere.

At the end of my road, a grove of trees encircles a lagoon that leads to the lake. One summer's night, late, Nick and I couldn't sleep. We got up from bed, wrapped ourselves in towels, and walked down to the lagoon and boat. Stars filled the sky. The lights along the edge of the lake kept us sane, but beyond that, our towels left on the dock, in the night and lake were ours.

How can I explain how it feels to live in such an environment so aesthetically overwhelming that the hearts and needs of people crowded in cities, hungry in flats, are put aside? In my school one day during the 1970's shootings at Kent State, there were those who supported the troops. "Shoot them radicals. Shoot them all!" swore one of my colleagues, and I realized how far away I lived from the world of ideas.

Access to the Lake Erie Islands beyond the town depended on plane or boat. Out there, wave rocking wave, rhythmic, threatening, consistent, we often traveled to the harbor at Put-in-Bay, docked, and went ashore toward an island culture that belongs in its own story. Returning on dark water, our boat riding the waves, we crossed the lake to the mainland shore and home.

How can I speak of its meaning?

There have been a lot of changes in the last few years. I hear tandems on the new overpass. Huge Lake cranes dredge lagoons for new marinas, for condos springing up like seeds in Persephone's garden and in their wake, people coming, as if this town were Hamlin and opportunity, the inexhaustible call of the peddler's piper.

Each year changes redefine and overtake the shoreline with stretches of construction, excavation, channeling. The water still ravages land, but excesses of people fight back, reclaiming shore, tough as weeds in our flowerbed. In summer, power boats crowd the lake. In winter, the snowmobiles parade across the ice all the way to the islands, the roar of their motors is lost in the force of wind, steady as Arctic explorers of unchartered territory. In a way, their determination demonstrates a kind of natural integrity.

A few years ago, an investor from Pittsburgh "restored" the local old hotel. Now, it's all pink and gilt with mirrors and rooms in the latest decor. I like it, but sometimes my early experiences here return in images of its old paintings, heavy walnut furniture and worn marble floors. Can gain and loss be one?

Dozens of enterprises line the lake shore boulevard. You can eat a Whopper in your car, or "get the best perch sandwich in town." In the parking lot, customers throw bits and pieces of food to the gulls, seduced like scavengers from the lake's freedom.

There's energy here, all right, raw and physical, and a creativity of sorts. New supermarkets, fast food franchises, pizza shops, real estate offices, out-of-town banks, new bank officials to replace old, neighborly administrators, marinas, sewage, cablevision, even a new logo for the schools ("We have to get out there and SELL ourselves"). Stores familiar for years to one location turn up somewhere else. Several gift shops open and close before the town gets used to their presence. I can't deny a power, sprawling and spreading and seeping into every empty place, unrelenting as water.

Masts...summer sails, accent tinted horizons. Luxury yachts cruise wters. Pleasures sumptuous as banquets create their own language. And something about the dynamics: Ohio football, the sparkle of metal on highways, condominiums arisen in place of trees, carnivals, promotion, physical and tough. A savagery and dignity of the lake have somehow been reincarnated in the people, as if a bond exists between human nature and the physical geography—almost as if the culture that has arisen from the lake is in control.

It's ironic. I have turned out, just as I once dreaded, like Mr. Phetzer and Mrs. Clark, evolved into the necessary discipline of public survival. Yet in some ways, I've escaped. I get a lot of complaints about how hard English is, but sometimes, someone asks for help. The phone rang about 12:30 one night.

"Mrs. Dunham, I'm sorry to call so late, but my boyfriend and I are having this big argument about Stephen Crane and we couldn't think of anyone else who might help..."

I can't believe it. I put the receiver down slowly. Michelle Keaton actually remembers Stephen Crane?

We're getting rid of the old literature books this year. They're thirty years old. The inside front of the books includes a list of names for each kid who used the book. I imagine their faces as they looked each September, lined up at my desk to sign in, ghosts of adults now in official positions, seated behind their own desks. They return like children around the table where I now sit compiling this year's sign-outs, end-of-year reports, grade adjustments.

All those students, all those years. So many changes seemed to have occurred in one generation with the media, music, the drug culture. We seem to have blended with the rest of the country. Several years ago, a few companies moved into the area complete with administrators and their families, one group from New England, another from the West. Smart kids—different influences. When the nuclear power plant was proposed in the mid-70's, a controversy opened up. Some of the environmentalists protested, and for a while

I went to meetings about the effects of nuclear steam on fish and animal life.

Then there was a lot of talk about legalizing marijuana because lots of people were doing it anyway, until one day in the 80's, sometime after the teen-age suicide epidemic, or in the middle of it, the country went on a health binge. Somebody got the idea of how to teach people to stop smoking and drinking. Not that it all worked that well, but it seemed Americans began to accept the ideal of personal responsibility.

When the Russians got ahead of us in outer space, everyone panicked over education, so these days, fashion has prescribed a new kind of pressure; accountability. Everyone is accountable: industry, individuals, students, teachers.

Sometime in the late 60's the Arabs raised the price of oil. It didn't take Ohioans long to figure out they didn't have to go far to get a good vacation. That's when a newer population arrived, and with it, more changes.

These days students travel all over. T-shirts from Oxford, Jamaica, Korea appear in classrooms. They want experience. Perhaps reading takes more patience than most possess. The film *Back to the Future* deals with a contemporay 16 year old traveling all the way back to the recent 1960's in an updated version of Orwell's space machine. I get shocked over how little the present generation knows about the past, until I remember how I viewed the history 15 years before I was born.

I have to be careful drawing any major conclusions. Teachers learn to like categories and answers. It's easy to be romantic about the past, harder to be accurate about the present. This day's generation will be reminiscing thirty years from now about the way things are today.

Something else. Too many places these days all look the same, like, if there's no Big Mac in the town, we'd better think twice about stopping there. We seem to have everything so slicked out, little room is left for secrets, those deviations of natural evolution, that old tongue of the lake. Have we lost our separateness in the transition?

The other night at one of the private yacht clubs, Nick and I were making our way toward the only empty spot in the crowded patio. As we passed a table around which five or six people were sitting, there in the darkness, so surprising, I heard voices talking of Goethe, Hesse, and Thomas Mann.

The group included an assortment of writers—a woman from upper New York, a journalist from Rhode Island, a novelist from California, a teacher from a campus nearby. On their way to the islands for a week of a writing workshop project, they had stopped here on the first leg of the journey.

We talked a few minutes. I realized how long it had been since I had conversed about language with anyone but students. I can't say whose fault that is, or if everyone has the same needs. In any case, that conversation awakened me to feelings too long dormant. I want to find them again.

I wonder what Sherwood Anderson would find to write about these days—or Faulkner, or Willa Cather? In this town of sunshine, commerce, prosperity, where lies the soul of the lake? What new secrets, nightmares, dreams are in its churning?

Port Clinton
1988

Dog Holler—My Farmhouse. Robert Fox

ROBERT FOX

DOG HOLLER

Robert Fox is a New York City native who moved to the Midwest in the mid-1960's, as he tells here, for reasons both simple and complex. Since then he has become one with his Southern Ohio neighbors as he has practiced farming, writing, teaching and editing among them from his Pomeroy, Ohio home. He has also worked for art, literature, and literacy from his position of writer-in-residence and literature coordinator of the Ohio Arts Council.

As a writer, Fox has produced a poetry and a fiction sensitive to the larger realities of the mind while tying them to real characters and places. His story collection *Destiny News* (1977) has been praised as "thrilling because they embody common emotions in a hauntingly real artistic framework" (Martin Lich). David Shevin finds his recent *Tlar & Codpol, Two Novels: The Last American Revolution and Confessions of a Dead Politician* (1987) as moved by "the certainty that our dreams have power." Mary Turzillo locates the book in its belief, "Fox seems to be telling us that the poet is a prophet, that he is more than an individual, that where he stands, the currents of history flow."

In our essay the poet-farmer is Fox struggling like many to make his farm in Pomeroy, a reality, and gaining in the process of enriching sense of place and people.

DOG HOLLER

I was born and raised in Brooklyn, NY but became an Appalachian. I did not do this according to a plan—I did not alter my speech or dress. Recently, a certain literary program director, whom I've known since I came to the Ohio Arts Council, confessed his surprise at my being a native New Yorker. He thought I was from Pomeroy, my mailing address. I'm flattered when my Appalachian friends say, "You're just an old hillbilly, like us."

Southeast Ohio became home for me. I lived there for twenty years, fourteen spent on my own farm, which I still own. When visitors came from New York, and even from nearby Athens, they wondered how two Brooklynites settled so far in the boonies. Our farm is located near Snowville. Sometimes when I told people where I lived they thought I was joking. They should have known better, with towns like Coolville and New Straitsville nearby.

Our farmhouse sits at a fork in the road sheltered from the west wind by three steep hills. It sits on a piece of bottom land the old-timers used to call "Dog Holler." The house is solid and square, built with yellow tulip poplar and oak, milled on the property, the windows graced with shutters, etched glass Victorian pictures in two of the doors, and gingerbread trim on the porches. The house looks south on a meadow, and there is nothing like the stillness, the sense of peace in the scene that faces the front porch swing on sunny days.

Echoes abound because of the hills, and when our children played on their homemade swings or by the creek, their voices carried across the bottoms to the next farm. In the early evening, in the stillness intensified by the whippoorwills, the hill on the east side of the house glowing red, it was easy to imagine what the hollow was like fifty years before the WPA raised the township road above the level of the creek, and built a sturdy bridge to the barn.

Settling in the hills of southeast Ohio made sense. I was drawn to the Appalachian countryside partially because it's the birthplace of banjo and fiddle tunes by musicians like Uncle Dave Macon and Blind Alfred Reed. I had been frustrated by my attempts to find a good college teaching job: academic life, the world of high culture and national politics (with Nixon in the White House and the Vietnam War in high gear) seemed corrupt beyond redemption. At the same time an educational subsidiary of a multi-national corporation reprinted a story of mine in a college text without my permission, and my agent said it was my fault she couldn't sell my work—I wasn't writing anything commercial enough; I made the right decision.

I had sworn in the 1960's that if Richard Nixon became President I'd move to Canada. I based my resolve on his activity as a Red-baiter in the 1950's when that was fashionable, and his record as Governor of California, where he and his Watergate staff-to-be carried out prophetic escapades.

Susan and I went camping in Canada in the summer of 1970, trekking from New Brunswick to Ontario. Despite the beauty of the land and the unexpected hospitality of the Canadians, it was still a foreign country. I had never felt as much at home anywhere as I did in southeast Ohio. You see, I was not used to strangers telling me their life stories in our first meetings. I was not used to being trusted and judged on the basis of what I was and what I stood for rather than where I came from, what my name was, what my father did for a living, where I went to school.

Unlike city neighbors, you didn't owe anybody for having done you a favor, nor did you collect IOU's. You simply did or asked for what was required without thought of compensation. I first began to learn about such ethics years before, when our car got stuck in a ditch in Perry County. An old farmer pulled it out with a log chain looped through the rust holes in the rear of his station wagon. When I offered to pay him he refused, saying, "You may have to do the same for me some day." It was a phrase I was later to repeat many times, pulling people out of ditches with my tractor or giving jump starts.

Ernest Wood, my neighbor whom I put up hay with in Dog Holler, was a wonderful story teller. He taught me how to set posts so they wouldn't come loose, and how to stretch fence so that calves couldn't work the strands. He was raised on his father's place up the road from me (Weber's farm and mine were one in the mid-19th century). Except for duty in World War II driving an ammunition truck in North Africa and Europe, and driving a produce and bread truck while living in Middleport, he lived in this hollow all his life. He told me in great detail how wheat was threshed in steam threshers by parties that travelled from farm to farm. Neighbors all knew and helped one another back then. "It's not like now where you don't know who's moving in up the road," Ernest said. "Back then if a man took sick, the neighbors harvested his crops, knowing he would do the same if they were down." He told me about the time Frankie Douglas, an old farmer on the Pagetown road, with a lilting, lyrical voice had broken his leg. The neighbors pitched in after their work was done to harvest his hay and corn.

When I first met Ernest I didn't think we'd get along. I drove out to the farm in the midst of a wet spell while waiting for the mortgage to be approved. The seller assured me the creeks hadn't flooded in the two years he had lived there. I thought if they would flood, now would be the time, for we'd had a week of hard rains. When I drove out, the creeks were high but not close to cresting. I was relieved as I drove past · the farm and backed in to the driveway by Ernest's barn to turn around. Ernest came out of his milkhouse and glared at me, standing rigid in his bib overalls, green baseball cap with the patch removed (he wouldn't pay for a cap to advertise someone's product) and blue windbreaker. I shut the motor off, got out and introduced myself. He wanted to know if I could weld like the man I was buying from, and was clearly disappointed when I told him I'd never farmed before. He glowered after me as I drove off. I may have been more disappointed than him, hoping for neighbors as warm and generous as Ward and Joan Starlin, whom we rented from in Amesville.

Ernest and I did not speak again until after the great flood, which ripped out the two-seater outhouse Johnny Morris had built only a few years before. The high, muddy water got into Johnny's old tractor, which was passed on to me with the farm, and the current ripped out barnyard fence and the water gap across the creek. I figured out how to set posts (not as well as Ernest would later teach me) and attempted to stretch wire from post to post, hammering the staples home and not understanding why the wire loosened. Ernest parked by the bridge and said it was none of his business, but he could show me why my fence wouldn't tighten.

Unlike a young neighbor who had all the answers and ruined everything he touched, I was willing to learn, and Ernest was willing to teach. That became an important part of our bond. I bought my first calf from him. He taught me how to cut and rake hay with my old equipment, and for helping him load, haul and stack his hay in the barn, he baled mine and helped me get it in. He baled with a New Idea square baler with its own motor, and with a towering Allis-Chalmers that made small round bales.

The advantage of the Allis was that the round bales shed water and you were not under pressure to haul the hay in before dew or if rain threatened. He baled mine mostly with the Allis and I followed along in clouds of chaff tying the bales, the one disadvantage of that machine.

The Allis was a mass of belts, gears, levers and trip springs. One of my memorable moments with Ernest came in the meadow across from my house baling hay when some gears dropped out of alignment. Ernest showed me how to pop the rods that bore the gears that turned the belts back into line, then fixed me with his blue eyes and said, "I'm learnin you so you can pass it on to yours."

This was the year before my son, the elder of my two children, was born. "I hope I have some to pass it on to," I said.

"Get busy," he said.

I looked over to the house where Susan, out of earshot, swept the front porch. I smiled at Ernest and then at the clear blue sky framing us, and the green hayfield with the pale cylindrical and cone-shaped bales in irregular rows. I expected then to live there the rest of my life.

Ernest was always ready with a story when, drenched in sweat and itching with chaff we took a break, telling me how they used to do in the old days, and showing me where he used to walk to school when he was a boy: the road through Ron and Cindy's place was once a township road, and just above their first meadow sat a one-room school house. Ernest told me in great detail what his mother packed in his lunch bucket, summer and winter, and his descriptions of shaved ham and home-baked biscuits always made my mouth water.

I helped him put up the three thousand bales he needed for his Grade B dairy herd and a few beef cows, and he baled my three hundred bales, some of which I fed to my few calves, and some of which I sold. He pastured on my place and I didn't charge him—he helped me keep my fence in repair. The milk we drank came from his herd of Holstein, Ayreshire, Gurnsey, Jersey and Brown Swiss. Sometimes the milk I brought home in glass jugs was a third to half cream. We separated it and sometimes Susan made blender butter.

The steep hills of southeastern Ohio have never been conducive to farming. Farmers hauled timber out of the ravines with oxen and plowed the cleared hills with horses, planting corn which they harvested with machetes. The red clay just never became good soil, and rather than encouraging soil building and conservation techniques, the government urged chemical fertilizer, pesticide and weed killer on the farmers to increase yields. This is yet another example of industry dictating government policy. I've seen good meadows corned and fertilized to the point where they couldn't produce decent hay, whereas an organic program could have become cost effective in about five years.

In his prime, Ernest put out hay and corn on shares (on other peoples' farms) and cut hay and plowed at night by the lights of his tractor, yet he never got ahead. He borrowed from loan companies and Production Credit to keep his old machinery "cobbled up," and did not get out of debt until he retired from farming and sold most of his equipment and acreage. Driving a bread truck and then a school bus hadn't helped him.

"You can't run a farm and work out," he told me, for our hay harvest was often interrupted by his school bus schedule. He told me I'd be ahead with a five acre place: enough room for a garden, some chickens, a steer or a pig. That's what he wanted towards the end, a small place in Harrisonville neighbored by the people he had gone to school with.

I learned quickly that I couldn't even make a subsistence living farming, and that I especially couldn't afford either the money or the time to engage in a soil building, organic program. The first Arab oil embargo struck during our first year on the farm. No sooner did we get cleaned up from the largest flood anyone had seen in the holler in fifty-six years (as far back as Weber Wood's memory went) than the price of not only oil and gas, but machine parts and hardware skyrocketed. At the hardware stores in Athens, the price lists of nuts and bolts would be marked in black magic marker, "All prices double." A few weeks later, "All prices triple." That crisis and the economy of scale put a lot of farmers in southeast Ohio out of business. Larger farms became smaller; ranch homes and trailers appeared in what used to be tillable fields. "Commerical Property For Sale" signs appeared in fields of ripe corn on the outskirts of Athens.

I hoped to get a little ahead selling eggs, hay, extra produce, but the best I ever did was break even. Still, there was a lot of satisfaction in knowing just how fresh the food was on the table. Egg yolks were a bright golden color and had taste, unlike the runny pale eggs sold in town. Lettuce, tomatoes, corn, early potatoes straight from the garden couldn't be equaled. And chicken and beef tasted like what I remembered from my childhood when my mother went to the butcher. He'd put on a fur coat, go to the freezer and return with a slab of his shoulder which he'd saw and trim for her; pullets hung by their feet and my mother would pick one and pay ten cents to an old man sitting on a stool to pluck it.

Butchering was the most somber of farm chores. Ernest and Norman Wood did the neighborhood butchering, having learned from their father, Weber, who had learned from his father-in-law.

Weber, who wasn't much over five feet, could drop a steer in a field and hand it from a limb. Ernest and Norman did only half the job and always worked as a team. Norman shot the animal, Ernest stuck it, and then one carved the upper half and one the lower. Each time the same. Weber was always along to supervise and tease, laughing aside to me how these boys (who were each old enough to be my father) could do only half the job. But the joking came later, when the carcass was hung and the job well under way.

The slaughter was performed with great seriousness not only to avoid injuries a dying animal could inflict in its death throes, but also to cause the animal minimal pain. I always admired Norman's patience how long he would sight down the barrel of the .22 rifle until he could place the shot exactly between the eyes, into the part of the brain that would kill instantly.

At times, waiting for the blood to drain, Ernest or Norman would say to me, as I watched the fallen animal thrash and kick, "It's just nerves—it don't feel anymore."

We took care not to make pets out of our livestock unlike our first next door neighbors who forced their six-year old daughter to eat Wilbur, their pig. Yet, Susan named our first calf "Beef-O"—a supposed impersonal designation. It was hard to see him go. But it was sad for me also to participate in the butchering of other unnamed steers who had followed me back into fenced pasture when I summoned them with a bucket of molasses-sweetened grain, or who came trotting off the hill in the evening when I turned the lights on in the barn.

Despite their lack of names, they didn't lack personalities. And these personalities weren't altered by neutering. In fact, I left my last little group of young bulls intact. They were a sweet-tempered group I called "my little bully boys." That's how I greeted them when they clattered into the barn for their ground feed, how I called to them in the caves when I hadn't seen them during the dog days of August. 'Good-by bully boys,' I thought, when I helped Owen Smith load them into the back of his stock truck bound for the weekly auction; after I began working in Columbus I could no longer keep my fence in repair.

The most ornery calf I had was a white-faced heifer that joined the bully boys into the back of Owen's truck. I bought the calf at the Athens stock sale and hauled her home in my International pick-up with an oak rack I built for it. An eleven year old boy on the loading dock played stock jockey and helped me load her. Though I tied the calf to the rack, she'd banged and bruised her head. When I got home she bolted, from the injury, I thought. She jumped the gate and headed up the meadow toward Johnny Morris's trailer. When I drove her back through the gate she jumped the fence by the chicken house and climbed to the top of the hill. This time I shut her in the barn. I understood then why a Hereford as clean and square-shouldered as this one was sold at the stock sale.

Our kitchen faced the barn, and that evening while doing the supper dishes Susan called me to the window. "Wait," she said. In a moment the cow's white face and hoofs appeared in the window of the stall and then disappeared. In another moment her face and half her torso appeared, fell back, and on the next try she plunged through the window, fell to the ground and was gone.

I told Weber how this heifer could not be contained by any fence or even in the barn and he replied, "Fox, what you need is a fork-ed stick to make a yoke." We then went across his driveway into my woods and cut a Y-shaped branch. We wrapped smooth, galvanized wire across the Y and went to get the calf, which stood across the road in the hay meadow, at the edge of the creek, staring at Johnny's trailer. We got her back to the barn, locked her in a stanchion, placed the yoke around her neck, tightened the wire, and she never got out of the barn again. Of course, I couldn't let her pasture, for she could still jump fence even if she couldn't wriggle through or under it.

Though I stopped raising beef cattle and missed seeing the calves up behind Johnny's trailer or silhouetted on the hill above the chicken house when I came home from work, I continued to raise what a friend used to call "an Appalachian garden," and raised baby chicks from my own eggs. I placed setting hens and about a dozen eggs in a cage I built from a motorcycle crate and covered with chicken wire. After losing a dozen chicks to minks once, I re-covered the cage with sturdier welded wire with finer spacing, which kept the rodents out, except for the coon or possum that tromped in the door once, killed the chicks and hen and escaped.

Possoms were rough on my full grown chickens, getting so desperate that one early dawn I saw a possom pull a rooster from a high limb of a dead elm. I took my 12-gauge to those rodents at every opportunity. My dogs wouldn't go near them. Once I found one at the dog food on the back porch. The blast scattered bits of ceramic bowl and possom pieces throughout the yard. I found paws at the edge of the garden weeks later.

I did not like having to take life, especially those oldest of mammals—one of Josh's books said they dated back to the time of the dinosaurs. Yet I also saw what those teeth, which were really part of their palates, did to chickens.

Groundhogs weren't as bad, but they could take a winter's worth of corn in not very much time. Traveler, our aged coon hound, had a last fling two summers before he died toothless at the age of 16. That summer he averaged two or three groundhogs a week. Knight, the black Lab who followed him, wasn't as good a hunter, but if you brought him in range, he'd pounce. He just didn't have the taste for groundhogs that Traveler had, who let them cure for several days before dining.

Johnny and Mandy Morris, who owned our place for over forty years, had been excellent gardeners and ran the garden clear up to the back of the house. When I bought the farm, the garden had been cut back to allow for more yard. I didn't need all that space, still, I gardened as close to the creek as I could, and substantially improved the soil in the lower half.

Weeds were my worst problem. I'd let pigweed and lambs quarters go to seed—I couldn't be out there every dawn with a hoe like the retired folks—and after a week of rain, the potatoes would be shadowed by a stand of timber. Josh had become pretty good with a hatchet from helping me split kindling and cut water willows, and he and I attacked the barky stems. It was hard to find the potatoes even among the remaining stalks.

Josh helped me dig as well as plant potatoes. He didn't even come up to my knee the first year he joined me in the garden. Later he raised his own corn and pumpkins. One year his was the only corn we ate and froze—coons and groundhogs got mine after Knight died. Josh was handy at shucking corn too, learning when he was three. Jessica joined me in the garden about the time Josh lost interest. She was a natural with a child's hoe just the right size for her, and she helped me plant lettuce, radishes, carrots, cucumbers and corn. She's had her own garden spot too, and raised some fine lettuce and green peppers.

Extremes of weather etched and defined our experience on the farm. After the first of two harsh winters, summers stayed drier longer. We bought an automatic washer after Josh was born and our demand was more than our old dug well would stand. Kenneth Welch and his son or son-in-law took turns hauling us a thousand gallons of water every few days. Since the well held less than five hundred gallons, I pumped the extra into a homemade cinder block cistern. A thousand gallons never lasted as long as I thought it should. Confident the cistern was still reasonably full, I'd stand soaped up under the shower only to have it sputter mud.

When the city water came in, Susan insisted we buy tap. One neighbor was even going to pay for my tap and install my water line, so that I would allow the right-of-way through my meadow; he needed the city water for his swimming pool. I allowed the right-of-way without accepting his offer, but insisted that one of the several springs in the bank across the road could be cultivated, and when the oil company that drilled our gas well returned to landscape the well-site, they dug out my spring for me. I ran the water line to the house in the same trench as the gas line, and despite the automatic washer and some of the most extensive dry spells I'd seen, we never again needed to have water hauled.

Our last water hauler was Felix Alkire, who would bring his wife to visit when he came with water. We sat on lawn chairs about the well. Ernest joined us once and he and Felix exchanged stories about Europe during World War II long after the well was filled.

We experienced our harshest winters on the farm in 1977 and 1978, when temperatures regularly dropped to twenty below. It took ingenuity and forethought to keep our vehicles running. Our fuel oil to the furnace gelled regularly, and our water froze as well. We made good use of the wood stove.

That first winter, I made the mistake of chasing my heifers who roamed onto my first next door neighbor's place in search of their bull, when they (the neighbors) defied country ethics by keeping a bull in a field with line fence. After running a few paces, I found myself short of breath, unable to breathe. I was gasping deeply for air as I made it through the back door.

That same winter, a sudden weather change caused the most unusual and lovely natural phenomenon I had ever seen. It occurred in February of 1977. Snow already lay on the ground. During the day the surface of the snow had been warmed, but that night it turned cold suddenly and strong winds blew blizzard-like flurries. As I drove home from pre-natal class, I thought I saw dark shapes in the brief moonlight rolling down the hills along the highway. As I approached home, I continued to see shadowy activity on the hills and the bottoms in between the flurries. Next morning I awoke to see the meadows filled with a variety of huge doughnuts and cylinders made of snow, and in the bright sunlight, I could see the tracks made by these natural sculptures as they formed.

Often I was out on the road in the winter storms. I kept my best log chain and a set of tire chains in the back of my truck, and made good use of both. The log chain pulled me out of drifts if I delayed putting on my chains. The worst storm I encountered occured in February of 1985, when my flight to Harrisburg was cancelled and I attempted to drive home from Port Columbus airport. I phoned Susan and we still had electricity. The storm hadn't yet arrived with full force in that part of the state. What normally was a two hour trip took over six hours. Most of Route 33 was one open lane of frozen slush. Hours after I started, when I arrived at the south end of Athens hoping to stop for coffee, the entire town was blacked out. The remainder of the trip was dark, except for my headlights and an occasional candle or kerosene lamp in a window.

When I couldn't make it up over carry-out hill, two neighbors came out with flashlights to help me put on my tire chains. I was an exhausted wreck by then and welcomed their aid. Without TV to watch, they were grateful for the activity.

Our electric power was off for three days from that storm. We were able to get fresh spring water from the gravity-fed hydrant I had installed in the yard, and we stayed in the kitchen with the gas oven on; our chimney could no longer handle wood.

Such battles with the weather were not insurmountable, but they seemed to add years. I understood better what it was like to survive in earlier times, and how the details of one's survival presented a day-to-day challenge. Such winters gave further importance to the first appearance of crocuses; I understood fully why Mandy had planted a growing season full of flowers that bloomed successively in unexpected places.

It took me two years to decide to leave the farm and the actual move was harder than I anticipated. It was a departure made more sad by the death of Ernest's wife Maudie Ethel, a month before we moved. Weeks later, Ernest too died suddenly.

I'm as comfortable in Columbus as I hoped to be. I was raised in a small walkup apartment in Brooklyn, in a better neighborhood than where my immigrant parents had lived before, across the street from the hospital where I was born. Yet, when I round the curve by Johnny's trailer, pass Weber's old place, painted and re-molded by its new owners, then see my barn, and the house with its slate roof and bright green flashings, I know it will remain in my mind as the home place.

Jim Galbraith (HARTLAND)

JEFF GUNDY

INQUIRY INTO THE "NEAREST OF THE ENERGIES OF THE UNIVERSE AND THE GREATEST WITHIN THE RANGE OF MAN'S NEEDS"

"I have spent my whole life in various parts of the Midwest: Illinois as a child, to Indiana for college, then to Kansas for four years of teaching before moving here to Bluffton, Ohio." Like most of our writers, he is also a widely published poet. His last chapbook "Surrendering to the Real Things" (1986) was published by Pikestaff Press. He has also been awarded a writing fellowship by the Ohio Arts Council.

In "Inquiry into the 'Nearest of the Energies of the Universe and the Greatest within the Range of Man's Needs,'" he has created an "Inquiry," his own essay form, perhaps best described under the open 'prose poem' form. In a series of journal type entries he moves us through experience toward a human understanding of the nature of fire. In the process—and the inquiring process is part of his content—emerges the importance of our place sense and the threat we pose to it. It is a moving and provacative piece, and one that enlarges our sense of place and the essay form.

INQUIRY INTO THE "NEAREST OF THE ENERGIES OF THE UNIVERSE AND THE GREATEST WITHIN THE RANGE OF MAN'S NEEDS"

"Wind and water are also primitive approaches to natural energies, but these change nothing while fire is a transforming agent."
—Walter Hough, *Fire as an Agent in Human Culture*

And the men?
They voted against
themselves again
and for fire...
fire
which voted for blackened stumps
and no more elections.
—Leonard Nathan, *"The Election"*

1.
It's the great fact of modern time, though mostly it happens out of sight. Remember visiting the coal-fired plants in junior high, riding on the school bus, sharing sack lunches, being led around through gray noisy forests of metal by a testy man in a hardhat? The great conveyors, the mountains of coal, the statistics, you and your friends oohing predictably in between trying to make wisecracks that would impress the cutest girls? Did they let you see into the firechambers? Did they talk about wind patterns and particulate matter? Did it occur to you that some things had not been discussed? Not to me.

2.
In the summer of '73 a guy I worked with at the sash and door factory somehow decided I had agreed to go with him to see the nuke plant at Benton Harbor one Sunday. He woke me up banging on the door of the dark apartment in the converted church where I lived and it took me fifteen minutes to convince him that I hadn't said I would go and didn't intend to. They have a nice picnic area, he said, it'll be a nice drive. I went back to my girlfriend.

3.
Uncle Vernon splashed something on the charcoal and struck a match. Get back, he said, then when I barely moved, Get *Back!* He let the match drop and the gasoline burst outward like a hot flower living at ten times our speed. Oh, I said.

4.
The use of smoke in worship, I learn, "seems to have arisen from the observation that this ghostly element of combustion dissolved in the air, thus supplying a messenger to the unseen." The message turns out to be more practical and direct than we thought; God may be sniffing and noticing out there somewhere, but the agitated molecules bouncing back into the biosphere, shifting the jet stream and the Pacific currents, are what cut the cake.

5.
The green letters appear on the screen like elementals summoned from the void, obedient only because I know their names. I shuffle and demand them, bored, using them like wrenches and screwdrivers. If I could track them back through the chips and processors, wires and transformers and lines strung across the dry fields like kite string wrapped on a ball, I would discover what I have lacked all my life, I would disappear willingly in the pure blaze. I know I would.

6.
The small exhaustions of the corn and soybeans should not fret me so. They have no interest in me, I have no power to help them. It's only this grim need to imagine the world as better than it is. A very loud crow demands most of my attention for a few moments, then a circling fly. Through the trees I see only a flat blue chunk of sky, giving up nothing of the stars behind it. Things die or persevere everywhere I know. Today, right now, I choose to sit in the shadow on the bank, but the dragonflies choose the sun and the river, and the fly chooses me.

7.
The latest theory, or so I hear, is that the oil and gas we claim to own are not prehistoric plants and animals cooked into black soup but leftovers of the earliest days of the earth, gathered in their pockets as the hot rock was cooling. There may be more than we ever dreamed. We may be able to keep the lights burning longer than we thought.

8.
The other latest theory is that the CO_2 piling up from all our burning is already changing everything, that we had better act fast if we don't want Saharas in Ohio and North Dakota, that we should leave the petroproducts in the ground and learn the "economy of fuel characteristic of uncivilized man." Try selling that to adolescent American males on Friday night.

9.
The farmers in Manitoba can look forward to planting early. Sooner than later we are able to change things we never dreamed. If we want to we can funnel Lake Michigan down the Mississippi to float barges or spray all of Texas from the air. Of course nothing is free. The doubters claim that the smoke of all our fires is circling and gathering like a great burning-glass, trying us in our own heat to see if we will take a temper.

10.
Say then that the gloomy ones are right about something, say the old weather we complained about so steadily turns out to be more and not less than we should have expected. Even so. We will not all die tomorrow. This could be the best and the last chance to change, as we have known we must change without accepting it for a long time. It could shake us out of our tedious and prodigal self-absorption, give us something to fight besides each other.

11.
Can we learn to love the earth with something approaching intelligence? Can we put the strength we have to work instead of blowing it up or burying it in silos like fatal treasure? Can we begin to trace the shining single net of things with fingers tender and alert enough to pull no thread loose to dangle, to walk light enough that the grasses lift themselves still whole behind our feet? Ah, we can.

12.
We have no choice but to think we can. It is not the war we expected. But it is the war the world has been trying to teach us to fight for thousands of years, and we are the enemy and the footsoldiers and the generals, and to win we must defeat ourselves first. We can learn to burn less, to burn clean, we can learn that when the smoke rises it does not just go away, we can learn the words it carries and make them say what we mean.

Winter Barn, Hoopeston, Illinois. Roger Pfingston

CRAIG HERGERT

BUT BABY IT'S COLD OUTSIDE: MEMORIES OF MINNESOTA WINTERS

Craig Hergert is a young writer from Slayton, Minnesota now teaching at Bowling Green State University in Ohio. His articles appear regularly in area publications, always with his understanding of the particular and his friendly humor. He has also worked as a stand-up comedian, folk singer, and song writer. His commitment to peace and justice often results in some pointed satire.

In "But Baby It's Cold Outside..." he ties past and present in a portrait of Minnesotan cold that is warmed by his cheerful nostalgia.

BUT BABY IT'S COLD OUTSIDE: MEMORIES OF MINNESOTA WINTERS

> Winter is icummen in,
> Leyden's sing Goddamm,
> Raineth drop and staineth slop,
> And how the wind doth ramm!
> Sing: Goddamm.
> Ezra Pound—"Ancient Music."

According to the *Encyclopedia Brittanica,* the name for winter comes from an old Germanic word meaning "time of water." Leave it to the Germans to goof up a name. The folks who should have been charged with naming the season between fall and spring are the Minnesotans. Minnesotans learn about winter the old-fashioned way: they survive it. I have survived twenty-four Minnesota winters, and I think two dozen is quite enough, so for the past four years I've been wintering in Ohio. You can't really call Ohio's postfall/pre-spring season *winter.* To be accurate, you'd have to call it a winter sampler. You find out what winter is like in Ohio, but you really don't experience a whole one. In Minnesota, however, a person can experience the real thing.

> If winter comes, can spring be far behind?
> Percy Byshe Shelley—"Ode to the West Wind"

If Shelley had asked that question in Minnesota, he would have been laughed out of the state. Spring can be and is far behind winter in Minnesota. Forget about that December 22 to March 21 nonsense. In Minnesota winter officially begins after the World Series and ends, God willing, some time in April. The two worst winters I lived through were in 1968, when I was 12 years old, and 1982, when I had lived through enough cold weather to think I didn't mind it. I was wrong. I still minded it plenty. During the winter of '81-'82, Minneapolis, where I lived at the time, got ninety-nine inches of snow. *Ninety-nine inches.* When I first heard that, I was rooting for one more inch so that we could boast about hitting the century mark, but the truth is I didn't want one more inch. I didn't want one more flake. Ever again.

Even worse than the amount of snow that winter, was the wind chill. Minnesotans are obsessed with wind chill in the winter the way we Ohioans are with humidity in the summer. "It's not the heat, it's the humidity," we'll explain to out-of-state visitors who stand sweltering before us, not caring what the exact cause of their discomfort is. Wind-chill refers to what the temperature feels like because of a good, stiff Northern wind regardless of what the bank thermometer says the temperature is. When I was home for Christmas break in December of '83, the temperature one night was twenty below, which, as a native Minnesotan, I laugh at—if, that is, my long-johns are on and the furnace is running. The wind-chill, though, was *ninety below zero*. I don't laugh at those numbers, even as a native Minnesotan.

My earliest winter memory is from when I was about five years old. My two-year-old sister, Kristi, and I were all bundled up and playing in the backyard. I have no idea what we could have been doing that would have been considered playing since I remember being awfully cold, but Mom said, "Go out and play," so we went out and moved around and figured that would satisfy her. Although my memory of this event is sketchy, I know that something went wrong. Kristi got hurt or upset or something and wanted me to take her back in. As I headed her for the steps of the house, I remember seeing the tears on her cheek turn to ice. When I saw that happen, I got her in the house *real* fast. For all I knew, other parts of her—or of me, for that matter—were going to be next.

It's probably quite telling that most of my specific memories of winter are positive. The negative ones, even the ones from the most severe winters, seem to have all melted together like a pile of April slush. The positive memories, meanwhile, remain as distinct as a snowflake.

The most joyous part of winter for a kid was school closings. I remember the night I saw my first episode of *Hawaii Five-O*. My parents were down the block at a friend's house, and there was a genuine Minnesota blizzard raging outside the picture window. My older sister, Sandy, a veteran of four more winters than I, made her prediction: "There's no way there's going to be school tomorrow." Few words ever sounded as beautiful to a twelve-year-old who hadn't yet finished the next day's fraction problems. We stayed up until ten—unheard of at the time—and I watched in wonder as, ten feet from the window and the storm, McGarret and Danno ran around Hawaii in short sleeves.

School closings were a special occasion, not just for me, but for my whole family. They meant that my dad, a sixth-grade English teacher, would be around for the whole day. And they meant that we would have potato pancakes with the elementary school principal. I have no idea how this family tradition started. On the morning of a school closing, Dad would call Paul Olson, the principal, and invite him over for a potato pancake lunch. Mr. Olson would accept, and Mom would spend the next hour converting a bag of potatoes into a mound of shreds. Mr. Olson, a small man with surprisingly explosive laugh, would arrive around 11:30 and sit in the dining room talking to Dad while my sisters and I were in the living room, watching the game shows that school normally denied us. Meanwhile, Mom was in the kitchen frying four potato pancakes at a time and bringing them out to the dining room as fast as they were ready. To me, potato pancakes with apple sauce and Paul Olson's laughter on the side were as much a part of winter as overshoes and parkas.

My foundest school closing, though, happened in the spring of 1968. The night before, there had been a freezing rain and by morning the roads were completely frozen over. Since it would have been dangerous for the busses to be out, school was closed. But around ten o'clock something wonderful happened: spring arrived on that very day. With the sun shining and the temperature mild, I ran outside to cash in on this free day of recreation and saw something I'll never forget. Because the streets were still covered with ice, there were no cars out, but there were kids out. Kids, a half dozen of them, from the other side of town were ice-skating on the street. It was like watching a pint-sized version of the Ice Capades.

In seed time learn, in harvest teach, in winter enjoy. William Blake—"Proverbs of Hell."

Those kids who skated on the street were merely responding to an instinct all Minnesotans have—the instinct to not only survive winter, but to conquer it. The cold doesn't keep kids indoors. When Mother asks, "Don't you want to go out and play?" the kid wouldn't think of saying "Are you kidding? In that cold?" The kid is out. The kid can handle the big chill. I expressed that instinct a little differently than most Northerners. Most of the kids could skate, and so they spent as much time as they could out on the town skating rink. Not me. I had skates, of course. Not to have skates would have been as unnatural as not having feet. So when I was ten, my parents bought me a pair of brown ones with thick, imposing blades. My ankles, though, refused to cooperate. They would both collapse, simultaneously, so that the blades were no longer on the ice but parallel to it, and my legs, following my ankles' lead, fanned out like Jerry Lewis's. Scott Hamilton I wasn't. But a Minnesotan I was, and so I still was attracted to the ice. Despite giving up on skates when I was ten, I played hockey when I was thirteen. As I recall I was the only hockey player who wore boots. Wayne Gretzky I wasn't either.

What I did enjoy was ice fishing, a winter sport which has more to do with winter than sport and more to do with ice than fishing. When I was fifteen and singing in the church choir, Earl Devine, a middle-aged basso profundo, adopted me as his ice fishing partner. Sundays after church he'd pick me up, outfit me with a snowmobile suit and fishing boots, and take me to Lake Shetek where we would stand in the middle of the lake for five or six hours, usually without the benefit of a fish house. Earl would drill a hole in the ice with a hand auger while I watched. For me, scrawny fifteen-year-old, to have handled the task would have meant the loss of an hour's fishing time. It took Earl only ten grueling minutes. The hole drilled, we could fish, sort of. Winter turns every aspect of fishing into a challenge—hooking a fish, and, especially, waiting in between the first aspect and the second.

Usually we wouldn't catch more than a dozen perch and after a couple of hours on the surface of the lake, they looked the way I felt, coated by a thin layer of ice. Once in a while, though, we caught something more, and that would keep us heading back, Sunday after Sunday. I remember one time when, my patience wearing thin, I had just about decided to sit in the car for awhile to warm up. Just then my bobber, barely visible since the sun had gone down a couple of hours ago, sank like a stone. Grabbing my sawed-off fishing pole, I was ice-fisherman enough to know that this was no perch. Seeing my commotion, Earl came over to help. After a few minutes of struggle, we pulled it out of the ice—a five pound northern pike. I was so proud I didn't notice what Earl noticed immediately. The northern was wrapped up in my line, but wasn't attached to my hook. It was attached to Earl's. We decided to chalk it up as an interception.

Earl and I had one more outing that winter, no northerns this time, just the dozen medium-sized perch. Then spring came, as it finally does, even in Minnesota, and we had to put away the ice fishing gear. But we didn't put the gear *far* away. In Minnesota, if spring comes, can winter really be far behind?

Bill Schnell

DIANE KENDIG

ON HOME SICKNESS AND HERE-SICKNESS AND THE LONGING FOR BUCKEYES

"I began in Ohio./ I still dream of home," Diane Kendig quotes fellow Ohio poet James Wright. She herself began in Canton, Ohio, studied at Otterbein College in Westerville, then taught at Cleveland State University and now Findlay College in the middle of the state. Her work as a writer-in-the-schools has taken her to all grade levels, kindergarten to graduate school, and into prison classrooms. Her English and Spanish training and her interest in human rights has lead to her book of translations, *"And a Pencil to Write your Name": Poems from the Nicaraguan Poetry Workshop* (1987). Her own book of poems appeared as *A Tunnel of Flute Song* (1980) from the Cleveland State University Poetry Center.

Writing from Santa Cruz, California, where midwesterners are likely to suffer from too much sun, she draws herself back through her place sense. She adopts an informal tone and a loose structure here to some very definite and personal truths. Like Garrison Keillor, the midwestern storyteller whom she praises, Kendig sews together a color quilt of good talk and sense and produces a warm yet realistic tribute to the places we each carry within.

ON HOMESICKNESS AND "HERE"-SICKNESS AND THE LONGING FOR BUCKEYES

I am writing this essay from Santa Cruz, California, where I am working for five weeks before returning home to Ohio. My desk here faces a hill topped with a redwood forest full of deer that glide into clearings and onto lawns at sunset. Some nights they hang out in the parking lot of the Bay Tree Bookstore up on the hill, for all the world like 17 year old kids hanging out smoking, trading stories about humans. From that hill at noon when the fog burns off, I can see the whole town, and beyond it, the ocean that spreads like a full blue skirt, furling and unfurling its white slip. Down there on the Boardwalk and the town mall some wonderful characters hang out, comfortable as the deer, and so colorful and loose, so jangling-jewelried with their guitars and petitions and songs. I walk among them, feeling like a *Prairie Home Companion* character miswritten into a psychedelic cartoon.

Despite the positive charm of this place, I miss my friends and my parents. I miss my Scottie, Emma, and our daily summer runs in the woods. I am homesick as hell, not for the first time in my life.

I was homesick for the first time at age ten when I went away to Camp Wanake, 47 minutes from home, for five and a half days. Even now when I read of children packed off to camp for the whole summer, my mind reels. I know that I would have died of grief at age ten if camp had lasted even one more day.

And not that I hadn't ever been away from home before. We had taken family vacations to Niagara Falls—where—Mom and Dad had gone on their honeymoon, to the Smokey Mountains, and, on one particularly long haul, to Florida, through all those strange Southern states where watermelons were 10 for a dollar and restrooms were labelled, "Whites," "Coloreds," and "Indians," a system that confounded us, especially since my father couldn't explain why it existed.

Otherwise all our vacations were pretty jolly. We were all together as a family, though, so the line between home and away never came clear for me then. I recall that for days after our return to our brick bungalow in Canton, my mother would say repeatedly, "Isn't it good to be home?" And my father would say, "It sure is."

Out of that Golden Age of Kendig-hood, I crossed the line to Camp Wanake and came to be known for generations of campers as "the most homesick kid" they had ever seen, even though I liked the place. It was full of wonderful, caring counselors, kids who were rather kind, and fun times. I was a model camper who learned all the routines and maintained my cheer. I also cried a lot. Huge, quiet tears rolled down my cheeks through meals and mail, through songfest and campfires, and I could no more stop them than I could stop the waves of nausea when we sang the third verse of "For the Beauty of the Earth":

> For the joy of human love:
> Brother, Sister, parent, child;
> Friends on earth and friends above,
> For all gentle thoughts and mild.

As a matter of fact, the songleader learned by mid-week to avoid that song altogether.

"I'm okay, I'm okay," I insisted to the counselors who tried to comfort me, to my mother, who, learning of my tears, said I would never have to go to camp again.

"But I want to go, Mom," I said. "I wasn't 'here'-sick, I was homesick."

My family ever after tried to maintain that distinction. "Heresick" is really hating where you are; "homesick" is missing home. "Heresick" is a darned shame; "homesick" is just natural, what you get from being from a home worth missing.

Occasionally I still experience homesickness in that all-encompassing way that I first experienced at age ten. More often I have the little twinges of absence. But when the real thing hits—the hurt to the bone, the blues of distance, the odds of presence, the huge surf of nausea—there is only one cure: a long, hard cry.

I had one of those cries here in Santa Cruz, 28 years after my first bout of homesickness, hundreds of trips away from home later. It was a long, self-indulgent crying jag that went on till 2 a.m. when I realized my husband's discomfort was exceeding my comfort. And besides, I was cried dry, the two weeks' tension in my shoulders was washed away by then.

During all this unhappiness in Santa Cruz, depsite all my happiness here, I have pondered a quote from Kim Stafford in his book *Having Everything Right: Essays of Place:* "Pascal said a strange thing: the sole cause of human unhappiness is our inability to remain quietly at home in our rooms." And I have to admit that it is my inability to remain quietly in my rooms which has led to my current state of homesickness. It led me, too, to Spain, where I felt as home as I do in Ohio. And it led me to Louisiana, a place as strange to me as North Africa was, only I fell in love in Louisiana with the man I would later marry—back in Ohio where declaring love felt safer than it did in the streets of New Orleans.

Certainly one way to avoid unhappiness is the saint's way of never leaving one's room. I've never learned that way, at least not yet. I keep leaving to find this longing for home that leads me back to remain again quietly at home in my rooms. And when I return, I hear my parents' voice in my head: "Isn't it good to be home? It sure is."

Besides, as Dorothy learned, there is nothing like the trip to Oz for making Kansas look a whole lot better.

Last March on a flight to St. Louis I read an article that concluded that the Midwest is not a place but a state of mind. It seems that a James Shortridge has polled 2,000 university students on the question of exactly which states constitute the Midwest. Curiously enough, students from Ohio, Indiana, and Michigan considered those three states to be part of the Midwest while students from *outside* the three states did not consider them to be part of the Midwest.

Stunned by the idea that I might not be a Midwesterner, I set about with my own poll of Missourians, beginning with my cab driver who told me he was a native of St. Louis.

"I just read an article that says no one agrees on which states are in the Midwest," I told him. "Which states do *you* consider part of the Midwest?"

"Well, I don't know the answer to *that*," he answered me in the rearview mirror, "but I'll tell you what I do know. I lived in Arkansas once, and it is not the Midwest. And St. Louis is."

That made a lot of sense to me, but when I told the story to my friends from Illinois, they laughed and said, "St. Louis isn't the Midwest."

Maybe St. Louis is not the Midwest, and I have given up asking what constitutes the Midwest, but that cab driver is right about at least one thing: we leave home to know it; we miss it in order to love it. There is nothing like coming home to the real home after living for months with the memory of home.

I still remember walking in the back door after my first time away at camp. The old familiar rooms and furniture were imbued with a magical strangeness, as though I had dreamed them all my life and suddenly woke to find them outside the dream. That second waking is more wonderful than the first. Kansas rivals Oz and wins. Our small home became so precious I never took it for granted again. When I returned from college at age 19, from Europe at 21, from Mexico after only two weeks just last summer, home reverberated for me with all the newness and nearness that Calderon's Segismundo must have known when he woke and declared life a dream, "and even dreams themselves are dreams." The prison or the palace—if only he could be sure which one was his home, he could wake up.

"I began in Ohio,/I still dream of home," James Wright once wrote. The annual James Wright Poetry Festival takes place in the poet's hometown of Martin's Ferry, Ohio, each spring when the dogwoods and fruit trees and maples are surprising the hills of the southeast end of our state with pinks, chartreuses, and creamy whites. One year for the festival someone stamped those two lines by Wright onto a t-shirt and sold them, and though I never wore a t-shirt before, I bought and wear that one. I wore it to the grocery store here in Santa Cruz the other day.

"Oh, are you from Ohio?" the clerk asked, reading my shirt. "Say, you're never going to want to go home, are you?"

Most Californians are so rightfully proud of their state, and it would be rude of me to tell one of my hosts that I already want to go home, so I smile and say, "It certainly is beautiful here."

"Yes, this is paradise," he says.

But I dream of another paradise where I'll be in a few weeks, enriched by memories of the redwood, elephant seal, and deer I've grown to love. Meanwhile I long for the relief of being able to remain quietly at home in my rooms and in my woods awhile, running there with my dog Emma through the Buckeyes and the pine.

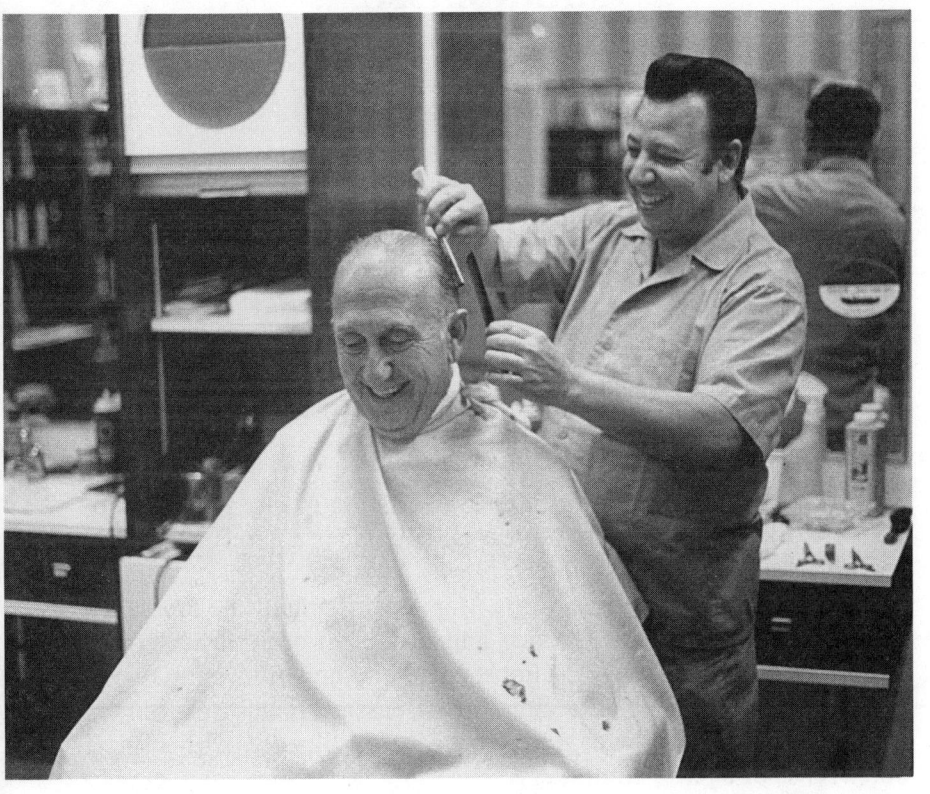

Rino Dovico and Customer. Mark Masse

MARK MASSE

THE CHAIR-SIDE HISTORY OF A MASTER CRAFTSMAN

Mark Masse is a young freelance writer from Rocky River, Ohio, whose works have begun to appear widely. He is a careful reporter, yet one who warms to his subject.

In "The Chair-side History of a Master Craftsman" he presents a nostalgic tribute to Rino Dovico and his Lakewood barbershop. . ."There is a Rino Dovico in almost every city and village in Ohio." Masse reveals how this once male rite-of-passage remains, if only in memory, as an experience where practicality blended with respect and a sense of ageless comradery.

THE CHAIR-SIDE HISTORY
OF A MASTER CRAFTSMAN

When I enter Rino Dovico's barbershop, he is in his usual spot crafting a customer's curly locks with the pride of a sculptor. His straight, shiny black hair is neatly combed, powder-blue barber's smock crisply pressed, black pants creased, shoes polished. The dark Mediterranean eyes are riveted while the glistening cutting shears click away with artistic precision.

It takes a few moments for Rino to realize I have arrived. But then he glances up, his full fortyish face warms with a smile of recognition, and he welcomes me with a nod and a simple, "Hi."

Rino's shop is clean and plainly furnished, well lighted and comfortable. I take a seat and wait my turn in one of the five faded green chairs with the chrome armrests. In front of me is the narrow table with the neat stacks of Sport magazines, a Golf Digest, Crain's Cleveland Business and the day's newspaper. Two empty antique ashtray holders flank the table. A pile of Playboys is stashed in a cubbyhole adjacent to the coat rack.

Mirrors dominate the walls that also display a hand-lettered price chart, a master barber's license and the latest Ridgid Tool Calendar pin-up girl. A small shelf with hair care products, a dark, silent portable television and an ancient cash register fill the far corner of the shop.

Adjacent to Rino's work station are two empty barber chairs, evidence of past partners from earlier, more hectic times. Easy-listening music flows softly from a radio as Rino makes small talk with one of his long-time customers—a gray-haired gent who returns monthly for a clean-up trim and a few minutes of honest conversation, part of the timeless tradition of Dovico's barbershop and others like it.

Rino Dovico is a modern man with an old-fashioned work ethic, a craftsman in an age of slick, superficial service.

Like other proud trades of the past, barbering is being replaced by trendy enterprises. Uni-sex salons have begun to dominate a scene once claimed by storefront shops with familiar, swirling, red-and-white barber poles.

The creeping displacement of the traditional barber reflects broader trends of the times. We live in an age of unseen "Super" supermarket butchers, harried department store tailors and part-time house painters. And when the meat is fatty, the seams come apart and the paint peels, the attitude is "take it or leave it." That's just the way it is.

That isn't the way it is with Rino and the vanishing breed of fellow tradesmen who consistently deliver a good product and so rightfully deserve praise and patronage.

There is a Rino Dovico in almost every city and village in Northeast Ohio. Mostly, they didn't graduate from barber college yesterday.

Rino's haircutting craft has been honed over two decades. He is a master barber who is at ease cutting short or long hair, the close trim or the shag cut. According to Rino, most of his customers come to him because they have hard-to-cut, problem hair.

"I make them look good," he says confidently. "Even the mayor comes here because he can't get his hair cut right anywhere else."

The folk who frequent Rino's shop are mostly a mature crowd. Younger men and teenagers typically go elsewhere, unless they need "an important haircut," such as for a job interview. Those fortunate customers who routinely return to Rino are treated to lively conversation, an occasional enchanting tale and an ever-ready ear.

On any given day, you're likely to overhear talk on subjects from sports and politics to real estate and romance.

A retiree, casually dressed in slacks, tennis shoes and pullover sweater, discusses selling his house and moving into a condo.

A blue-jeaned divorced husband in a blue mood shares his frustrations and anger over being separated from his kids.

A middle-aged man of great girth launches into good-natured kidding about Rino's barbering ability and his high-priced, 'You'll-be-back-in-10 days' haircuts.

Rino takes it all in stride, playing the raconteur and counselor to those who sit in his chair.

When the topic of women comes up, Rino becomes animated and his high-pitched voice begins to chatter, spiced with an Italian accent. A boyish giggle often finds its way into the conversation. As Rino tells it, back in his native Italy, he was quite the footloose, sportscar-driving, soccer-playing rogue. He loves to reminisce about his halcyon days as a nimble ladies man.

"I would never go out with just one girl at a time," he proudly recalls. "I could date three girls and have them all thinking I was going steady."

Each time I go to Rino, I learn a little more about the man.

He entered the barber trade reluctantly. As a high school student in Italy, he tried his hand at haircutting after unsuccessfully attempting auto mechanics, machine trades and carpentry. (In Europe, teenagers must take some form of vocational training during part of their summer vacation.) But, becoming a barber was the last thing on Rino's mind when he was a teen, filled with dreams of romance and soccer glory.

After being graduated from high school, he journeyed to America to join family in Cleveland, but the adjustment wasn't easy.

"When I first arrived in New York, I saw people rushing around, all the traffic and big buildings. My heart became dark," he says in an uncharacteristic, melancholy musing.

The dark days didn't last long. Rino became a plasterer on his uncle's Cleveland construction crew and began earning a living and learning American ways. He worked on construction jobs for almost a decade, until the dry-wall industry emerged and plastering became too expensive and time consuming to compete for business.

When the building contracts disappeared, Rino, by then a married man, had to seek other means of supporting a family. A friend casually mentioned he was looking for a barber to join his shop. The man could guarantee $200 a week and asked if Rino knew anyone to suggest. Rino suggested Rino.

For 18 years, Rino Dovico has owned his Lakewood Continental Barber and Styling business at 14701 Detroit Ave. The tidy shop is tucked in a corner of the first floor of a low-rise office building.

Although he has built a modestly successful business, Rino wants to guarantee more financial security for his wife and three children. He has acquired a real-estate license, taken adult-education classes and even contemplated pursuing another business career.

I began compiling my chair-side history of Rino four years ago when I stumbled upon his Yellow Pages listing. My hair-care twist of fate has been well rewarded.

As one of Rino's regulars, I get my spirits lifted while having my ears lowered. In good times and in bad, my barber has been there, sharing talk, laughter and more. A year ago, he even helped with some needed grooming advice for the groom.

"You come in about two weeks before your wedding," he said, deftly sidestepping the hair drier cord with athletic grace, "then a trim the day before. I'll make you look like a movie star when you get your ball and chain."

There are other, more mystical payoffs for visiting Rino Dovico's barbershop. His place is a vehicle for time travel—a setting in which memories of youth are replayed. I grew up in a town on the outskirts of New York City where the monthly barbershop visit was a treasured custom. A flat-top cost a buck and a quarter back then, and what a deal!

My brothers and I would rush off to renew acquaintances with our friendly neighborhood barbers, Sal and Dominic, while attempting sneak peaks at those forbidden fruits of puberty—the girlie books, buried like treasure among the Life and Look magazines.

Although we would certainly get scolded if we got caught in our pubescent perusing, the risk was well worth it. In retrospect, going to the barber was so highly valued because it represented one of those rare, approved expressions of boyhood independence.

After I grew up, and long before I met Rino Dovico, I took haircuts for granted. During my college years in the '70s, my hair bushed wildly and I avoided barbers altogether. Later, I turned to girlfriends for "freebies." But now, as in my youth, I look forward to my barber visits.

I like being taken care of by a man who takes pride in his craft and his customers. A sitting with Rino means more than a haircut. It's an opportunity to see a master at work, and a chance to shift gears, swap stories and savor a slice of tradition amid the ever-changing American scene.

Jim Galbraith (HARTLAND)

KAY MURPHY

THE LATHS OF MEMORY

Born in Paris, Illinois, in the midst of World War II, Kay Murphy has transplanted her Midwestern roots to other parts of the country where she has taught—Danville Community College, the University of Illinois, the University of Utah, Goddard College, and now to New Orleans where she is an associate director of the writing program at the New Orleans Center for Creative Arts.

Her first book of poetry, *The Autopsy,* appeared from Spoon River Poetry Press (1985). Her style is quiet and quick, drawing us up close to real people and places. In "The Laths of Memory," she re-enters the brave world of her grandparents and binds herself and us to their way of being—with the land.

THE LATHS OF MEMORY

*If you liked, you could call me a writer
who goes to work with a lathe.*
Robert Walser

The last image I have of my grandfather comes from the Christmas of 1986, two days before his 89th birthday. Although the heat vent had been closed over years ago, I always slept upstairs when I was home, and even though my parents lived in the same small midwest town as my grandparents, it was my grandparents' house I called home. On this particular morning I came down the stairs to find the door closed—my only resource to heat—and my grandfather sitting at the kitchen table in a fog of nicotine and staggering furnace heat. He had closed the door in order to keep the heat in the kitchen two reasons.

One was his poor circulation. He was cold in the dreadful, humid summer as well as in the dreadful, dry winter. Even during the hottest August days in Illinois my grandfather wore long white insulated underwear, top and bottoms, gray green perma press pants, and a long-sleeved plaid shirt. In the winter the pants became corduroy and the shirt, flannel, layered with a flannel-lined jacket. Over his knees draped a dirty multi-striped afghan my grandmother had knitted long ago, the one on which their pet Chihauhua slept before she died. In front of him would burn a small space heater with which the family swore he would burn down the house. But that was all in the living room in his chair with the split vinyl arms and cigarette burns. This morning he was in the kitchen, his other spot in the house, in rearch of the coffee pot, his foil-lined ash tray before him, his small open pocket knife with which he cleaned his nails, gazing up at me over the tops of his glasses because the lens were too dirty to see through. For my grandfather, and I smile as I say it, took an allergy to bathing in his last years. And although my grandmother would nag him, grab any clothes he would reluctantly remove, and throw them in the washer or the fire depending on their condition, seldom would she get him in the shower. He complained that it was cold in there and, besides, the water hurt. Sometimes Grandmother would carry the small space heater into the bathroom and turn it on an hour before his rare baths. It was on these occasions she would grab the underwear, which I'm sure always disappeared in the rusty barrel in the back yard with the trash.

The second reason my grandfather closed the door to the upstairs that very cold December morning was to save on the heat bill. My grandparents had an elaborate system of whose money went where, and although I never fully understood it nor asked about it, I gathered that my grandfather's money went to pay the utility bills. When he was younger he would walk around the house turning the lights off behind us, but as he got older he merely requested that we turn off the light in the kitchen if we were through and turn off the light in the dining room if we were through in there. My grandfather would never have to yell at us to do anything. And he certainly would not have yelled at my grandmother. It simply seemed impossible not to do what he asked, which wasn't much. On this particular December morning he had several stacks of silver in front of him. He could tell you the exact amount of money he had received for any job and the exact amount anything he ever bought cost him. My grandmother, who everybody but me thought was mean to my grandfather, gave him all of her quarters. And I was with her more than once when she asked the sales clerk to give her an extra dollar's worth of quarters. There are several secrets about my family that I think nobody else knows, and that may be one of them.

My grandfather always seemed to pick up odd jobs here and there. And I guess if he had a trade it was lathing houses. I still don't quite understand what lathing is, as I don't understand so many things about my family, but I was told that it has to do with the support of a building. Probably before such things as pre-fab hit the country. I know that he traveled around the state at times. And that he had a level, a long piece of wood with a bubble in the middle with which I used to play, holding it up to walls, down to floors, up table legs, and along door frames. My child's logic determined that his work needed precision, which would also account for his exactitude in money matters. And that the strips of laths under the wallpaper, under the stapled ceiling tiles, represented the position taken by my grandfather in his own home. For it was my grandmother who embellished the rooms, who provided the entertainment with her caustic wit and love of language, and how drew most of the love. At least from me. For it took me years, right up to my grandmother's prolonged illness and death, to realize that I was one of her few champions, that others did not think or feel about her the way I did. And even now as I write this memoir of my grandfather, it is her presence which invokes me, which shines through the darkness of my memory. But as I think back on it she was always trying to divert my attention to my grandfather. Although I confess I believe that if I had shown too much attention to my grandfather, she would have soon found a way to win me back. But she had no fear, I was here from as long as I can remember. And I set these words down now only to try to understand how my grandfather and the Midwest came into play in my life and in my imagination, the former which deserted me for death and the latter which I deserted for the South and a better job. Both of which continue to inform my life choices.

One of the ways in which I entertained my grandfather was to play gin rummy with him, the rules of which are unlike any other card game invented. A sure sign my grandfather was sick was when he wouldn't play gin rummy. My grandmother hated cards and pretended she didn't understand "deuces and trays." I heard rumors that in his younger days my grandfather was a gambler and perhaps a bit of a drinker and ladies man. I choose as most of us do what to believe and what not to believe. And my grandmother and I both believed it all to be true, although the rest of the family thought it was a manifestation of my grandmother's senility. Once when my grandmother, by all accounts, including the nurse's, who looked at me and shook her head hopelessly, was dying, she pulled me down; and said, "Whatever you do, don't hold a grudge." I haven't yet lived long enough not to, and I don't believe she did either. But all of this lay buried like the laths of the walls, plastered over with time and stapled into little smiles. So my grandfather and I played gin rummy in the dining room and he probably cheated me although I never caught him. And my grandmother sat in the living room and read aloud what was important to her from the daily paper that she thought he and I should hear, beginning with the obituaries. It was in this way that the conversation always turned to death and my grandfather would go to bed.

One period during my childhood my grandfather drove a school bus. Later, in high school, I wanted to recondition an old school bus and travel around the country with my best friend. And for a time he worked for the state, but only when the Republicans were in because the jobs were all political. During campaigns he would drive around and pick up voters and give them a half pint of whiskey after they came out of the booth. For this 89th birthday, his last, I wrote to the Greetings Division of the White House and my grandfather died blissfully believing that President Reagan and Nancy had personally sent him a birthday card. During hard times, he got my husband—a Democrat—a job with the state during a Republican reign. And later he got my cousin's husband a job and a boon feel on his back, paralyzing him. And during much harder times he helped me and my three children to receive county aid. In younger wintery times he would get calls in the middle of the night to plow snow from the roads for the morning traffic. He would get up after answering the phone and assuring my grandmother that no one in the family had died (although one January night that is what the phone call was about), pull on all his clothes, perk a big pot of coffee and fill his thermos, pull on his coat and hat and gloves and step out into the severe midwestern night. Sometimes he'd have to shovel the car out when the road grader wasn't parked at the house. When he retired, he got a state pension, but when he died, my grandmother did not get one penny of it.

My grandfather also served in WWI. He was discharged before my grandmother and he ever dated. There was a buddy system at the time and he enlisted, underage, with two of what later became his brother-in-law. He was in France. He later had a hearing problem which seemed to wilfully come and go. I drove him up to the veterans hospital in Danville, Illinois, once to see about getting him a hearing aid. He confessed on the way up that he was riding in the back of the truck headed for the front lines when he and one of his buddies jumped the truck to escape being shot and a mortar shell went off right beside them and he had trouble hearing ever since. At the veteran's hospital he bragged that I was his granddaughter and that I knew all the doctors there. It was true I had worked there for a couple of years, but I hardly knew any doctors. He talked to everyone and had a grand old time. When he had to be taken to the other end of one of the wards, I asked him if he wanted to ride in a wheel chair and he had no loss of pride in letting me push him up the long corridors. On the second trip we picked up the hearing aid. He wore it home, took it out of his ear and laid it on the dining room dresser. When my grandmother addressed him, he said he could hear her fine. He never again put the thing in his ear. He had a nephew who looked very much like him, who was hard of hearing, who shouted something fierce when he talked, his hearing aid resting comfortably in his shirt pocket.

For all of his life my grandfather suffered from nightmares carried over from the war. One night I was sleeping down stairs because my grandmother had had surgery and I was staying there taking care of her. She was sleeping in the living room on a hospital bed and I was on the couch. My grandfather, who had a hospital shuffle by then although he had never been in the hospital, came running through the house at top speed heading for the front door in his long white underwear. When grandmother and I woke up and yelled at him, he said he was going outside to help Fern, his oldest daughter who lived across the street, carry a chair. It was the middle of the night and the middle of winter. When he woke up, he slumped back towards the bedroom at his usual slow pace, and my grandmother told him, "Straighten up, Elmer, you're a young man yet." He was about 85 at the time. When I fell back to sleep I had a nightmare and woke up screaming Help! Help! My grandmother, unable to get up, sighed, "Oh dear," in the most resigned tone I'd ever heard in her voice. The events of the evening summed up pretty well the emotional and physical dynamics of the trio. It was clear the wrong one was incapacitated. My grandfather was a member of the American Legion for over sixty years. On the fourth of July celebration and other parades he carried the American flag until my grandmother called them up and told them to get a younger man for the job. He attended in uniform every military funeral in the town. He was lowered into the ground to a 21 gun salute. He received a pension from serving in combat but when he died my grandmother didn't get any of it. Never did she get any of his social security, because she had made more than he did.

My grandparents were married by the justice of the peace on April first 1920. I asked my grandmother if she wore a flapper dress, because no pictures were taken of the marriage. Although she had told me she wore out a pair of shoes a week square dancing on Saturday night, she answered that she "wasn't that kind of a girl." They had as witnesses an army buddy and his French wife who couldn't speak English. Then the four of them took the train to Terre Haute to the buddy's house. When they woke up the next morning, my grandmother said a pet pig ran through the room squealing. Forty-two years later I spent my own honeymoon in a motel in Terre Haute without the glamour of a French woman or a pig.

My grandfather stood about six foot four and was slim, like his father before him who had a handlebar moustache and looked in the tin types as if he should shoot it out in the old west. You learned not to ask how tall my grandmother was. His mother was very short. Both of his parents had sharp dark eyes. His father eeked out a meager living by walking through the woods digging up sassafras roots, shaving them into small strips, bundling them with twine and selling them at the local markets. This was supplemented by a large garden. My grandfather followed in his footsteps, literally. Many an evening I had red stained fingers from boiling the roots of the sassafras for tea. The most interesting detail I heard about my great grandmother was that she was nearly blind near the end of her ninety-four years but that she could still thread a needle.

Because my grandfather's work was not steady and because my grandmother worked in a paper factory until she retired, my grandfather did most of the cooking. He would go out and shoot a rabbit or squirrel during the day, come home and clean it, and cook it for a long time, stirring up some milk gravy and boiling new red potatoes from the garden, then browning them. I would pick the buckshot from the legs and spoon on the gravy onto my bread. The evenings would get dark early, although the snow lighted the rooms some times. If it were Saturday night, my grandfather would turn on *Gangbusters* on the radio. And often we listened to *The Lone Ranger* brought to us by Cheerios. Sometimes he played a small French harp smaller than his mouth. Sometimes we would play checkers, but my grandmother told me to watch him because he would cheat me. I couldn't imagine an adult cheating a kid at checkers. I watched him but I never caught him at it.

On that morning in December my grandfather was looking up at me from within his circle of smoke, and although I was nearly nauseous from the heat and smell of nicotine, I perhaps saw him for the first time, counting his money, his cigarette held high between his boney stained fingers, graceful as a woman. He smiled when I came down stairs and uttered a sort of grunt for a greeting. He had the little portable radio behind him by the coffee pot, the one I had bought him the Christmas before. It was spattered with grease from sitting in the kitchen. I don't think he ever played it. And it had been a long time since I had heard him play his favorite song, "Good Night Irene" because the record player had been sold in one of my family's perpetual garage sales. I poured myself some of his strong, filmy, day-old coffee, started a new pot, and sat down to listen to some of his stories about how he'd lathed the best houses in Champaign and Charleston and Peoria and Gary, Indiana. He remembered the house numbers and the streets where the houses were and asked me if I knew some of them, and, yes, I lied, but he never caught me at it. And if I'm lying here, no one will catch me for I'm the only one who lathed these walls of imagination with their stories. My grandfather's mind remained accurate as the stack of coins before him on the table while my grandmother's swirled like a midwestern blizzard rendering unfamiliar the shapes and colors of even her own house. Now they're both gone. They can neither verify nor clarify these words. And I'm left with a legacy of snow and a pen for a shovel, sitting her in the suffocating heat, the nicotine still burning my eyes and nose, the thick coffee scorching my tongue, half listening, if the truth be known, to my grandfather's stories, half listening for the springs of my grandmother's bed, scratching my way through my childhood, across this page, like a path which is unmistakably vanishing.

Downtown, Sweet Springs, Missouri, Carolyn Berry

JOE NAPORA

POETRY IN THE MID(DLE) (ST) (DEN), AND...

Joe Napora was born in Ohio in 1944 and already has a long record as a poet, essayist, and activist. His years in New York, San Francisco, and Canada have brought him back to his Ohio roots where he works in a library and continues his work for civil rights, peace, and anti-U.S. aggression in Central America. A poetry reading by Joe Napora is always an encounter with human issues of peace and justice as well as a finely wrought poetry. His essays in *Poetry in the Middle: Notes on Land and Language* (1981) reveal his continued exploration of the nature and significance of an American poetry of place.

Joe Bruchac has praised Napora's writing as "carefully constructed and as organic as that newly planted corn plant." Among his many books of poems, the most recent are *Scighte* (1987), *Journal of Elizabeth Wilson* (1987), *To Recognize the Dying* (1987), and *Bloom Blood* from *Three by Three* (1988).

George Myers Jr. writes of Napora, "this mid-western author pries loose academia and Romance as all that is malignant on the body of contemporary literature and land politics." In our essay Napora explores the path to a total ecology that includes "earth and sky and breath," in a poetry of the body which is the place.

POETRY IN THE MID(DLE) (ST) (DEN), And...

I have far from exhausted my interest in the idea of poetics gathered from explorations of the meanings attached to the term "middle." I am still interested in the mid-point / place / time, what Ed Dorn refers to when he wrote, "The middle is just the frontier between both ends." But I am also interested in being-in-the-midst of, the poetics of inclusion, immanence, and the poetics of the discarded and fragmentary, the midden. And as it was before, I return to where I started from, oYo, or Ohio, the middle-border state.

Near to where I live is a county park. This is a county noted for its neglect of human services—welfare, schools, roads; this park is no exception. I would like to think it is a purposeful negligence to preserve the park from being overused, abused. The potholes keep the fast cars out. The uncut grass discourages large picnics. The small picnic shelter appears to encourage a gathering, but what is there for people to do? And the sign that announces "Indian Mound Trail" points to a maze of 30-year old pines with no clear path leading out of them. This place, officially neglected, nearly deserted, and ambiguous in its intentions, it is one of my favorite places.

The Indian mound nestles in a surround of brambles, bushes, and young hardwood trees, a slight and natural uprising out of the earth, or so it appears. But it is a manufactured, not a natural, upheaval, perhaps only 6 or 8 feet at its highest, 25 feet around, nearly circular. It was probably made by the people we call Adena, and is roughly 2000 years old. From what I know about the Adena culture, I suspect that the mound contains burials, successive burials, the bodies left for the scavengers and the picked bones gathered together in bark vessels and covered with earth. This is a place bound in with time. It interests me, draws me to it, because it defines for me the surrounding landscape. It endures, and it is feminine.

Next to the park is a cemetery. It is April and the graves and the pine wreaths hanging on or leaning against the headstones are marked with flowers—purple, yellow, blue, and pink plastic carnations. The trees, except for 3, a maple, and 2 spruce, have been cleared and 25 or more obelisks mark the space, define it in vertical thrusts. The largest monument, at least 30 feet high, is an erection, a memorial to Gideon Samuels: Born Jan. 5, 1815 and Mary DeCamp wife of Gideon Born June 18, 1818, Died Aug. 24, 1889.

I think of the Indian burial mound as part of the land even as it, as a made structure, stands apart from it, and there are these phallic monuments pointing up away from the earth. There is a language here. It speaks of our arrogance, mis-direction, and a false security in a belief of permanence. I did not invent the plastic flowers which challenge decay; these fake flowers are very real. And across from the cemetery is a run-down shack that the wind blows through, and from the road the sign is barely visible but though some of the letters are worn it obviously reads, "Private Property." And the cemetery says: inheritance, wealth, patriarchy; it says, "Property of the Private Parts." And I wonder about our parts, our poetry part of ourselves, is this language not also a sign of its dying?

Cognition in us is from the first knowledge of death, knowledge of the power of death.
    -Alphonso Lingis, *Excesses, Eros and Culture*

The complete death-rebirth process always represents a spiritual opening. People who go through that experience invariably appreciate the spiritual dimension of existence as being extremely important if not fundamental. And at the same time their image of the physical universe changes. People lose the feeling of separateness; they stop thinking of solid matter and begin to think of energy patterns.
    -*Stanislav Grof, in Unconscious Wisdom*
    by Fritjof Capara

My proposal is simple. Writing is death. Speech is breath. And poetry is both and neither.

William Carlos Williams almost gets it right, when he tries to write the wrong in a written poem moving toward song, he *says,* "Say it! No ideas but in things." Which saying is only a thing as it is written but proclaims its shadow, which if it was said it could not cast: "Write it! No things but in ideas." And thing and shadow create relationship. I am not thinking of the obelisks and the shadows they cast. That was Ezra Pound's way—the unwobbling pivot, the erect phallus as the sign of the creative act. Poetry and pricks. I am probing another relation.

Death is necessary for immortality, obviously, and obviously not sufficient for it. The frost heaves and the land breathes; these obelisks wobble with the earth's continual moving. The future fails. The phallus falls. And stays down. No poetry compensates for this fundamental impotency. The book goes unopened. The unopened book, like so much of our poetry, is a rebuke to the writing that comes only from misplaced desire, for survival and sex and expression. The writing that sustains arises from the total body, and more specifically from the middle. I am drawing upon the yogic tradition, tantra, the force of kundalini and the chakra system.

The first three chakras are necessary, absolutely, but keep the body as limited as is our poetry. The fourth chakra, the heart center, the middle chakra, integrates matter and spirit. Each chakra is also a middle, vortices where spirit becomes dense into matter, but it is the fourth that unites the total body and the larger body system, environment and community. Anahata is the fourth chakra, the center for relationship, love; breath is its expression. *If poetry arises out of the dark, death awareness, the universal universal, it is love that connects it to the living community.* Eros points beyond, it fills in the void of the single voice out of and into a chorus, community. It is here, this connection of the single voice with the communal, that poetry can be compared to magic, fundamental transformation. Substitute in this quote from Starhawk's *Dreaming the Dark* the words "poetry" for "magic" and "language" for "consciousness":

When we practice magic [poetry] we are always making connections, moving energy, identifying with other forms of being. Magic [poetry] could be called the applied science that is based on an understanding of how energy makes patterns and patterns direct energy. To put it another way at its heart is a paradox:
Consciousness [language] shapes reality;
Reality shapes consciousness [language].

Back to the mounds. Researchers in the mid-1900's estimated that Ohio had over 5,000 burial mounds, enclosures, earth effigies, maybe 10,000. Now we are left with gaps, emptiness; we are only intimate to our non-knowledge about them. The mounds, even those partially remaining, become voids in the landscape, reminders of love lost. If we are open, we can experience the pull of Eros. Eros reaches us to the beyond. The force of our desire pulls us outward. The beloved stands out of our reach. We put words to paper, as we strive to fix the process of our love. At that moment we are actually present but at that moment at the creation of the material, we are only virtually present. Our artifact lives without us. There is an anxiety present here. Almost our entire culture—which is a mirror for the pervasiveness of imperialism—is dependent on virtual presence, writing, videos, tv, records, movies. Poets do readings to convince themselves that they are real. And write poems to convice themselves that they will abide. But neither is so, but both. Poetry resides in the middle—both living and dead, spoken and written, oral and visual. The middle is the expression of the body, the unseen body. The element of the fourth chakra is air:

> ...air in the form of breath represents the vital energy of life. The Hindus call it *prana* (from *pra,* first, and *na,* unit), the Chinese call it *chi,* the Japanese *ki.* Under any name, this energy can be moved throughout the body through proper control of the breath, and in doing so parts of the body are nourished and "charged" by its essence.
> -Anadeo Judith, *Wheels of Life*

Charles Olson spoke of poetry being an energy transfer from poet to audience. He didn't speak enough about how and where the poet received the energy. Looking at energy as *ch'i* helps to reveal more about Olson's explanation of negative capability, the poet as receptor, open to the unknown without the interference of the ego. *Ch'i* is a force for involvement in and balance with the social and cosmic order. And, as Olson said it, breath is the vehicle; and written poetry re-enacts, approximates as it can (and it can only approximate which does not mean it is inferior), approximates the speech as it is guided by breath. The poet is nourished by audience, returns language to the community and is less of a creator than a maker or form maker of a shared content. Language becomes current as it becomes a currency, a medium of exchange, with the emphasis on flow. In the medicine of the East, disease is only a blockage of the flow of current. The paradox and the danger is that all writing is a form of blockage, stasis. So the poet, while using writing, must continually be pushing writing into the impossibility of the speech act, out of virtual presence into real presence. It is, I believe, at this place, physical, psychic, even spiritual place, where the poet re-enacts the energy that is the poem. At the same time it is full, it is an empty place. The place, again, of paradox. In *Journey Without Goal, the Tantric Wisdom of the Budda,* Chogyam Trungpa writes about this awareness of cosmic energy, which could, even should, be about the energy of our poetry:

We are not talking about centralizing energy within ourselves, making ourselves into little atom bombs and then exploding. Working with energy in a trantric sense is a decentralized process. That is a very important point. We are talking about energy as something spreading, opening. Energy becomes all-pervasive. It is all and everywhere. If we centralize energy in ourselves, we are asking for trouble. We will find that we become like baby snakes who are vicious and angry but still very small. Or we may find that we are like extremely passionate, horny baby peacocks. So it is important to remember that, in Buddhist tantra, energy is openness and all-pervasiveness. It is constantly expanding. It is decentralized energy, a sense of flood, ocean, outer space, the light of the sun and moon.

We have had enough of the concentration of energy that capitalism feeds on, is only possible because of, the same concentration of energy that has produced our vicious and angry, and extremely passionate, horny baby peacock poets, poets more interested in filling themselves than acknowledging their emptiness, emptiness that makes poetry, even political poetry, possible.

It would be a legitimate question to ask, what has this commentary about energy and its possible connection to form and the form of the poem have to do with landscape? I am tempted to answer with this poem from another book on Buddhism, Robert Aiken's *Buddhism and Zen:*

> The bamboo shadows are sweeping the stairs,
> But no dust is stirred.
> The moonlight penetrates the depths of the pool,
> But no trace is left in the water.

The question demands more, or rather, a different type of answer. Our poetry is at home in this middle place between speech and writing, and perhaps it is through the idea of "home" that we discover what it means to be connected not only with land and the body and the body politic but connected in specific ways to specific landscapes. Yoga, yoke, joining, is a being-at-home with the body. The larger body, the social body, the body connected with each individual body and with the body that is the earth, demands for its being-at-home an expanded sense of place and the individual body's relation to it. Is there a midwest poetry with a distinctive form and a form distinguished by its relationship to the land? I have only inclinations of the character of such forms for they would be continually shifting, shifting into the realizing that form is no-form, as landscape is no-landscape, no landscape that is not also the undercurrent, the *ch'i,* or *ki,* the relationship that makes possible the aperception of things. And at the same time, such form would be the same, the same as the form of the body, which is our human universal. A poetry born of the body, brought to expression through the awareness and activation of the heart chakra will exhibit its peculiar affinity with this aspect of the organism—earth and sky and breath—its affinity for this total ecology, and the human history defining this environment, and the responsbility for political action, which is the expression of the body's integration into the place we inhabit, the place we in the midwest are fortunate to call the heartland.

Ohio Barn. Julie Koba

ROBERT RICHTER

LAND LESSONS

"I'm a dryland wheat farmer on the high plains of western Nebraska where I've rented what's left of a family homestead for a dozen years or so—fourth generation out here, going on fifth with my kids. This isn't something I can make a living at. Here by choice and for the spirit of it. And for the time to write."

Robert Richter is also one of Nebraska's finest prose writers. His *Windfall Journal* (1980) includes his poetry and prose, and his coauthored *Plainscape* reveals his rootedness in regional history. His essays and features on issues of political, economic, and environmental concerns have appeared throughout the Midwest. His essay "Badger Flats and the Topography of Spirit" which appeared in *Prairie Schooner,* resulted in his being nominated for both a G.E. Foundation Grant and the Don D. Walker Prize.

In "Land Lessons" he expolores how it is we come to "learn the landscape." This impressionistic portrait of growing up on the land is both mythic and real—a midwestern archetype. His sense of place theme reveals the elemental way in which the land is taken into the body of a person. Richter's simple directness is shown in his humble self-portrait, to which he adds, "Most of the time, I'm farming summer till, pushing snow or tending trees, raising kids and a few other animals." His lyrical yet earth-bound prose moves with the rhymes and rhythms of the land.

LAND LESSONS

Out here in the agricultural heart of the country we can live so long on the land we almost forget how strong a part of our own heart the earth is. Like heartbeats or breathing, it has been with us from the beginning, gradually so familiar that a sense of its significance can easily fade into a careless neglect.

We learn land from the first. For a young boy growing up, a first sense of terrain might be learned by foot, wandering at the edges of fields his father attends each day. He gets to know what the dirt is like to the touch and taste. Later on he might learn the landscape by bicycle, getting home to school and back finding ways to go to avoid the steepest streets or to coast a long block through a tunnel of trees. He learns how to pick directions and measure the characteristics of one route to others, and he eventually comes to know the territory close to home. It's a time of getting the feel for the detail of the ground he covers while growing, its shapes and angles, what houses lay along what winding street, where a casual ride home can turn into a fast-tracking trail with a few good jumps, taking all the skill he's got to ride it out to the bottom.

Then gradually awareness grows with those journeys away from home, to grandparents' places or an auction somewhere, to another town where the stores and pace of traffic are different. The longer he lives in the region, the more trips taken. Directions change and spread. He rides a lot of buses, in a lot of back seats, going to ballgames, school activities, to a movie in another town, fishing at hidden lakes, spending more time on the region's roads. He comes to know at least a little about the highways into the sandhills, some of the towns scattered across the south table, some scenic route around a heavily trafficked highway, the gravel roads of his own county. The river valleys and lake regions, the corn country and where the plain breaks open into wheat as far as he can see, the bends, dips and rises in the road all become as well-known as the landscape of his day-to-day living.

But when you're young and after you've been at the window a while and have an idea of the ground's condition the way you're going, those rides can lull you into daydreams and dazes with the hypnotic hum of monotonous movement. And what you're learning then about land, maybe without sensing it, is how immense the horizon everywhere seems to be and the kind of personal time it costs to cross distance and space. You learn about how big the land, this land right under your feet, really is and how much of it keeps filling the ride across it, the time, the life you call yours.

During those rides, or between them, or in moments of sleepy unawareness, a boy goes on growing. His life fills not only with land but jobs and family and friends that cross the country with him. The ground a person covers becomes as familiar as his own face in the mirror, so much a part of what he is it submerges in the mind, as unconscious as a habit. There are rides now when he might not see the land at all, being with troubled thoughts, bothered with weather, or listening to the radio. A passenger might be listening to something he's had to say of times and places and other roads through his life. Meanwhile, his rides rush on. They are part of routines and schedules and times that just seem to get busier, more hectic and demanding. And the land changes so slowly it's hardly to be mentioned.

But maybe some summer night, later after a ballgame, before he heads for home cross-country and another day, he lingers over a few beers to talk about the game with friends, about life in general, work, weekends, who's moving where. Everyone's around enjoying the summer night's company, the jokes and fish stories, the talk about trips taken. A town father tells of fishing the sandhills lakes. Someone asks how to get to Egan Lake, how the fishing is. Soon everyone listening knows the way, what the road looks like, landmarks, who to see about the fishing, where the perch and bullhead hide. Over his shoulder two farmers talk about hail alley in the southwest corner of the county, how the thunderheads build and darken so intensely there in no time at all. Voices around him compare grasses and the season's weather to last year's. There's talk about where a man took out a tree claim to add two acres to a circle of corn. And talk about the time it takes to go over a field, what it does to the soil, how close to the surface the water might lie, what may be beneath even that. Though he may not realize it yet, if a person listens randomly around himself, the talk he hears will somehow pertain to his terrain. These lives are part of the territory. Tomorrow they all will head different directions again, out on the land to put in a day's work on it, take away a day's worth of living. The times and lives are busy and so much contained in the character and contours of terrain.

And maybe not the next ride, but sometime on a journey when he reaches a rise and looks down the Platte Valley, seeing how the lights lay like welcome beacons along its shadowed curve; or when he sees a vast sea of sandhills and senses a meadow lake just below a certain shade of light a ways away; or just in an idle gaze across the shimmering crops into the mirages the sun melts on a summer road, making a maze of the land he's learned so silently; in some random ride he will suddenly feel again how full of this land his life has become. And if for a moment he feels every heartbeat, every nerve tingling, the air of the plain in his breath, he will sense what it means to know terrain. And not just from horizon to horizon, lowland to hill to valley to vast plain, but from the highest whisps of cloud where the air percolates and filters the sunlight, down through the dusty sky, into the plants and rootzones, to the minerals and water, to the molten core of the life-giving earth. As intimately as knowing his own emotions, his memories of boyhood and first times learning the land, like knowing himself, he'll know the road he's riding, the direction and distance and how all these features fit him. And all the time he is passing on over it. Going on, growing older, knowing somewhere up ahead only the shape of the landscape lasts.

HEARTLANDS— 153

Gary Ainley

MICHAEL J. ROSEN

UNDER THE SIGN OF WONDER BREAD AND BELMONT CASKETS

Michael J. Rosen is an Ohio native who has published poetry *A Drink at the Mirage* (1985) and a children's book *Fifty-Odd Jobs*(1988) while working as literary director of The Thurber House, the writers' center in the restored Columbus home of James Thurber. He is an active force for writers and writing in the Midwest.

In "Under the Sign of Wonder Bread and Belmont Caskets" he does a lot of juxtaposing, not only of the mixed images within his Columbus childhood, but within an overall comparison and contrast between his Columbus past and what was his present existence on the West Indies island of Grenada. What emerges from the panoramas of these two geographies (physical and emotional) is a fundamental human awareness of himself and others within the creative flow of time and place.

Rosen's gentle and often self-mocking humor calls forth our identification and allows for the larger human insights that make meaning out of the ordinary.

UNDER THE SIGN OF WONDER BREAD AND BELMONT CASKETS

In January of 1978, I moved to a small island in the West Indies. I had lived in Columbus, Ohio, for twenty-six years and had never left nor thought of leaving the country, except for the time in Teen Camp when our bus passed Buffalo, New York, and we visited a nation distinguished solely by the fact that twelve-year-olds could purchase cherry bombs and bottle rockets four days running in order to relinquish them at the American border on the fifth.

Now, for the first time in my life I inhabited a place where weather was cast into two definite seasons, the wet one and the dry one. Beyond those major fronts, no forecasts troubled the airwaves with minor valuations. In the Midwest, thousands of miles north, the local media had made the transition from news anchor-who-also-watched-weather to certified staff meteorologist, and yet, I could only imagine the weather above the house where I grew up, cast in magic markers and Velcro, its severities ably represented by the drawing of a big umbrella over Mr. Winter's head, or the adhering of fluffy Colorform—not cumulus—clouds.

My parent's air-mail letters confirmed this quaintness. Quite possibly their handwritings' ingenuousness embodied it. In truth, I had never read anything my parents had written besides phone messages or *please-excuse-Michael-from...* notes. My father wrote on memos from his office; my mother, on tissue-weight stationery she must have had printed just to write to me. Yet the contents of their letters converged into a reading of weather and its sidekick, health, as it influenced the local population. Perhaps they assumed it would only make me miss them more were they to report on anything other than the greyish winter in Columbus.

Every part of my lush and arid, foreign surroundings estranged me from the mild suburban life with which I'd been familiar. In the slant of my parents' shy but jocular sentences, Columbus sounded unexceptional and staid. Yet when I told stories from my years in Columbus I detected a different cant, at least in the responses of new friends. Apparently the modest Midwest and my parents as its forecasters, legislators, and developers teetered between an unheard-of sincerity and a heart-felt giddiness.

My first night in the Caribbean was spent in an open-air auditorium with the rest of the island's new residents, learning of the specific dangers of this foreign environment. "Never sleep under manganero trees," the island's minister of health recited, "Their sap is rain-water soluble and caustic." And he continued for an hour: "Don't wear blue jeans in town: They symbolize anti-government loyalties....Beware of fire coral, sea urchin spines, and barracuda in schools....Never swim at night or alone or anywhere on the south side of the island where the smell of blood from the slaughter house attracts sharks." He also cautioned us about sexual contact with the natives, consuming any form of meat or chicken in the markets, and many other dire and dispiriting facts that fell first into dread, then into disuse, and now into some part of the brain I had once been able to diagram with enormous satisfaction.

But that February, Ohio experienced the severest blizzard within recent memory—even that of my parents'. My father mailed me a picture of my old car's roof barely breaching a four-foot bank of snow, and my mother's head and waving hand frozen in a picture of the snow-blocked picture-window in the dining room. He bought expensive film for the Polaroid he was never comfortable using and sent me a whole portfolio of the neighborhood's month-old abominable snow sculptures that showed no signs of melting. Among those takes, he included a valentine that the new key-punch operator at his office had generated. "The local news," my mother wrote, "is just a list of what's cancelled." My father jotted a few lines about a man in Mansfield, Ohio, who had spent a week marooned in the cab of his truck. And both of them sent clippings about the prayer meeting in the state rotunda, where Governor Rhodes petitioned God to please turn up the world's thermostats.

On Grenada, there were sudden downpours that would drench a sunny, scorching afternoon for two solid minutes, although all signs of rain would evaporate or suck into the dry earth within the next two minutes. I was experiencing the most temperate and personable weather I had ever known. The island flaunted its balmy gifts the way a tourist might, with the gaudiness of pink conches strewn across a black-sand beach, with a wildness of guava, lime, papaya and coconut trees too accessible not to claim as one's own.

Exempt from Ohio's blizzard, I was not oblivious. During that month I started my own letter-writing binge. I was gathering, in dozens of weekly letters sent mostly to Midwestern friends, a new perspective on the place where I had been born and reared, the place I returned to six months later, and the place where I am now living and writing.

When I tried to imagine something more general in which to include my home's geography, I visualized a dittoed worksheet, a lovely-smelling blue outline of a heart-shaped state, crazed into eighty-eight fragments. Memorizing the names and whereabouts of each county was our year-long, fifth-grade project. (Eighty-eight was a number just under a million, and it had taken our entire elementary school six months to fill the front-hall showcase with bottlecaps just to help us comprehend the magnitude of *that* number.)

The year before, we had memorized the capital and location of each state in the United States. The year after that, we made a dent in memorizing the rest of the world's countries before Mrs. Gardner permanently snagged, in its overextended position, the world map, one of the blackboard-size rolls suspended beneath the cursive alphabet. After a spell during which precious board space had been compromised, the custodian removed the whole pedagogical apparatus. Mrs. Gardner intended its return but, from that day forward, our room had no movie screen, no solar system, no topography to show America's ocher rocky parts or the deep-violet swirls of her oceans. Nonetheless each of us had our own country, assigned to us like our own undiscovered heritage.

Our explorations had to include export products and natural resources, but a will toward extra-credit supplemented cold facts with warm, almost authentic baked goods the room-mothers heated in the teachers' lounge, hotel brochures with pictures of people swimming outdoors among snow-covered mountains, and multi-colored salt maps.

I was assigned Saskatchewan, a province as foreign to our classroom as Uganda or Samoa. What filled me with enormous pride was the Trip-tik from Columbus to Saskatoon, Saskatchewan, that my parents requistioned from AAA Motorists Club. I'm sure part of my delight came from the fact that no one else in my class had included such an insert in a report folder's pocket; but part came from the fact that I had received a free tourist's guide, set of roadmaps, several sight-seeing booklets, and a three-volume, page-by-page, Magic-Marker-highlighted trip to somewhere neither I nor my parents had any intention of ever going.

The fact that I had driven through several other Ohio counties (besides my own, Franklin County) didn't help with the previous year's county quiz, for the relative difference between a county and a country seemed to be held in that lone, additional letter. As for traveling through other states, which we did on our yearly vacation to my aunt's in Massachusetts, I had no vivid sense of anywhere else, any place I could have grown up had my ancestors settled there. I had no real sense of the place in which I *did* grow up. Though I hadn't read Ohioan Louis Bromfield then, I certainly shared his confusion about our state, "...the farthest west of the east, and the farthest east of the west, the farthest north of the south, and the farthest south of the north...."

I had seen Ohio, and then Ohio, and then Ohio regardless of the states passing our windows as we spotted silos and bridges on our Autobingo cards. Even though Columbus boasted that it was "Half-a-Day Away from Half the USA," it took us two days of traveling until we, at last, reached Aunt Renee's.

The world has changed slightly, but I named it then after people I knew, places that were inconceivable if the homes of relatives hadn't been there, bigger than the dot or the star beside the city's name on the map. So with a child's sense of the world, we children knew that Aunt Renee's meant Massachusetts "near Norman Rockwell's studio"; Great-grandma's meant Florida, "with a swimming pool not twenty feet from the ocean"; and Cedar Point meant an amusement park featured in everyone's genealogy.

Aside from fourteen-hour trips to Aunt Renee's, the only other traveling we did took twenty minutes or under. It took twenty minutes to reach the kids-under-twelve-pay-what-they-weigh smorgasbord. It took Mother eighteen minutes to drive to whatever shopping mall had just opened. A twenty-five-minute drive delivered us to the Columbus Zoo for a yearly visit with the first gorilla ever born in captivity. For, while our home was located in the midst of Circles and Courts named after the developer's relatives, numerically-titled freeways and main streets provided the tangents that could speed us downtown to Lazarus and The Union Department Stores. These arteries whisked us as easily past the county roads to acres of farmland striped with corn, dotted with cows, basted with the hills and valleys of telephone lines.

We were clearly suburban, something tucked *under* the stature of urban, since ours was one of the first houses built, according to my parents' warnings about tetanus and lockjaw, "in the middle of a rusty barbed-wire cow pasture." What we children understood of this middle-ground between the swelling city and the shrinking country, was the lot by lot confiscation of the unmowed, grassy fields as our neighbor's houses broke ground, and the gradual disappearance of specimens for the nature center we'd assembled in our two-car garage.

The pleasures of leaving our neighborhood for "a Sunday drive in the country" must have been different for each member of our family, although for all of us, it meant no time limits, destination, or directions. And most importantly, it always meant being with the other four members of our family, in one place, and for a longer interval than our weekly comings and goings sanctioned. The unspoken adventure of the occasion was following unpredicted precipitations—weather, road signage, grumbling stomachs, suggestions from the Sunday paper or someone's recollection or something seen from the car window. I'll concede that my father, the only one of us who knew how to read or correctly refold a road map, might have possessed a greater figure for our wandering.

Thinking of that unwieldy map, I would spread the morning's ready-to-mail letters across my desk in Grenada, sliding the variously shaped envelopes until, fitting against one another, they created the crazed and seceeded world of places I loved and missed. I upset my parents when I wrote this in a letter. "We call relatives our roots," I said, "because each person keeps a place from being washed away in our absence."

Snorkling idly, nervously, above a Caribbean—no, an otherworldly—architecture of brain coral and sea fans, I was reminded of the Sunday drive that happened to end at The Blue Hole in Castilia, Ohio, where, through the smeared and scratched glass bottom of a rented boat, we observed bluegill and beer cans swirling in a pit of khaki water. Floating in the Caribbean water, a blue the Blue Hole must have had in a distant part of its collective unconscious, I understood that the actual destination for each drive had been the opportunity to be together, as though family were, itself, a place, and a Sunday drive in the country would bring us there. A definition of my particular Midwest was evolving as a place without definition, as a region that could contain a journey a child might have squiggled across a map.

Our routes would take us along U.S. 40, a road my father maintained stretched clear across the continent like the crack in my salt map of Canada. But how could we believe him, when what we saw of The National Road was a familiar procession of wacky neon and vernacular architecture—the Bambi Lodge, the Robert E. Lee, the *Clean Rooms with Free TV and Telephone?* "Come to Columbus, and Discover America," the city boasted those years, and each motel contributed its far-fetched, foreign theme to our singular locale—a colonial inn, a Western dude ranch, a tropical paradise, a streamlined 1957 Thunderbird. And yet all was naturalized by the one neon word they shared, a "VACANCY" that flashed like a warning light as we zoomed past.

Beyond the motels, and seemingly en route to anywhere we drove, stood Lynn's Fruit Farm, where we drank endless cups of combination ciders, like apple-cherry and pineapple-apple, from dispensers we could work ourselves. Even then I knew the word "spoiled" applied as much to the bushels of bruised apples that would be squeezed in the cider press, as it did to my brother, sister and me, dashing from spigot to spigot, downing as many kinds and cups of cider as it would take to give us a stomachache that evening.

In that same autumn season, the trees called to my father to pull onto the berm so we could collect leaves from the roadside gully. Somehow they had turned colors we couldn't imagine anywhere but outside our suburb. And yet my father applied the names of trees planted on our new block to these massive, majestic species. We gathered leaf specimens so perfectly edged and colored they announced, like the finding of a four-leaf clover, a quintessence of Nature's power. By a happy coincidence, there were always black walnuts to stain our hands yellow, a grazing horse to feed the sugar cubes that my father produced like a magic trick from his pockets, wrinkled green Osage oranges (large and tropical as anything I could now imagine growing in the Caribbean), and milkweed pods to release from the windows of the moving car in a steam of profligate wishes. Regardless of what we hoarded, Mother could throw out the entire cache before the following Sunday without our noticing, without dimming our enthusiasm for the next week's purveyance.

We passed pottery stands encircled with opalescent strands of reflecting globes, barracaded by towers of flower pots, attended by queues of tiny black jockeys, enraptured St. Francises, and pairs of kissing Dutch children. But most curious to the five of us, driving past the statuary without a single vote to stop and browse, were the herd of deer, the brace of ducks, and the dray of squirrels. Here we were in the country, where, just driving past, we often spotted deer ("Deer X-ing" signs, anyway), usually ducks, and certainly squirrels. But here, too, were houses settled among these creatures—families who set salt licks for the deer, who scattered bread crumbs for the ducks, who shot rock salt at the bulb-digging squirrels—populated with stoneware models of these same creatures nestled in life-like arrangements in their yards. "Perhaps they attract real ones like decoys," my father hazarded. "Maybe the people still don't spot the real ones *enough,*" my mother suggested. "Probably the real animals don't come that close to the house anyway." But once in a while, we sighted real people on their porches and the look on their faces said, "Go ahead and race by, you city-slickers. But see how lucky we are to live among all of God's creatures (and, in some niches, even God in the guise of a miniature Virgin Mary or Jesus of the Sacred Heart)."

On the beach near my room in Grenada, a border of unchartered fishing boats hemmed the tame surf into a swimming hole with more fishes than I'd ever seen in all our Sundays of fishing in Ohio. The fishing holes we frequented as a family pooled into a single spot in my memory: the creek on the grounds of a farmer's grazing field across from National Trails Raceway. Oddly, the sound I associate with fishing is not the peace and quiet of cricket wings and cicadas sheltered beneath the sound-proof canopy of half-dead trees leaning over a shoreline, but the engine-gunning of funny cars and the indecipherable slur of the broadcast speakers that circled the raceway. We never asked how my father had discovered this amazing fishing hole, or when he had received permission to boost us all over the fence posted "No Trespassing," or why the grazing cattle wouldn't stampede us on our trek to the creek. We trouped across the field with our gear—radio, folding stool, tacklebox, comic books, snack sack, wading boots—and set up our afternoon camp.

Once or twice we prepared for the day by setting the car's floor mats on the driveway after a rain to catch nightcrawlers, but usually we bought the bait at a nearby Eskimo Igloo that sold soft ice-cream, licorice-scented doughball, worms, candybars, and minnows. Worms came in an earth-filled cottage-cheese or Chinese-food takeout container, offering Mother the chance to say, "Who's ready for a little lunch?" while giving a couple shakes to the bait.

My father or, to everyone's amusement, my sister would gore a worm on the hooks, and we'd each cast a line into the water, or as often, into the nearby cattails or one another's hair. For the two minutes, the five of us made a motionless and quiet model of what we imagined the sport required. We could have been a diorama in the Ohio Historical Center, a future scene that might be labeled, "For recreation, Columbus families often journeyed into the wilderness with bamboo poles and primitive carvings of small fishes called 'lures'...." This sustained moment filled my father with a sense of family spirit that must have resembled, in his mind, our hushed and huddled five-some sitting on the synagogue pew during the High Holy Days. After that initial family frieze, "fishing" had to include roaming the banks for fossils, rummaging through the tackle-box, dueling with cattails, skipping shale across the fishing lines, overturning the tacklebox, and fighting with one another because, alas, the fluorescent-orange corks and red-and-white bobbers marked the spot from which ripples of boredom issued.

Periodically we checked to see if my father or mother had caught anything and had forgotten to call and show us; *they* checked to see that none of us had fallen in. At different points in the long afternoon, my father would claim to need one of us kids to help him or spell him, and during those returns, a bobber on one of the four or five lines would suddenly sink and rise and flutter—do all the things that our fixed gazes had apparently prevented. We'd grab the pole, reel with the kind of fervor that would either install a backlash in the winding spool or a proud smile on our father's face. He would be leaning with the lowered net as though he expected something that could feed a family of five, and my mother would have jumped up from her folding stool with such excitement that the transistor radio would tumble into the water. And there it would be: a flailing carp, a barbed, chubby catfish, or a slick white bass. Stepping lightly on the fish, my father would pry the hook free, slide a huge pin through its mouth and gills, and, before lowering the stringer of fish into the creek, let us each feel the impossibly heavy heft of the day's catch.

For all our childhood years, my father performed the sport of turning the interminable experience of catching fish into an immediate one. He and Mother kept to themselves the fact that he had caught first the fishes we reeled in, that he had pulled them in, secured their hooks, and slid each one back into the water, so that the bobber's second dance appeared to his children like a vision of Man and Nature in bounteous harmony.

We didn't need to learn to fish. My father had learned to fish and we had taught him that it was relatively futile to think we could learn anything about lures or the science of flycasting or the virtue of patience. His happiness fell into place beside ours, his wife's, his three children's. When we were old enough to share my father's surefire fishing secret, it was never discussed or declared; he was gone fishing before we had even awakened on Sunday morning—by himself or with an old fishing buddy he had known before his family was born.

This figure of the family featured prominently in the idea of my suburban Midwest as I tendered it in conversations in Grenada where tonic water is more costly than gin and drinks were mixed in the opposite proportion. Unlike the metropolitan or agrarian or coastal or southern childhoods of my displaced American friends, Columbus provided a place where play and pasttime, hobby and happen-stance, appeared to be the reigning climate. Experience had no obligation or destiny. Mastery of an activity was seen as an option (another merit badge, a camp elective) rather than a survival skill.

For our family, fishing decidedly did not mean eating fish. We didn't subsist on fish or sell it for our livelihood. Moreover, we wouldn't have considered cooking one even for what Mother called "a change of pace." We would go to the drive-in Sunday night and order breaded fish sticks, oblivious to the presence of pound-size bass circling in our trash can/holding tank, or a quartet of live carp wrapped in the Sunday paper in the refrigerator's fruit bin. On Monday, my father would give the fish to an appreciative but distant cousin who wouldn't feel obliged to invite us to the feast.

Our other agricultural experiences were likewise limited. Beyond the planting of roses, those delicate annual bushes, my mother's desire for plants of any kind was sated by the dried and dyed bamboo tree that her interior decorator had arranged behind the recovered loveseat. The premium concept in market produce wasn't homegrown, but frozen or canned, the remarkable opportunity of the always-on-hand and ready-to-cook. (And canning didn't mean actually immersing vegetables in a boiling water bath; nor did freezing mean a quick blanching and freezing in the garage freezer.) We did have a freezer, for a one-time, supposedly money-saving purchase of half a butchered steer, and the occasional no-limit-per-customer sale on Mountaintop Pies.

I sowed my first graden at the age of twenty. Before that I might have correctly visualized how a carrot grows from the packages in our vegetable bin, and an onion, from the way the ones in our cupboard grew tendrils of green leaves. But the sights of Brussel sprout nodes, a blanching head of cauliflower, or the yellow-blossoming, ground-creeping zucchini, were shocks for which nothing in my parents' grassy lot had prepared me.

One year, we did aspire to grow a 350-pound pumpkin from seeds harvested from one of the award-winning giants at the Circleville Pumpkin Festival. Throughout the closed-off town square, we had sampled pumpkin in the guise of all of our favorite foods (burgers, waffles, fudge and milkshakes), and had circled the fenced-in intersection of Circleville that displayed mounds of every kind of shapely and misshapen squash and gourd. Then, just as we were leaving with a crookneck squash as large as my younger sister and a sack of gourds that soon would dry into maracas, my father purchased five of the prize-pumpkin's seeds and jotted down the grower's tips for proper cultivation.

That spring we found the seeds in the basement (itself a colossal feat), and sowed them in a bare spot our dog had previously prepared at the back of our yard. Just as the grower had instructed, we predestined the one bloom from all the vines' possible choices to become our prize-winning pumpkin, and committed ourselves to drenching it with five gallons of water everyday. Long before it might have reached the 150-pound stage that would have required the roof we had pulled from the delapidated dog house to shield it from the sun's rays, our only pumpkin shrivelled and rotted. That fall we purchased a manageable, suburb-size pumpkin, carved it into a jack-o-lantern, and placed it on our porch beside an evergreen in which my father had hidden an old intercom, so that the flame-eyed ghoul could laugh and scream like Vincent Price at all our trick-or-treating friends.

What I understood as my father's ambivalent relationship with the seasons was absent from his well-spaced letters to Grenada. The blizzard so dominated the state, that my father was as defenseless as the city's salt truck and snow plow. And once the siege was over, there was only the walk from the driveway to the front door to clear, and even less to write about. His determination typically exhibited itself at critical moments, when fervor would be frustrated by the element at hand. We shoveled snow when the weatherman predicted six more hours of snow, we raked leaves when the trees were still laden with color, we plucked dandelions when our neighbors' yards were grey with the seed-headed weeds.

During the erratic years our sour-cherry tree chose to bear fruit, we knew it was time for dinner not by the smell of a baking cherry pie, but by the sound of my father's car turning into the driveway, honking at the tree of cherry-robbing starlings. Weren't these the same birds he had fed all winter, trudging across the snow in his fishing boots and bathrobe to refill the suet and seed feeders he'd hung in same cherry tree's boughs?

As children, all our other practice at rural life occurred in day camp. Every summer from the age of four to fourteen, and then for the next ten years as a counselor, I inhabited a wilderness tempered by picnic shelters, nature trails, and capture-the-flag fields. None of these was an overnight camp that involved actually leaving Columbus for some pastoral setting or sports complex. By bus, camp was the typical twenty-minute drive. We encircled our woodsy campsites with burlap and two-by-fours, heated sloppy-joes and banana-boats on tee-pee fires we'd built without the benefit of our wadded-up lunchbags, stitched pieces of leather into pocket-comb cases, and took lessons in swimming, archery, canoeing, sailing, and horseback riding.

In Grenada, some friends my own age had never seen a horse more vividly than in pictures, while others had attended riding camps and learned all about English riding and *dressage*. After five years of riding lessons at my camp, I was awarded the much coveted Pegasus Award, a wallet-size card with a loop of gold-ribbon pinned to it. What elevated my riding style from that of the hundred other day campers', I can only guess, for several of us could perform the few requisite maneuvers like distinguishing between clockwise and counterclockwise canters, and keeping both hands off the saddlehorn.

Our riding sessions represented the entirety of horse ownership. Each of us was assigned our lone charge for the four-week session to brush and card, bridle and saddle, feed and water, and then, for an hour, walk, trot and canter. The stables was an enormous facility with enough horses so that the morning-, the afternoon-, and the alternate day's-campers could each have the responsibility for a horse. And yet, as fierce as our group's commitment, after our four-week session was over, only a few of us returned for the second session, and I don't recall hearing that any of us returned to the stable until the following June, when it appeared that the old stable of horses had been sold and a fresh stable bought.

Just narrating those years of horseback riding on a Caribbean beach, cast them into a spoiled and unspoiled light I'd never seen before. On an island where the closest thing to a horse I'd sighted were the donkeys, braided with bougainvillea blossoms, parading in front of the hotels, it dawned on me that hard-mouthed Ranger and spirited Veteran and docile Li'l Lil were all the same Tennessee Walker, and that in each riding class, names were assigned to campers and not to horses. Although the riding instructor used the horse's name when a correction had to be made, weren't we the ones who had made the error, who had recognized the called name, and who would have to hold the reins tighter or squeeze harder with our thighs?

Of all my out-of-the-suburb intervals, horseback riding brought me closest to life and death forces. Sure, we had all seen lifeguards towing younger campers from the diving well. My own hands had puffed with poison ivy, my eyes, swollen shut. I knew about the danger of heat exhaustion and swallowed the nurse's salt pills when it reached ninety-degrees. But nothing had the sting of mortality as the week we had seen, through the bus windows, a dead horse—some camper's, wasn't it?—a horse who had fallen into the creek from the very bridge we were crossing into the stables.

The year after my Pegasus award, my horse Sparky refused my typical version of neck-reining after a morning in the corral. Later, when we had come to the center of a field, she sank to her knees and slowly rolled onto her side, pinning my leg in the stirrup. A team of adults managed to half-coax and half-pry the immobile horse from my leg. Hysterical, I rode to the tack room hugged between the riding instructor's arms and legs, as she tried to convince me that Sparky would recover from the colic in a week or so. But that was after camp had ended. How would I know? All I could visualize was the sick horse abandoned in the emptied field, as though I had caused whatever "colic" was—my heaviness, the cinch I'd pulled too tight, my child-shaped saddle hugging its heaving chest for dear life.

If it weren't for the challenge of individual achievement, so dramatically different from the teams in which we competed at tent-building, ballgames and paper-bag dramatics, our hours on horseback could be as easily corralled in a letter's paragraph or a mocking aside, as our motley posse was, within the white fence of the stables. Our experience existed safely between earnest horse-assisted work and a pony-ride in a shopping center's parked car corral. And perhaps it is there I detect my first conscious inklings of self-confidence. Despite the presence of instructors, hired hands, and fellow campers, a personal, barely translated relationship existed among a horse, a child, and a rough swatch of the knowable world.

At a distance of thousands of miles, each image from the Midwest, as I held it up for my new friends to consider, looked precious as a souvenir with its locale wood-burned or glittered across it. Qualities sounded like quirks; opportunities, like crazes. I began to worry that anything—an object, a scene, a love—at a distance of memory or miles, must resemble a little photo at the end of a keychain viewer, reduced but enlarged again by the present eye. How could I keep anything I remembered about the Midwest from sounding like a tourist attraction, even an unattractive one? Do we live our lives once as ourselves, then repeatedly as everyone else?

In fact, I could place the scenes and the objects surfacing in my memory of Columbus just opposite the items I was planning to bring back from the island: frond baskets of nutmeg and tumeric (misnamed "saffron") straw-embroidered with words "Spice Island,"coconut fudge and coconut tanning oil, unconscionably large bottles of duty-free French colognes, unpunctured conches from six months of culling. Which of them, once I had left the island, would seem anything but garish and sentimental? Is it the ocean I hear in a conch or any breeze to which the ear will fasten a remembered echo?

A tendency to trivialize or tout wasn't something I cultivated. Like any place, when the Midwest became conscious of itself—that it was an original, significant, historical territory—pride set about to mint and market that quality. Such communal recognition requires the additional qualities of kitsch: too much or too many, under- or oversized, and always in the wrong place. Our family made more than one pilgrimage to Olentangy Indian Caverns which, whatever else it reported to preserve—frontierism? the wonders of geology?—was a generously brief tour of damp rooms lit by low-wattage bulbs whose theme colors were adapted from the feathered Indian headdresses hung in the gift shop over the plastic arrowheads and beaded belts.

Old MacDonald's Farm might have commemorated our long-standing domestication of livestock; still, we showed our respect by sliding around haylofts, chasing baby goats, and milking cast-concrete cows whose water-filled, rubber udders made perfect squirt guns.

And the Ohio State Fair impersonated every aspect of Ohio's self-consciousness. Just entering the fair through the legs of the "H" in the thirty-foot tall "OHIO" admission gates cautioned the visitor that whatever lay ahead was sure to be out of proportion. Something—the August humidity?—had swollen the whole fair, the nation's largest state fair, into near parody of itself. And each booth and building was infected with the same giddiness that came from driving all the way to the state's capital, or the same titillation, from viewing Chief, who, at 1203 pounds, was committed to gaining another 132 pounds to become the world's largest pig.

The fairgrounds woke from its hibernation at the center of a city with a million residents, people, who, according to an immense *Readers Digest* survey in 1958 preferred Westerns and quiz shows above all other television programs (thirteen of the twenty-five most popular). The fair straddled this ambidextrous viewing habit, creating an unofficial body of the both kinds of frontierism, a past and a future Midwest, two painted flats with openings for visitors to frame their own faces and be photographed. (Was this another flat—a painting of a headless man at a desk scattered with childhood snapshots—through which I was peering, years later, at my own fair attendance?) Ideology balanced technology, tradition balanced innovation, and nothing balanced the will to excess.

Besides honoring the exceptional in arts such as sheep shearing, corn-relish canning, stoop-masonry, crazy-quilting, and chicken hybridization, the fair featured Ohio's industrial advances. These were highlighted along the midway where, each year, the rides swelled higher, spun faster, ran shorter, and sported longer lines—all technological marvels to a child my age. But the Buckeye Building was the temple of free enterprise, and inside the darkened barn, crowded rows of exhibitors proclaimed that every discovery, of every magnitude, should have a table on which to display its literature, free samples, and register-for-a-free-year's-supply card. Curious, prodigal, peculiar, the displays drew more gasps than the oddities of the side show: a space capsule bank molded before your eyes, a silver-cleaner that removed tarnish in one quick dip, a computer-generated personality analysis.

The move from Columbus to the West Indies focused this Midwetern integration. In Grenada, the primitive abutted the progressive; native heritage, against modern heracy. The only harmony I could detect appeared to be the afternoon hour when no one worked. Although there were no dairy cows on the island to spark it, a vivid memory of mine featured the Ohio State Fair's particular combination of country craft and scientific advance: the butter sculptures inside Dairy Barn. Since the early nineteen-hundreds, one of three men has sculpted nearly half a ton of fresh butter into the shape of a cow. Since I can remember, the exhibit has always included the cow, her calf, and a featured third figure to reflect a contemporary theme. What began as a modest culinary whim—the molding of a butter pat into a curlique or flower—has become a seasonal occupation, predicated on the impulse to combine the staple with the caprice into an artistic medium for popular culture. Annually, the sculptors transformed Ohio's own butter into Ohio boys like Bob Hope, Coach Woody Hayes, racecar driver Bobby Rayhal, Jack Nicholas, and Neil Armstrong (waving a flag on a moonscape made of butter—*not* green cheese), into the non-Ohioan Darth Vader, and into a butter child in a wheelchair, reaching for a butter butterfly that dangles out of reach.

At Grenada dinners in the school cafeteria, I laughed with my Caribbean friends as I described the sculptures I had seen. The paradoxical combination seemed as oddly conceived as the dessert the native cooks had prepared especially for us Americans: gelled imported Jello (primarily a protein) dissolving around chunks of indigenous papaya (containing an enzyme that breaks down protein). But the humor had the glow of homage. And didn't it sound varguley holy for a man to create a cow from the very butter the man had created from the cow?

If it wasn't holiness or wholesomeness, perhaps it was just the spirit of adventure that gave such added license to the spirit of Columbus entrepreneurs. Certainly the most common form had already taken hold—the way gardeners say certain weeds take hold—on the lawns in our own neighborhoods: houses that existed in a state of perpetual garage, yard and tag sale. (A mild, biennial form had even attacked my mother and her friends. Indeed, the first profit I had ever "made" came from contributing things my parents had bought me or I had bought with my allowance to our garage sale.)

Nearby homes expressed their commercial aspirations by hanging a "Beauty Parlor Supplies" or a "Dogs Groomed" sign in what was clerly a dining-room window. More extenuated longings in Columbus founded multiple-business establishments. Our city preserved the idea of "both," as though a Midwestern career choice meant heads and tails, and even multiples of each. We frequently passed Kennedy's, a single facade labeled in huge block letters: MARINE ACCESSORIES, FISHING SUPPLIES, HUNTING GEAR, CAKE DECORATING. Another neighborhood enjoyed the convenience of The Glorious Corner, an ex-gas station offering its services as a Revival-Hall/Soft-Serve-Ice-Cream-Stand/Thrift Shop/Dry Cleaners. An easy drive away stood Odero Sinoh's, a Beverage Drive-Through/Party Mart/Lounge/Auto-Leasing Company. What other service could a neighborhood require?

Before my birth in Columbus, that same imagination created Big Bear, the nation's first supermarket. Alas, I was born decades too late to see the trained bear lumbering along the (then) strangely accessible aisles, pawing particular comestibles into a cart, thereby testifying to the ease of *going* shopping. That mindset spawned Town and Country, the nation's first shopping center, a stretch of individual businesses that offered, more than windows decorated with the latest goods, a vision of the future. And that heady will-to-patronize established Columbus as an official All-American City, which meant that in the minds of corporate and commercial ventures, we were the ideal headquarters, test market, and trial base. Fast-food chains like White Castle, Wendy's and Rax began their successes with people I knew, perhaps even with my own mother, who would even meet me outside the school cafeteria with an enviable hot lunch from Wendy's.

I hadn't realized the extent of my own immersion in commercial testing until I learned that my Caribbean acquaintances had never consumed a childhood cereal of sugary flakes and dehydrated bits of ice cream. They had never purchased chocolate- or vanilla-flavored gum as we had for an enthusiastic but unrepeated chew. Flubber, that purple cube of wiggly plastic that appeared at Kiddie Korner just after Fred MacMurray's success in "The Absent-Minded Professor," was never found in their living room carpeting or sibling's hair along with Silly Putty and Goop—nor in their trashcans when, a month later, Flubber was withdrawn from the market for causing rashes.

Would Americans buy film from a shed-size ladybug settled in a pizza parlor's parking lot? Would families use a toilet paper roll that released a rose fragrance when a sheet was torn free? Would mothers prefer Coca-Cola in a family-size jug? Would husbands buy more Stroh's beer if the can was white instead of gold? If a corporation wanted to know the answers, people just like my family, living in Columbus, Ohio, could tell them. Our size, our age, ethnic and income distribution represented the national as a whole—we *were* the All-American City.

My first authentic glimpse of industry was our school visit to a commercial bakery. Downtown, the aroma of baking bread was as pronounced as the looming letters of "WONDER BREAD" that rose, one glowing red word over the other, above the adjacent neighborhood. Most of the time we could only see the one word "WONDER" revealed between the blockade of downtown silhouettes. At night, the word loomed beside the other prominent white factory lights that proclaimed "BELMONT CASKETS." As far as I knew, Columbus produced bread and coffins, the slices that covered the cheese and tomatoes packed in my school lunch, and the tombs that Boris Karloff and Bela Lugosi occupied every Saturday afternoon during a triple horror feature. Together, those two large, legible phrases of the skyline extended the city's hospitable greetings—or was it a warning?—to travellers on the downtown freeways.

The Wonder Bread factory, the very place that baked the bread which helped our bodies grow in twelve essential ways, created a flush of excitement second only to the Invisible Woman and her series of illuminated organs at the Center for Science and Industry, our other school field trip. "Overly refined," "mass produced," "preservatives," "unwholesomeness"—not a negative quality entered our minds or our tour, for by the end of our visit we had possession of a food more miraculous than manna: the identical family-size loaf transformed into a miniature loaf each of us could take, just for visiting. As it happened, those precious slices of white bread moulded before I'd let my mother profane two pieces in a sandwich.

This was the time period when marketing strategies, packaging, premiums, and associated entertainment, eclipsed their own commodities. Before becoming a writer with the occupation's typically attendant obsessions, my favorite mail was the small sample package. It didn't matter if the product tucked inside was non-spotting dishwasher detergent, creamier hand cream, secretly disguised sanitary napkins, or country-fresh air freshener—each was special because it was improved, new, or advanced; unannounced, free, and miniature; and because *you couldn't buy it at the store even if you wanted to!* How had we been singled out to deserve these treats? And what could we do to get more? The samples had been sent to us just for living where we lived, on Bolton Avenue, in Columbus, Ohio.

With a vividness that borders on permanent damage, I can recall the thin, squishable packets of Herbal Essence Shampoo that arrived frequently enough that my mother never needed to purchase a bottle. These were the years when the peace symbol, spray-painted on overpasses and bathroom walls, was never mistaken for the Mercedes-Benz logo, and our late awakening to ecology urged us to compensate by rinsing our hair with scents from the green world.

Correspondingly, our family meals found inspiration in invention. "Freeze-dried," "evaporated," "instant," and "condensed" became the essential catch-phrase qualities just as "vitamin-enriched" and "like Grandma used to make" had been for previous generations, and swayed Mother toward purchases much more frequently than did our taste buds. We children relished the idea of TV dinners, particularly if we could eat them on TV trays while watching "Peter Pan" or "Soupy Sales" on TV. To witness the cooking of a boil-in-a-bag dinner, provided an evening's sustenance. The thrill of whacking dinner rolls' cardboard tube on the edge of the Formica, eclipsed the sensual experience of warm, aromatic bread.

Something probably went caterwaul in our sense of appreciation, but pleasures no longer issued from the simple consumption of something wonderful, but from its convenience or novelty or a tangential prize or contest. Real value in a purchase was determined by what other thing was thrown in, redeemable, or discounted. Our glassware came from fill-ups at the gas station, our dish towels from jumbo boxes of detergent, our toaster-oven by changing banks, our toys inside or on cereal boxes, our walkie-talkies and electric carving knife from pasting grocery stamps into little booklets.

We were real, hard-working, sincere, prospering people entitled to these real values. And by virtue of this, we could win incredible things. In fact, according to the posters at the drug store and the letters in our mailbox, we might already be winners. Disc jockey's were combing the city at random, ready to give prizes to our license plate!

All we'd have to do is pick up the phone and call. The host of "Bowling for Dollars" telephoned someone in our area every Saturday afternoon with dinners-for-two at restaurants with table-side cooking. And if we hadn't registered, sent in a postcard with our names, or filled-out an entry blank, we could always identify with the winners. They were people like us. An afternoon with the flu, and I watched contestants on "Supermarket Sweep" running down the aisle of a store just like our Big Bear, raking the tinned hams and cigarette cartons into their shopping carts just like the bear himself. I watched the women on "Queen for a Day" receive all the unaffordable things like Oneida silverware, and a new electric clothes dryer, and even a certificate from the Spiegel catalogue. People from Ohio were on that program; they had even filmed a week's episode at Veterans Memorial Auditorium where my parents had taken me to a concert by The Supremes *with* Diana Ross. But beyond actual participation, I could hear, in round after round, a list of personal tragedies that far exceeded anything I'd ever experienced, and I could hold an elbow in one hand and use my other forearm like the applause meter that appeared on the screen, measuring, for myself, each heartbreaking, disaster-ridden, poverty-stricken degree of desperation. And then I could feel the glut of prizes, heavy as the queen's crown and cape and armload of roses, smothering any residual grief beneath its weight. By the time "Flippo, the Clown," was broadcast, I had watched "Let's Make a Deal," "The Price Is Right," and "The Newlywed Game," and the things we didn't own, the answers and tragedies and opportunites I didn't possess, occupied my bedroom like the germs that were keeping me home from school.

We cherished the experience of icing cupcakes with ready-to-spread canned frosting, withdrawing money from a sliding drawer at a drive-through teller, and borrowing books from a green bus that pulled into the school playground once a month. Between a pair of panning searchlights, we shopped for cars in lots occupied with barbecues, a hot air balloonist, midget clowns, and a woman frozen in a block of ice. Supermarkets solicited our attention by inviting an amusement park to settle in front of their doors. Which store for new school shoes? The ones where we could receive the next in the series of Buster Brown toys and our parents could peek into a small step-up X-ray machine with no foresight into radiation's dangers, and confirm how snuggly their babys' feet fit inside the booties they had selected. An innocence was applied, like an unconditional guarantee, to anything advanced. And Columbus appeared to be as advanced as any place in the world.

This minor, applied technology was a second point of perspective through which I could imagine the Midwest. Further comparison with Grenada brought an overlooked poignancy to the trials and tests "suffered" by Columbus families. On the island, labor was the age-old, time-tested product, and could be purchased for fewer East Caribbean dollars than batteries or spray starch. Most American students easily afforded someone to garden, iron, shop, cook, clean, and drive.

The demonstrations I experienced as a child had nothing to do with rebellious blue jeans and civil rights, although Columbus had made little enough progress in that area. Our attentions were trained on domestic demonstrations. To witness was to want. "Try our new smokey cheese on a cracker?" a woman just like my mother would ask, piping an orange stream from the nozzle of an inverted can. Was she the same Ohio housewife who had never dreamed of being in a commercial but said *OK* to this one because her family truly preferred this brands above the others? Crepe paper streamers waving in an air conditioner's breeze, a fried egg sliding from a hot skillet sprayed with PAM—these fascinated us children the way movie stars did our parent's generation. What could be more enchanting than watching an appliance perform a herculean labor like vacuuming a clear path in a pile of spilled straight pins. Comparatively it was an easy task to imagine how it might smooth the dents or our footprints on Mother's new shag.

My desired but never-acquired favorite was a blender--an Osterizer, I think—that must have had the sound of a tree clipper, although no one would notice this at the time of purchase amid the general din of the Buckeye Building. I hadn't imagained what use our family would have for the powerful machine, but I *had* sampled a strawberry milkshake concocted from egg shells, celery, and beets poured by the smiling man into the same kind of tiny cup from which I had drunk by "Don't Forget Sabin on Sunday" polio vaccine. *Indispensible,* I remember the aproned man saying into the microphone around his neck. "But it's indispensible," I implored my mother, feeling the kitchen of our new house grow steadily out-dated and out-moded. How had she resisted the knife we'd seen together the previous day at the fair, the one that glided through a brick-hard package of frozen spinach and and diced whole onions in a few deft strokes? "The only tears you'll cry are tears of joy," the demonstrator promised. Was it our imagination or our conscience that took a cue from an onion's ability to draw tears? We trained ourselves not to look away, but to look forward, forward to owning such aids to modern living.

At my desk in Grenada, I wanted the objects and experiences I was recovering—in letters, conversations, and revisions of memory—to remain independent and intact. Yet I knew I couldn't help but do as the word "recover" implied: hide each one again beneath memory, even beneath the memory of a memory. The danger with the things that recollection has chosen is their willfullness. Deserving or not, each hopes to be a symbol—at the least, a symbol of what we've forgotten.

At a desk now, in Columbus, Ohio, I have hoped that my recollections of Grenada and the Midwest I began to describe there would resist similar tidiness. Is it possible to see the native and the derived qualities, the species and the spectacles, that formed some version of a Midwestern sensibility as opposing only the way magnetic poles oppose, creating a force that suspends each charged item between the values of its field?

It *is* tempting to say: My reason for leaving Columbus was to be a physician *and* a writer; my reason for returning to Columbus, to be a writer. But what is so reasonable about a single reason?

I had enrolled in a medical school with students who, shunted along an uncertain foreign route, possessed a singular determination: to pass the entrance exam into an American medical school. Unlike my colleagues, I subsisted on British novels, composing letters, writing journals, and toying with images for poems and my first stories. In a far-too-conscious part of my mind, there was a compound image of myself: family physician by day, writer at night, with the additional hope that one vocation's hours would illuminate the others. "The choices are yours," replayed in my head. "Whatever makes you happy will make us happy." Weren't those the voices of a test-market city, a free sample of Midwestern indulgence, a personal challenge to go where no one I knew had gone before?

I left Grenada in late May with the rest of the medical school. The rainy season was beginning. In Columbus the weather service announced a high-pressure system and unseasonable warmth. I wrote St. George's School of Medicine for a leave of absence. That summer I made the decision not to be a doctor, and, at that point, not to be a writer necessarily, but to begin doing things writers did. Columbus, in the person of my parents, greeted this decision with the same open arms that had embraced the idea of my being a doctor, and had annually embraced a child's fickle experiments and fascinations. I'd like to hold them open there, if I could. I'd like to hold all of my suburban Midwest in a similarly open gesture of encouragement, discovery, and watchfulness, and think of myself, now, as a combination butter-sculptor/pumpkin grower/part-owner of an Appaloosa named Pegasus, minding my own small business under the sign of Wonder Bread and Belmont Caskets.

Quarry Swimmers, Bloomington, Indiana. Roger Pfingston

SCOTT RUSSELL SANDERS

STONE TOWNS AND THE COUNTRY BETWEEN

A native of Memphis, Tennessee, Scott Russell Sanders grew up in Ohio, and though he has lived in many places since, he declares, "My imagination has always remained tangled in the woods and creeks and towns of the Ohio River Valley." Now living in Bloomington, where he teaches literature and intellectual history at Indiana University, he frankly admits, "I am committed to the making of art about the Midwest."

That art has resulted in ten books, including the recent novels *The Invisible Company* (1988) and *The Engineer of Beasts* (1988), the historical tales of *Wilderness Plots* (1983), and the prize winning essays from *Stone County* (1985) and the *The Paradise of Bombs* (1987).

"Stone Towns and the Country Between" is taken from *Stone Country*, his book about the Indiana stone cutting country. Here he records in a finely textured film the panorama of place while slowing for rich close-ups on the bumps and grooves of its details and characters. He is most drawn to the workers and their tools, their memories and talk of better times. He reads the landscape with a sense of wit and significance. As we walk past main street shops, stroll down side streets with their open midwestern yards, encounter a local festival, a sense of life emerges that is as resilient as the quarry stone. We end in the town cemetery with an image that holds it all—"looms the jaunty figure of the cutter, frozen in stone at the peak of his pride." Sanders moves us homeward into the bold intention of the place.

STONE TOWNS AND THE COUNTRY BETWEEN

Water-carved chunks of limestone flank driveways and rise from flowerbeds, pale and knuckled like the vertebrae of dinosaurs. Landscape architects send trucks long distances to fetch them from quarries and creekbeds, but the local people drag them home behind tractors or in sagging pickups. The backroad name for them is "waterwarts." The prize ones are pierced with holes, letting air and sunshine pour through and making the massy rock seem riddled with light.

In the tulip bed at the center of Jim Medley's driveway turnaround, out Red Hill Road from Ellettsville, a fan-shaped waterwart stands on edge. The hole through it, large enough to swallow a cabbage, gives it the look of a great staring cyclops. "Daddy calls it his potty stone," Medley tells me. "If we still had a privy, I believe I'd try it out. You'd never find a smoother seat."

Shaped like a dolmen, the sign welcoming you to Ellettsville is a rough-hewn limestone slab balanced across two stubby uprights. Carved beneath the town name are the words: "Builders of American History."

A hand-lettered notice in the town's main pizza joint proclaims: NO TOBACCO CHEWING. A wooden peacock with a spray of real iridescent feathers hangs on the wall alongside posters of rabbits, clippings about local football games, and baskets filled with dried flowers. The cigarette machine supports a terrarium and a clutch of baseball trophies. At lunchtime the men play Donkey Kong and PacMan on the video boxes while their orders cook. They eat from varnished picnic tables, and keep their heads warm under visored caps: FARM BUREAU CO-OP, TRUCKERS OF AMERICA, JOHN DEERE, ODON CLOTHING COMPANY, LUBRIPLATE, HYDROPOWER, MAIL POUCH. In the parking lot, the bumper stickers on their trucks say: EAT MORE POSSUM, KIDS NEED TO BREATHE, I'D RATHER BE DANCING, IF GUNS ARE OUTLAWED ONLY OUTLAWS WILL HAVE GUNS, NUCLEAR WAR IS BAD FOR CHILDREN, NUKE THE WHALES, I LOVE GRANDMA, HAVE YOU HUGGED YOUR DAD TODAY?

Where Jack's Defeat Creek crosses Ellettsville's main drag, the Village Inn greets you with a round clock labeled "Time to Eat." Indoors, a sign over the cook's window gives you a cheery "Hi, Neighbor." The walls are decorated with the horns of bulls, wickerwork fans, and placards bearing words of wisdom. One saying comes from Will Rogers: "Politicians are the best men money can buy." The waitresses are grandmotherly in age and manner, making you feel like a long-lost grandchild who's dropped by for a meal. Their hair is piled in billowy mounds the color of gunsmoke. Their hands and voices are in no hurry as they serve you "The Stone Cutter's Breakfast"—omelet, butt steak, fries. For dessert they bring coffee thick enough to hold the spoon upright, and a wedge of peanut butter pie.

On the highways, billboards promote fast foods, herbicides, pesticides, fertilizers, cigarettes, Army, Navy, National Guard, Savings Bonds, booze.

Signs along the edges of cornfields announce the brands of seed: PIONEER, BIG-D, TROJAN, AGRIGOLD.

Religion leaps at you from the roadsides: FAMILIES THAT PRAY TOGETHER, STAY TOGETHER; JESUS SAVES; GO TO CHURCH THIS SUNDAY; GET RIGHT WITH GOD. Words painted in day-glo yellow on the window of a gas station holler two hard questions:

**IS YOUR   IS GOD
BATTERY   IN YOUR
SAFE?   LIFE?**

A sheet of plywood lettered in red and nailed to a tree demands:

HURTING?

then answer its own question:

GOD CARES.

The churches come in more brands than hybrid corn: Primitive Methodist, United Methodist, Regular Baptist, Separate Baptist, Southern Baptist, Old Dutch, Seventh-Day Adventist, Whole Gospel, God of Prophecy, on and on. A street sign on the drive leading up to a pentecostal assembly in Peerless advises:

**DEAD END
CHURCH**

Two photographs have been thumbtacked to the bulletin board just inside the door of Summitt's Grocery and Post Office, the only store in Stinesville. One shows a candidate for sheriff, grinning around a fat cigar; the other shows the local raccoon-hunting champ, his feet hidden by an avalanche of ring-tailed pelts. Beside the photographs hangs a calendar with the names of villagers printed on their birthdays and anniversaries.

Whatever anybody in Stinesville has to say eventually gets said at the rear of the store on a bench between the woodstove and the cash register. I sit there, jugs for ears, beside the proprietor. Forty-nine, with a steel-colored brush of hair like a scouring pad, Bob Summitt possesses the rounded bulk of a man who has sat for quite a few years within easy reach of ice-cream bars and soda pop. Today he is red faced from having sat all morning on a mower. As we talk, he stokes himself periodically with pinches of tobacco. The soft-drink cooler is at my elbow, and every time the door opens I catch a refrigerated breeze.

It opens often this July afternoon. While Summitt rests up from mowing, his wife waits on the needs of the town. Jumper cables, cheese, a stump puller, bread, pint of chain-saw oil, fire extinguisher, aspirin, sliced ham. She is a brisk, soft-spoken woman, her steel-gray hair cut short to match her husband's, a pair of black, round-framed glasses giving her an owlish look. Whenever boxholders come in, she fetches their mail without being asked. People sort out the letters from the bills on her counter and sit down beside us to read anything noteworthy. They also read the newspapers that are stacked on the bench, or catch up on the news in the perennial fashion, by talking.

Summitt began work in the mills as a laborer, shoveling stone dust and scraps. "No matter who you was, you started out with a shovel in your hands." Eventually he apprenticed as a planerman, but one week after completing the apprenticeship he was drafted. By the time he came home, in 1959, his hands had lost the feel for tools, and business in limestone had sunk very low. The old men, with decades of seniority, would not give up their places. Young men like Summitt, in order to work at all, had to shuffle from mill to mill, and had to put up with the shabbiest equipment. "When I quit working stone for good I was down in Indian Hill, and they put me to using these wore-out steel tools. Three passes, and they needed sharpening. I'd never worked with anything but carbide tools, and down there only the old guys had them. If they wasn't using them, they'd hide them in the dirt just to keep me from getting my hands on them. Well, one day I was using them soft tools and broke three pieces of stone, and I got so blame mad I never went back." It's no wonder that stone has gone under, he says. The owners never modernized. They stuck with the old equipment and old methods while other industries were keeping up with the times.

He knows for a fact that stone from his planer was used in a lot of famous buildings, but can't name a single one to save himself. The names were all there on the job tickets, but he hardly ever bothered to look. "To tell you the truth, what I looked for was 3:30 in the afternoon and a paycheck on Friday." After quitting the mill he worked all over, doing everything under the sun. Eighteen years ago he took over the store and post office. "And if I knew who my boss was I'd put in for retirement."

In two hours of sitting there, I meet two dozen people, every one of the men a former stone worker, every woman the wife or daughter of one, every kid the grandchild of one.

"When I was a boy," says a butter-voiced man with a cowpoke's face, "the quarries and mills were all there was. That's where your daddy worked, and that's where you worked, as soon as you got big enough to work at all." He lied about his age so he could start young, at sixteen, hooking stone. "Now there's a job where you've got to trust people. So long as the guy at the other end of the block has dug his hole and set his dog right, and so long as the derrick runner and powerman do what they're supposed to do, you're just fine. But if anybody blinks, you could be dead."

Paydays were celebrated with poker and craps, the cards played on stone, the dice on bare dirt. Many a week's wage was lost in a single roll or deal, and if the loser was married he would catch sand and hellfire when he slunk home. Once, a man who had grown too old for the quarries came back for the weekly game. After a year's work at squaring logs for railroad ties, he had saved up twenty dollars. In three rolls he lost every nickel. Whereupon he stood up, dusted off his hands, and declared, "Easy come, easy go." The police raided the game one time and made a big stink about it. The next week a new spot was cleared in the woods and the game resumed.

After the quarries near Stinesville closed down in the early 1960s, the gambling continued, but the paychecks came from elsewhere. Leaving stone, the men went to work fixing cars, airconditioners, televisions. They patched holes on the highways, pumped gas, screwed parts together on assembly lines, swept floors, drove trucks, whatever they could find to do.

When a mousy old gent creeps in to buy an ice-cream sandwich, he mumbles that he doesn't know anything about the quarries. He's well up in his sixties, toothless, wearing a moldering Chevrolet cap and the mournful expression of a beagle. His eyes aim at the floor, as if on the lookout for dropped keys.

Summitt prods himself gently. "Who you think you're fooling, pretending you never been in a quarry?"

"Oh, sure," the old man concedes, his voice a faint trickle, "I worked for a few years on a channeler." Like most of the stone men, he's hard of hearing. He whispers because he is afraid of shouting the way deaf men do. I lean close to listen. As a boy, he used to carry his father's dinner bucket from the farm house to Wallace Quarry. There was a regular beaten path that all the children followed. His parents knew exactly how long it should take him to cover the distance, and if he was late at either end he caught the mischief. Since the trail cut right through a strawberry patch, in the season when the berries came ripe he ran most of the way in both directions, to leave himself time for picking and eating.

Along with three of his four brothers, he fought in Hitler's war. One of them was killed, shot to pieces in Italy. When the casket was sent home for burial, the surviving brothers knew there was no body inside. "I saw them battlefields. They buried whatever scraps they could find right on the spot." But the boys assured their mother that the slain brother was in the box, safe and sound. Almost crazy from grief, she wanted to open the casket to make sure. "That's why they send an MP along, to keep people from prying it open and finding out the truth."

Every man I've talked with today spent some time in uniform, usually the Army's olive drab. Some of the old mossbacks fought in the Great War; the balding men fought in the Second World War and Korea; and the young bucks (whom we can see buzzing their motorcycles and jacked-up cars past the window) fought in Vietnam. "You didn't think about whether you was going to go," the butter-voiced cowpoke tells me. "It was like starting in the quarries and mills at sixteen or eighteen. When you come of age, you just signed up and they handed you a gun."

Across Main Street from the store, in a tiny park, there is a war memorial, with enough names on it for a town five times as big as Stinesville. From over here you can see that Summitt's Grocery and Post Office occupies what used to be the Odd Fellows Oolitic Lodge. Built of wood in 1891, and after a fire rebuilt of limestone in 1894, it is linked to three other abandoned stores, all dating from the 1890s, all bearing the names of various Easton brothers. For obscure reasons, the Eastons opened four dry-goods stores side by side. During the town's heyday, between about 1890 and 1916, some twenty businesses flourished here, and the population crept over seven hundred. There were four taverns, and trains brought thirsty folks from all the surrounding—and tavernless—villages. The streets were so thick with people you could hardly walk. But in 1916 the town's largest mill burned down, and Stinesville's fortunes began to slide.

Many of the citizens eventually slid into Mt. Carmel cemetery, west of town. Except for a single wedge of pink granite—which looks out of place, like a cardinal in a flock of sparrows—every marker is limestone. Most were professionally carved, but a few, for children, were hacked out by hand. There is the usual forest of sculpted tree trunks with the limbs lopped off. On one of these a mallet and sledge have been carved right onto the branches, as if forgotten there when the job was done. The marker for the Titzel family is capped by a steam locomotive, complete with coal tender, all in lichen-covered limestone. In the sinkholes of the cemetery grow towering arborvitae, spindly cedars, blackberries, frilly topped wild asparagus. The weeds are knee high, except right near the stones, where lily of the valley and periwinkle hold their own. The weeds keep me from seeing a fat blacksnake until I've almost stepped on it. I freeze, and his lordship slithers under a memorial slab.

Many houses in the stone towns have an evolutionary air to them, no longer as fine as they once were, not yet as fine as their owners hope to make them. Warped clapboard shows around the edges of aluminum siding. Porch roofs lean on two-by-fours, waiting for fresh mortar on their limestone posts. Replacement windows, smaller than the originals, wear collars of milky plastic. In winter, bales of hay snug up against the foundations for insulation; in summer, the hay mulches the garden. Silvery new stovepipes rise next to crumbling chimneys. The woodpiles are half the size of the houses. Gnarled antennas dangle from roofs, while in front yards the gauzy dishes of satellite receivers snag images and sound from all the world.

Yards in limestone country are decorated with plaster donkeys pulling carts, mirrored balls in tints of green and blue, wagon wheels, plastic flamingos, figurines of black servants (some with faces painted white) holding lanterns, statues of alert deer with ears pricked forward and tails uplifted, wooden ducks whose wings revolve in the breeze, model windmills with spinning vanes.

Gaunt rusting towers of real windmills loom between farmhouses and barns. The houses are frame, blazing white in the sunshine, rising two stories above limestone basements to gables filigreed with arabesques of wood. Metal-roofed porches clasp the ground floor in shadows. The barns are hump-backed, tin-roofed, with sides the color of burgundy. The cornbins are tall gleaming cylinders or squat blue tanks, their pointed roofs giving them the look of rockets on launch pads. Round bales of hay clump together in the fields, as if for company. In the farm lots women hang up clothes and men thrust their arms into the entrails of machines—tractors, bulldozers, trucks, cars—and kids make up games out of sticks and stones and dirt. Middle-aged cars, cannibalized for parts, rest on blocks of stone in the side yards. Elderly cars, gnawed down to fenders and chassis, sink beneath briars in the gullies of pastures.

The old state road heading north from Oolitic has been cut in two by a quarry. The townspeople must detour miles around the hole to visit their neighbors in Needmore. But they are used to shaping their lives to suit the needs of the great god limestone. The name of their town derives from the egg-shaped particles—the oolites—they saw in the rock. At one time nearly every house here belonged to a family whose menfolk worked in the quarries and mills. Too poor to build their houses out of anything except wood or tarpaper or concrete blocks, they used limestone only for stair treads, sidewalk flagging, pillars on porches, lintels, benches, birdbaths.

Since the road was cut, most of the gas stations have given up the ghost. Hoosier Avenue Liquors has taken over one of them, and appears to be thriving. Another one houses Stone Capitol Pest Control. And still another one, across the highway from the Living Word Church, is occupied by Stone Kingdom Realtors. The sign out front shows a pyramid with a mystical eye at the apex, but the realty business has winked shut. From Oolitic Rent-All a radio blares, advertising *Hot Rod Magazine's* Super Nationals auto show in Indy, a "picnic of power" designed to "celebrate America's Love Affair with the Car." A few steps away from the Living Word Church, kids scramble and yell in the school yard. The boxy school itself hunkers down in a smear of blacktop, looking grim and bleak, like a grout pile at a quarry. Bas relief panels up near the roof depict a globe, an open book, a lamp of learning—and a basketball passing through a net.

Many of the women in Oolitic, having learned from the Bible that their hair is their glory, walk down the sidewalks under mountainous beehive hairdos. They look as though thunderclouds have gathered on their heads. In a town with one grocery, they can choose from four or five beauty parlors, including Raintree Hair Company and Tigress Lair Salon.

Banners draped from lightpole to lightpole across Main Street advertise the Oolitic Summer Festival. The newest attraction stands out front of the town hall: a pasty-white limestone statue of the World War II comic book hero, Joe Palooka. About eight feet tall, dressed in boxing gear—shorts, cape, high-laced boots, taped fists—he's a big-chested brute, rock ribbed and square jawed, with a shock of hair draped over his forehead and bullet holes for eyes. For years he stood south of Oolitic in a park run by the Fraternal Order of Police. But the cops couldn't keep vandals from defacing him, so he was moved into town for safekeeping. In preparation for the summer festival, he's been sandblasted and his muscles have been touched up, but he's still an ungainly brute, long trunked and short legged, a Neanderthal in limestone.

Zigzag country roads follow the section lines, turning ninety degrees at the corners of fields. Roads topped with crushed limestone turn blazing white in summer, like pathways of snow. Driving them, you trail plumes of dust behind. In winter, under real snow, the roads merge with the fields. You keep on the hidden gravel by aiming midway between the fences—barbed wire strung on creosoted poles, rusty wire stapled to fat stumps, single strands charged with electricity, mossy limestone walls laid up without mortar, split rails, hedges. Cedars raise their green flames above the fence rows and flicker in the brown woods. Along frozen creeks the sycamores bristle like pale whiskers in black beards. Last year's stubble shows in dotted lines across the corn fields. Crows pump by overhead on raucous errands, the pitch darkness of their feathers deepened by the white of winter. Flocks of starlings dash ink strokes against the sky. Farmhouses float in the oceans of snow like islands, like mirages.

In front of trailers, low-slung ranches, prefabricated boxes, and suburban villas—homes whose owners punch the clocks in town—memories of farming still show in the choice of mailboxes: some are shaped like miniature barns, some like silos, some like corncribs; they're propped up by milkcans, hand pumps, plowshares, augers, upended cultivating disks, horseshoes welded into iron lace, chain welded into serpentine curves. Inevitably, some mailboxes also rest on pillars and piles and pyramids of limestone.

Some roadcuts near Red Hog Hill, south of Bloomington, were dug not with drills and dynamite, but with channelers, because the limestone was too valuable for blasting. In roadcuts near Harrodsburg, rock hounds with hammers and battery-powered drills prospect for geodes. Where the geodes are thickest, they have burrowed in several feet. Every now and again the overhanging ledge collapses, strewing the highway with jagged debris. Recently a chunk the size of a dump truck tumbled down and blocked two lanes of traffic. The rock face is sixty or seventy feet high, eroded at the top. Mud seams creep down between the upthrust knobs of stone, pouring out rust-colored deltas of clay. Crown vetch, pink with flowerheads in June, and yellow clover snag their roots in every smidgen of dirt. High up in the roadcuts the crystalline faces of exposed geodes shine from the gray rock like diamonds set in tarnished silver.

On the highway leading into Bedford from the south, the Chamber of Commerce has erected an antique derrick. The billboard affixed to the mast announces that you are about to enter "The Limestone Capital of the World." Back in the boom years, there were thirty or thirty-five mills cutting stone in Bedford; today there are two or three. Despite this dwindling, the townspeople still call the place Stone City, and the high-school teams still go by the nickname of the Cutters.

In the middle of June a carnival forms a ragged noose around the courthouse. Hawkers invite you to try your hand shooting basketballs and airguns, have your fortune read, drive leashed motorcycles or dented dodge-um cars, fill your stomach with sugary goo and then empty it again by riding the whirligig rides, all as part of the Bedford Limestone Festival. But there is no whiff of limestone anywhere in the festival itself, only bored barkers, horseshoe contests, a beauty pageant, a celebrity bake-sale, a bike-run-trot-walk fundraiser for a local child, and, to finish it off, a buffet dinner and dance at the Elks Club.

On the courthouse square the banks look prosperous, but other enterprises are ailing. Across the intersection from the Stone City Bank is the Greystone Hotel, once a hive of limestone wheelers and dealers, once a place where moneymen made decisions about the skylines of cities, now a dreary hulk with a caved-in roof and lobby—glimpsed around the NO TRESPASSING signs—buried in fallen plaster. Nearby is the ruin of a fire-gutted cinema. You walk under the marquee, through a gap where the popcorn machine used to be, under a web of twisted girders and into open air. The emblem hanging in the doorway of the pillared Masonic Temple is broken and dangles askew. Three plaster owls, dyed an implausible brown and blue, have been stuck on window ledges up under the portico to discourage pigeons. But the pigeons flock around and bespatter the temple anyway, cheeky birds, oblivious. Around the square a few shops get by: The Ice Cream Klinic, Kloset Boutique, Smoke Stick Gun Shop, The Corral Video Games ("No Foul Language"), Greystone Gift Shop, Living Waters Ministry, Puffy's Tavern, and a bakery just called—in red neon—Bakery. But many stores are empty, their windows covered with paper or glazed with paint, and several display flame-red GOING OUT OF BUSINESS signs.

Railroad tracks run along the west side of the square. When a train lumbers through, the town stops dead. At one time, hundreds of flatcars loaded with stone rumbled over these tracks every week. Now the trains haul aluminum, plastics, automobile parts, livestock, coal. The milled stone that still leaves Bedford rides by truck, because the railroad beds are so broken down they will not bear the weight.

The county museum, in the basement of the courthouse, devotes a single glass case to limestone (there are a dozen cases devoted to dolls and cutlery and high-button shoes; there's an entire room stuffed with the memorabilia of war), and even this display is all but hidden by a photocopying machine, which the genealogists keep busy churning out family trees. In the gloom you can see a handful of limestone artifacts: a wreath, an angel, an eagle, a bust of Will Rogers, a plaque showing an Indian in a cactus landscape, and several of the pointy balls—like the bristling seedpods of sweetgum or sycamore—that apprentices carved to prove their skill. The finest piece in the case is a miniature statue of a stone cutter, holding a mallet in one hand and a chisel in the other. The sleeves of his jacket are rolled up over ropy forearms. He wears a railroadman's cap, an apron, a handlebar moustache, and the jaunty look of a man who knows exactly how far he is from the center of the universe.

Walk south from the courthouse square to Green Hill Cemetery and you will find a full-scale version of that miniature. Lifted high on a pedestal, the figure of a cutter lords it over the acres of graves. Not a memorial to anyone dead, the statue is a tribute to all diggers and cutters of stone. Many of the bluebloods from the industry are buried nearby—Ingalls, Elliot, Perry, Matthews, Reed—whose names are engraved in ritzier stones, in granite and marble. Near the foot of the stone cutter's pedestal is the monument for Louis Baker, sculpted to represent a carver's bench with a section of pediment on top and all the tools of the trade—calipers, square, chisels, hammer—scattered about. As you drift toward the oldest part of the cemetery, where the dates of birth run back before the Revolution, you leave marble and granite behind and enter a forest of limestone. The most eloquent of all these markers is a raw monolith, uncut, undated, tilting as if toward sleep and bearing only the faint initials "T.W." There is a primordial feel to this rough pointing finger of stone, as if it rose from the very roots of grief and praise. And over it all—over monolith and Grecian temples, over carvings of cupids and hound dogs and doughboys, over peony bushes, marigolds, and begonias, over plastic flowers and the lords of industry—looms the jaunty figure of the cutter, frozen in stone at the peak of his pride.

Dennis Horan

DAVID SHIELDS

WELLS

David Shields is a California native who graduated from Brown University, then studied at the University of Iowa's Writers' Workshop where he lived from 1978-1983. His novel *Heroes* (1984) deals with some of his autobiographical roots. His second novel *Dead Languages* will appear in 1989 from Knopf.

His personal essay "Wells" is a poignant recapturing of those basketball days of our youth when play was for real and the losses became a part of us. Shields brings the methods of fiction to the simple realities of our ordinary lives. His writing picks up the emotion within the breath and pulse.

WELLS

—There has always been some strange connection for me between basketball and the dark. I started shooting hoops after school in the third grade, and I remember dusk and macadam combining into the sensation that the world was dying but I was indestructible. I played all the time, in all seasons, instead of other sports, played until my sad, mousy, immaculate mother stopped long enough from showing houses to take me home. In fifth grade I developed a double pump jump shot, which in the fifth grade was almost unheard of.

Rather than shooting on the way up, as everyone else did, I tucked my knees, hung in the air a second, pinwheeled the ball, then shot on the way down. My friends hated my new move. It seemed tough, mannered, teenage, vaguely Negro. I don't know how or why I started shooting differently. I must have grown weary sometimes waiting for Mom to drive by or Dad to return from his unsuccessful tennis road trips, or maybe it was my attempt to copy the Drake Bulldogs I watched at Veterans Auditorium. The more I shot like this the more my friends disliked me, and the more they disliked me the more I shot like this. It was the only thing about me that was at all unusual and it came to be my trademark, even my nickname. DC—Double Clutch.

One afternoon I played Horse with Cindy Larsen and she threw the ball over the fence, saying, "I don't want to play with you any more. You're too good. I'll bet one day you're going to start for Drake."

Cindy had by far the prettiest eyes at Valley Elementary and a grin so infectious it made me grin whenever she looked at me in math. She had a way of moving her body like a boy but still like a girl, too, and that game of Horse is one of the happiest memories of my childhood: dribbling around in the dark but knowing by instinct where the basket was; not being able to see Cindy but smelling her deodorant mixed with dirt; keeping close to her voice, in which I could hear her love for me and my career as a Drake Bulldog opening up into the night. I remember the sloped half-court at the far end of the playground, its orange pole, orange rim, and wooden green backboard, the chain net clanging in the wind, the sand and dirt on the court, the overhanging eucalyptus trees, the fence the ball bounced over into the street, and the bench the girls sat on, watching, trying to look bored.

The first two weeks of summer Cindy and I went steady but we broke up when I didn't risk rescuing her in a game of Capture the Flag, so she wasn't around for my tenth birthday party. I begged my parents to let Ethan Saunders, Jim Morrow, Bradley Gamble, and me shoot baskets until sunrise. My mother and father reluctantly agreed, and Dad swung by every few hours to make sure we were safe and bring more Coke, more birthday cake, more candy. There is no safer place in the continental United States than City Park Playground in West Des Moines. His occasional high beams were the only intrusion into the all-dark court we ruled for one night.

In shifts, two or even three of us slept on benches like baby bums and we had the usual disagreements about the last piece of cake and someone's dishonest count in 21, but all of us stayed till dawn. Around five in the morning Bradley and I were playing two-on-two against Jim and Ethan. The moon was falling. We had a lot of sugar in our blood and all of us were totally zonked and totally wired. With the score tied at eighteen in a game to twenty, I took a very long shot from the deepest corner. Before the ball left my hand Bradley said, "Way to hit."

I was a good shooter because it was the only thing I ever did and I did it all the time, but even for me such a shot was doubtful. Still, Bradley knew and I knew and Jim and Ethan knew, too, and we knew the way we knew our own names or the batting averages of the Cubs' infield or the lifelines in our palms. I felt it in my legs and up my spine, which arched as I fell back. My fingers tingled and my hand squeezed the night in joyful follow through. We knew the shot was perfect and when we heard the ball, a George Mikan special, a birthday gift from my sweet mom, whip the net we heard it as something we had already known for at least a second. What happened in that second during which we knew? Did the world stop? Did my soul ascend a couple of notches? What happens to ESP, to such keen eyesight? What did we have then, anyway, radar? When did we have to start working so hard to hear our own hearts?

As members of the Borel Junior High Bobcats, we worked out in a tiny gym with loose buckets and slippery linoleum and butcher paper posters exhorting us on. I remember late practices full of wind sprints and tipping drills. One day the coach said, "Okay gang, let me show you how we're gonna run picks for DC."

My friends ran around the court, passing, cutting, and screening for me. All for me. Set-plays for me to shoot from top of the circle or the left corner, two spots I couldn't miss from if I tried. It felt like the whole world was weaving to protect me, then release me, and the only thing I had to do was pop my double pump jumper. Afterward, we went to a little market down the street. I bought paper bags of penny candy for everybody, to make sure they didn't think I was going to get conceited. We walked home in the cold rain of December. Still wanting something after eating our candy, we knew we would live forever.

The junior varsity played immediately after the varsity. At the end of the third quarter of the varsity game, all of us on the JV, wearing our good sweaters, good shoes, and only ties, would leave the gym to go change for our game. I loved leaving right when the varsity game was getting interesting; I loved everyone seeing us as a group, me belonging to that group, and everyone wishing us luck; I loved being part of the crowd and breaking away from the crowd to go play. And then when I was playing I knew the crowd was there but they slid into the distance like the overhead lights.

As a freshman I was the JV's designated shooter, our gunner whenever we faced a zone. Long-distance shooting was a way for me to perform the most immaculate feat in basketball, to stay outside where no one could hurt me. I'd hit four or five in a row, force the other team out of its zone, and then sit down. I wasn't a creator. I couldn't see a spot or wedge an opening, but I could shoot. Give me a step, some space, and a screen, then watch the ball tuck into twine.

Throughout my freshman and sophomore years the junior varsity coach told me I had to learn to take the ball to the basket and mix it up with the big guys underneath. I didn't want to because I knew I couldn't. I already feared I was a full step slow.

The next summer I played basketball. I don't mean I got in some games when I wasn't working at A&W or that I tried to play a couple hours every afternoon. I mean the summer of '72 I played basketball. Period. Nothing else. Nothing else even close to something else. All day long that summer, all summer, all night until ten.

The high school court was protected by a bank of spreading yew. Orange rims with chain nets were attached to half-moon boards that were kind only to real shooters. The court was on a grassy hill overlooking the street, and when I envision Eden I think of that court during the summer—shirts against skins, five-on-five, running the break till we keeled over.

Alone, I did drills outlined in an instructional book. A certain number of free throws and lay-ins from both sides and with each hand, hook shots, scoop shots, set shots from all over, turnaround jumpers, jumpers off the move and off the pass, tip-ins. Everything endlessly repeated. I wanted my shoulders to become as high-hung as Bob Pettit's, my wrists as taut, my glare as merciless. After awhile I'd feel like my head was the rim and my body was the ball. I was trying to put my head totally inside my body. The basketball was shot by itself. At that point I'd call it quits, keeping the feeling.

A fat, older guy named Doug Beacham started coming to the court every afternoon. He drove a red pickup, stroked his moustache, and told dirty jokes none of us were sure we completely understood. He would tell me, "Basketball isn't just shooting, DC. You've got to learn the rest of the game."

He could barely bend over to tie his shoes but he had the sweetest corner shot you'd ever want to see. I couldn't stay with him in Horse. In real games, though, he didn't do very well because he needed an hour and a half to launch his jumper.

He set up garbage cans around the court that I had to shuffle-step through, then backpedal through, then dribble through with my right hand, left hand, between my legs, behind my back. On the dead run I had to throw the ball off a banked gutter so it came back to me as a perfect pass for a layup. He was teaching me the rest of the game.

The varsity coach was wiry and quick, and most of us believed him when he mentioned his days as a floor leader at Purdue. He never said much. He showed a tight smile, but every now and then he'd grab you by the jersey and stand you up against a locker. Then he'd go back to smiling again.

The first few games of my junior year I started at wing for the varsity. In the first quarter I got the ball at the top of the circle, faked left, picked up a screen right, and penetrated the lane. My defender stayed with me, and when I went up for my shot we were belly-to-belly. To go forward was an offensive foul and backward was onto my butt. I tried to corkscrew around him but wasn't agile enough to change position in mid-air. The defender's hip caught mine and I turned 180 degrees, landing on my leg. While he apologized, the referee said I was probably permanently crippled and called an ambulance. My left thigh tickled my right ear. I shouted curses until I passed out from the pain.

I had a broken femur and spent the winter in traction in a hospital. My doctor misread the x-rays, removing the body cast too early, so I had an aluminum rod planted next to the bone, wore a leg brace, and swung crutches all year.

In the summer the brace came off and Beach tried to work with me to get back my wind and speed, but he gave up when it became obvious my heart wasn't in it. I wasn't fast enough or angry enough. Senior year I was ninth man on a ten-man team and kept a game journal, which evolved into a sports column for the school paper. I soon realized I was better at analyzing basketball than playing it. Like thinking of witty repartee six hours after the party's over, I could concoct the perfect move only after the whistle had blown the ball dead. I'd finally found my water level. There is nothing sadder in my experience than understanding this is as far as your talent can take you and no further.

I was pitiless on our mediocre team and the coach called me Ace, as in ace reporter, since I was certainly not his star ballhawk. I could shoot when left open but couldn't guard anyone quick or shake someone who hounded me tough. I fell into the role of the guy with all the answers and explanations, the well-informed benchwarmer who knew how zones were supposed to work but had nothing to contribute. I'd become a fan.

That summer I went to the county fair with Cindy Larsen, who had finally forgiven me for not rescuing her in Capture the Flag. She still didn't know anything about basketball but she did know she wanted a pink panda hanging by the scruff near the basketball toss.

The free throw line was eighteen rather than fifteen feet away and the ball must have been pumped to double its pressure, hard as a bike tire. Your shot had to be dead on or it would bounce way off. You weren't going to get any soft rolls out of this carnival. The rim was rickety, bent upward, and was probably closer to 10'6" than 10'. A canopy overhung both sides of the rim, so you weren't able to put any arc on your shot. With people elbowing me in back, I could hardly take a dribble to get in rhythm.

I won around twenty-five pandas. I got into a groove, and when you get into a groove from eighteen feet straightaway sometimes you can't come out of it. Standing among spilled paper cups and September heat and ice and screaming barkers and glass bottles and darts and bumper cars, we handed out panda bears to every kid who walked by.

Doing good deeds was high on Cindy's list, and passing out pandas was probably about as simple and good a deed as she'd seen in a long time. She ended up going to Carleton and becoming a labor lawyer in Minneapolis. I got a letter from her recently that said she works with a lot of terribly important local politicians, but I can't help wondering whether she looks at them with as much admiration as she looked at me the night we gave away stuffed animals.

I still like to roam new neighborhoods, tugging on twine, checking out the give. I like jumping up and down on concrete courts, feeling young again. In Cranston, Rhode Island, there's a metal ring that looks like hanging equipment for your worst enemy. In Amherst, Virginia, a huge washtub is nailed to a tree at the edge of a farm. Rims without nets, without backboards, without courts, with just gravel and grass underfoot. One basket in West Branch, Iowa, has a white net blowing in the breeze and an orange shooter's square on the half-moon board. Backboards are made from every possible material and tacked to anything that stands still in a storm. Rims are set at every height, at the most cockeyed angles, and draped with nets woven out of everything from wire to ladies' lingerie. Every type and shape of post, court, board, and hoop, and what I've finally realized is they're all the same thing, the same view over and over: from Port Jervis, New York, to Medford, Oregon, the same deep wells.

John Ameling

TONY TOMMASI

DUCK SPRING

TONY TOMMASI admits, "I'm a New York native transplanted by patience, will and affection to Quaker Iowa. Sometimes I write about a guy who drives an ambulance, sometimes about a distant injured daughter, and lately I've been reaching on paper for the experience of the rolling land." His stories, poems, and essays have appeared in a variety of national magazines.

"What does it mean to be a midwestern writer? When new neighbors greeted me shortly after I moved here, more than once I was asked why I'd come to Iowa from the City. I'd say, lamely, 'look around you.' I guess I don't really know the answer. Here, while writing a letter to a friend who knows about sunshine and darkness, I saw the spring ducks as a way to find out."

In a brief yet vivid personal description, Tommasi captures subject and content in an essay as telling and still as one of the photographs assembled here.

DUCK SPRING

From the large windows of the dining hall we looked out on the river's edge, past the neat green slope of lawn and the paved walk. Trees still young stood evenly spaced just beyond the morning shadow of the campus union building, their leaf buds a haze of dusty gold green. On the far side of the wind-shimmered water, the slope was beginning to bulge in soft new colors: pale white, burgundy, and several distinct shades of charttreuse.

Architectured outcrops of brick and concrete sprawled across the further bank and climbed the slope—broad level structures, windows glittering, or featureless slabs and pedestals—edges sharply visible among the lacework of leafless branches. Winter was clearly gone, as the ducks had been telling for weeks, their numbers and activity increasing rapidly.

We take breakfast occasionally, sitting by the windows among the few early stragglers before Sandy would go to open the office over in the hospital. Even on icy mornings (though we hadn't seen the river frozen over) when we could watch a few ducks huddled near the stone base of the footbridge, or walking sparely into and out of groups, we marveled at their ways of dealing with the hardships.

Sometimes we would think, seeing a solitary brown speckled bird hunkered down under a slatted bench, "Too bad you stayed on when the smart ones left for the Gulf"; or when one lost its footing as it lighted on a sheer, glazed surface, recovering its strained dignity with a shudder and a flutter, we might shake our heads and laugh, "Seems to be shrugging its lapels and adjusting its necktie." In their bad times, worst times, our vision of them never lost our sense of the comic.

And then shortly after the freeze began to crack, and the iridescent-emerald necked mallards began arriving in larger groups, we laughed aloud over one morning's omelet at the spectacle of seven or eight males in constant dizzy pursuit of a slender female. She skittered and shuttled left and right and ahead, the gang of suitors stumbling and knocking into each other like a comic platoon of draftees executing close order drill. From time to time with a peculiar inevitability, she would panic into a faulty sidestep and one or two would clamber awkwardly across her sideways, or topple headlong into a tumbling cluster. A lucky guy would claim a brief glorious mount, and after two or three triumphant flaps of his wings and a wide-beaked inaudible cry he would flop inelegantly off her back into the surrounding riot to stagger or lie momentarily dazed as the parade would shift quickly back up to speed while he shook himself, regained his composure and sauntered off casual and unremarkable.

As one male would drop aside, one or two newcomers would materialize—either wanderers from one or another group of sitters several yards away, or random gliders attracted from the sky by the flurry of wheeling, weaving and clattering repeatedly over the same dozen square yards of lawn. The newcomers (it was our impression) seemed willing to tag along at the edge of the company for several turns before working their way up to striking range, as if catching on to the rhythm of the reel.

And she—the focus, the belle—she had her own hilarious presence, never taking the air as we watched, perhaps because that avenue had failed earlier, or because she could get hurt far worse that way. She seemed to us to have three earthbound moods: harried desperation, stolid resigntion and powerless indignation. From time to time, though quite rarely, we saw her suddenly stop and wheel to face her nearest pursuer, squawk expressively and seem almost to stamp her webbed foot. The whole group would halt for a kind of stunned heartbeat, and just as suddenly the rush would be on again, her neck outstretched, eyes wide, the corners of her mouth stretched back tight, wings spread slightly for balance, her body's darting waddle straining into a twisting, rolling, jerking torrential rhythm, a nightmarish flight with no hope of escape or rescue.

When she was caught and pinned, mounted and surrounded, she lay more or less flat on her belly, offering no apparent resistance, even when one of the claimants climbed backwards onto her head while another clasped her successfully for his one or two seconds (no more, ever) of mind-shattering joy. Some of the others milling about would for the brief moment appear to be merely passersby, nodding to one another or gazing off into the distance—toward the river's ripple perhaps, or the sky, or one of the other groups settled mute and unconcerned along the edges of the farce's ragged stage.

And just as abruptly the dance of rolling thunder, of racing, shrieking stumble would explode again. Eventually the company spun beyond the nearby space, off around a corner of the building, and was gone from sight. (We were left with such meanings as we wished, as always.)

Perhaps a week later, we set our trays down at one of our usual small tables by the broad window and watched, as we took our first bites of breakfast, a number of birds—perhaps two dozen or so—feeding industriously if disorderly on the new green shoots of the lawn, nibbling and tugging lightly, moving easily around the broad expanse that had been the earlier scene of hilarity and gender politics.

Without warning and as startling to the ducks' consciousness as to ours, a large ivory tan dog crashed into and through the center of the largest clump of birds, scattering them, knocking some down and aside. Instantly, a flurry leaped aloft—not far but beyond the dog's reach—and were quickly beyond the range of surprise. The dog looked like a mix of labrador and golden or other kind of retriever, thick bodied with a massive head. He had lunged into the crowd snapping and, overshooting his target, he braked, skidding on the dewy grass and twisting back toward his victim.

The attack was too sudden to be seen clearly, but amid the tumble and rush and mad flapping we saw one bright green whirl and flutter, a shape trying to right itself, to resolve itself, to regain its feet, to push off into the sky, to leave the pondering for later, for others—like us, the watchers. One wing was arched upward, the other appearing to have crumpled under his body, which was tossed in a half roll upon itself. Probably the dog's sidelong snap had broken a bone. The wing stretched up and out but the dog was there and the green neck and head were within his jaws and the killing was done.

It took as long as it took for several window sitters to cry out "Oh!" or to sharply take in a breath, and the gasp was followed immediately by a young male voice drawling "Great catch!"

Then there was silence. A few flat metallic sounds of utensils laid back on tables and trays. The dog dropped the mallard at his feet and looked about, sniffing the air and the ground and glancing at the ring of ducks. They were respectuflly beyond him but standing and setting in apparent neutrality in their safety. He stooped to gather the dead bird in a better grip in his jaws and loped briskly away in the direction he had come, as those ducks in that quadrant courteously gave him the way without fuss or frenzy. I had not taken my eyes for long from the scene, though when the dog was gone I gazed blankly, wordless, at the place he was last.

When I looked back at the survivors, they were not agitated or even particularly inactive, as though nothing had happened. No sign, no marking. And on our side of the window, low voices, some undeniable glares in the direction of the young man whose voice had made recognizable words, but no attempt to establish fellowship among the witnesses. Perhaps even a kind of embarrssment in the aftershock and some difficulty getting back to the meal before us all.

Jim Galbraith (HARTLAND)

SUSAN ALLEN TOTH

SWIMMING POOLS

Born in a small town, middle class family in Ames, Iowa, in 1940, Susan Allen Toth has celebrated the joys and pains, the ambiance and ambivalence of that life in her three autobiographical books—*Blooming, A Small-town Girlhood* (1981), *Ivy Days: Making My Way Out East* (1984), and *How to Prepare for Your High School Reunion: And Other Midlife Musings* (1988). In a memoir style that is as entertaining as it is reflective, she speaks candidly yet warmly of a broad, middle range of American experience. Maxine Kumin has described *Blooming* (from which our selection is taken) as "an important book on coming of age in the breadbasket of America, it is also a delicious, witty, insightful autobiography."

In a finely textured style, Toth presents a frank and vivid sense of personal experience as both her subject and theme. "With a journalist's ear and a novelist's touch" (NYT Book Review) she captures and conveys the sense of what it was like to grow up in the heart of the Midwest. Toth admits, "My memories of growing up in Ames are as true as I could make them. . . I have always wanted to write this book. . ."

SWIMMING POOLS

We were talking, my friend and I, about our children. Almost every day for nine years we have called each other to exchange anecdotes, complain, congratulate, and reassure ourselves that we aren't such bad mothers after all. That day I was complaining. I was suddenly bone-tired of worrying, fussing, arranging. I gritted my teeth as I told my friend how I suddenly, desperately, didn't want to listen to piano lessons, fix dinner, scrape dishes, run a bath, comb tangly hair, fix the wobbly night-light. I went on and on, cataloguing weariness, winding down in a disheartened gasp.

"I know, I know," said my friend soothingly, as she always does. "But think of how much easier it is now than it was three years ago. Remember when they were two? Or when they were just crawling?" We were both silent for a moment, evoking those breathless days. "I was just thinking today," my friend went on, "as I saw Katy riding down the block on her bicycle, that this spring she is finally launched. She can ride a bike, and she can swim all the way across the pool. Now I think she can make it on her own. As soon as the baby gets a little older..." Her voice trailed off too, and we began to talk of other things.

After we hung up, I pondered what my friend had said. Is that what it means to be launched into life, to be able to ride a bike and to swim? The bike I understood quickly, because I remember myself on my first blue fat-wheeled Schwinn, weaving crazily down the sidewalks at first, then soon riding in gangs down the empty streets, riding to school and to stores and to the park. But swimming? Why should a girl know how to swim? Even here in Minnesota, land of ten thousand lakes, we may not get to one of them in a whole summer. None of our friends owns a boat. Jennifer's social life would hardly be damaged if she stayed out of the water. Yet, like my friend, I hurried to sign up Jennie for Water Babies when she was an infant. I shivered through endless hours in the YWCA pool as she clung and tugged fearfully at my swimsuit. I was overwhelmed with pride when I saw her finally leave my arms and swim all by herself two feet to the side of the pool. What had she mastered? The ability to save her own life? I would not always be near her; if she were fishing, on a yacht, in a sailboat, could she now swim to shore? Was I happy because I had given her the self-sufficiency to survive one of the myriad dangers she will face in the years ahead?

Or was I pleased to see her swim because I now felt she had begun to master her own body? Because she could make her muscles move in a coordinated way, force them to do what she wanted? Was she learning to enjoy the way her body moved? Did I see in her early flappings and splashings some promise of grace? Was I foreseeing her physical pleasure in being a woman?

I didn't know then, and I still don't know. Since that conversation with my friend, I have wondered about the ways in which I myself was launched many years ago. My friend is intuitively right: though born and raised inland, I connect many of my most vivid memories about growing up with water. When I dip into the past, I often come up gasping in a swimming pool.

I always ask for a window seat so I can see the swimming pools. As we descend over the suburbs, I stare like a child with nose pressed to glass at the brilliant blue eyes that stare back at me from the ground. They blink in the sun with affluent pride. What would it be like, I wonder, to live in a neighborhood where every yard had its pool? When I was growing up, our town had ten thousand people and only three swimming pools for us all, so that on hot days we were packed like Vienna sausages into the water. The pools I see below me look empty and lonely, unable to convey the intense excitement and fear I remember. My own swimming pools were three enchanted places, each casting a different spell, and we girls growing up in Ames passed through certain rites there.

All this was besides the swimming lessons. Girls didn't have many other lessons to worry them. Nobody owned horses, except a few farmers, and we didn't mix much with their kids anyway. A few girls took dancing from a dark-haired lady downtown, and once a year they gave a recital in the high-school gym. Draped in flags or dressed like soldiers, they tap-danced vigorously as their teacher played the piano. A few star pupils, all much older than we, were ballerinas who spun through a spotlight carefully wielded by the teacher's son. Their layers of net, painstakingly sewed together like giant nylon pot-scrubbers, whirled as they danced so you could see lots of pink, perspiring legs. It somehow seemed not quite socially acceptable. But instinctively we agreed that we ought to learn how to swim, and so every spring we signed up for Saturday morning lessons at the college pool.

Why we were so determined to swim would have mystified any outsider. The nearest lake of any size was a two-hour drive, far away in the corner of the state, and few of us knew anyone with a cabin there. We simply wanted to hold up our heads at Blaine's Pool, the town's only public swimming place, and to do that we had to know how.

Entering the college gym was like edging into a strange and vaguely threatening world. Partly, of course, we were in awe of any place that belonged to college students, those noisy, reckless grown-ups whose fraternity parties and pep rallies often lit up the lives of those of us who lived near the campus. As we entered the dark brick building, and descended the cold tiled staircase, a smell of old sweat, dampness, chlorine and mildewing towels seemed to creep up the stairs and beckon down the halls where we were not allowed to go. Here in some hidden labyrinth the Iowa State athletes "worked out." From one of these doors, opening off a hall we couldn't see, they emerged to the open field next door into a chorus of cheers. Walking outside the stadium walls on Saturday afternoon, I could often hear the cheering rise and fall like a giant inarticulate voice."OOOOOH," the voice cried, "AAAAAH." Then it would be silent, as though the giant had fallen back into his cave. These shouts of incomprehensible pleasure or disappointment seemed to hover in the air as I now found my way to an empty locker and started to slip into my swimming suit.

Even changing into a swimsuit was part of the physical education of swimming lessons. I wasn't all that shy; after all, I had a sister. But still it was unsettling to get undressed in a line of other freckled, tanned or pale bodies that looked so critically different from mine. Even though my best friend was famous for her golden hair, I was still surprised to see that the little fur of hair between her legs was blonde too, not brown like mine. I had thought everybody's was probably brown.

As I unfastened my cotton-knit band that masqueraded as a bra, I looked surrepitiously around at the other girls. Some of them had actual breasts. I looked away again quickly. I only wore my "bra" because recently one of the cruder boys in our seventh grade had told me he could see my titties through my sweater. I wasn't sure what he meant, until he pointed. Then I held back tears, and embarrassment, until I could get back home for lunch and demand that my mother take me out right away, that noon, to Younkers to buy a bra. I wondered why she hadn't seen that I needed one. As I pulled my swimsuit up to fasten it, I looked down at myself and felt once again that somehow all the bumps fell in the wrong places.

All this examination of bodies, furtive as it was, made me feel as though there were something faintly medical about the college pool.

We had to splash through a footbath of gray, smelly disinfectant before we trooped down the inner stairs to the pool. This footbath, we were informed, was to guard against all kinds of fungi, like athlete's foot; I wasn't sure what that was but knew that it must be very personal, infectious, and unpleasant. I associated it in my mind with rumors I had heard about something called syphilis. Even today, when someone mentions v.d., I sometimes think of footbaths.

Once we were assembled, shivering, along the pool edges, sniffing the chlorine and watching the black marking bands on the pool floor waver through the gently moving currents, I was in a daze. Stripped of my dignity, cowed, I held my knees tightly and listened to Big Mike O'Donnell tell us what we would do today. Big Mike was the college swimming coach. We all thought he was very handsome and a fitting imperial figure to strut up and down the pool sides, surveying us struggling swimmers. He had a muscular, hairy chest, usually covered by a sort of terry shirt left unbuttoned, and he wore trim black racing trunks that contrasted with our variously flowered swimcaps, bright cotton suits, little skirts and ruffles. He was obviously efficient, powerful and knowing, a man to be feared as well as admired. As I slipped with a gasp into the cold water, I would look up with eyes blurred by chlorine and see Big Mike sternly patrolling above me, poking a long pole into the water. If you misbehaved, he would rap you on the head. But if you were in trouble, or seemed about to drown, he would extend the pole to you so you could grab it and get pulled out.

I suppose there were women's swimming teams somewhere in those days, but I could never imagine them practicing in the college pool. Big Mike was the men's coach, and I always thought of his precincts as a man's pool. Later in the day boys we knew would come to take their swimming lessons. We knew, because one of them had told one of us, that they swam naked. Without any suits at all. I never thought much about male bodies: I had no brothers, I had not yet been exposed to art, and I simply could not picture all those boys in the pool. I would shudder a bit and feel very cold. I was glad I wore a suit.

Sometimes after lessons we could stay and watch the advanced class, older high-school girls who practiced diving and fancy strokes. Once I was very late in getting dressed, and on an impulse I climbed up the back upper stairs to the tiny gallery overlooking the pool. There I could see six girls, dressed in identical one-piece striped suits, all with dolphin insignia, performing a sort of water ballet. They were Big Mike's synchronized swimmers, special protegees, and he even occasionally smiled at them as they dipped and dove, turned and flipped, kicked in unison like submerged cancan dancers. I stared, entranced, until Big Mike glanced up and saw me. He frowned, waved his hand, called something, and I backed away. But I carried home with me the vision of those lovely, beautiful bodies, all grace and precision, moving in the water as though they were sleek fish.

When summer finally came and I was ready to go with my friends down to Blaine's Pool, how I longed to be able to swim like a fish. My lessons always seemed to leave me half-finished, almost passing advanced beginners, or just a few backstroke lengths short of moving on from intermediate. It wasn't so much that I wanted to swim like Big Mike's special girls, I just wanted to look like them in the water. As I tried on swimsuits at Younkers, sucking in my stomach, I looked in the mirror and saw nothing there but plump discouragement in a bright shirred Hawaiian print. All the elastic in the world wouldn't transform me into a dolphin.

But I bought the suit, hoped I would magically turn sleeker, and agreed to make the first trip to Blaine's. School was out, and a few weeks might have passed between the last classes and the first really hot day. None of us girls had seen any of the boys, except during chance encounters at the ice-cream store, or downtown, or perhaps at a Sunday matinee. Many of them had summer jobs, earning real money, and they were glad to emerge on the weekends to show off their new muscles and their purchasing power. They all knew that Blaine's was the place to do it.

Even the setting of Blaine's Pool made it a place apart. Outside the city limits, it was dug out of the ground in a small hollow surrounded by a scraggly woods and a dirty, meandering river. Blaine's had a remote air about it, a kind of isolation. As one of our mothers drove, very carefully, down a steep hill that curved sharply, we heard the noise of splashing and confused shouts, screams, and the lifeguard's whistle before we could see the pool itself. We bounced up and down on the back seat, giggling and chattering in high-pitched voices, until the mother, made nervous by the hot rods that zoomed past her up the hill, snapped crossly. We subsided and clutched our rolled-up bath towels in anticipation.

As we pulled into the parking lot, where the mother would pick us up a few hours later, we all strained to see what faces we could make out at the poolside, in the bleachers, or at the pop stand. Much of our anticipation depended on just this uncertainty. Who was here? Would Bob O'Brien and Lon Sell have already come? Or gone?

Were we too late? Or too early? Was that Tommy Sandvig on the diving board? The mother was probably glad to escape from our gasps, pointings and smothered cries. No matter whose mother she was, though, she never commented on this aspect of the swimming pool ritual. By eleven or twelve, we were all expected to have boyfriends, or at least to want to have them. Blaine's Pool was a proper place to find them.

I sometimes think I learned about sex at Blaine's Pool. Oh, not the hard facts (it was years before I knew what they really were, and there are still some days when I don't feel too sure). So what jagged bits of knowledge did I take home from Blaine's, along with a bent locker key and someone's used Tangee orange lipstick, rescued from the dressing-room floor? Mostly stinging bits of intense physical sensation. Looking back to those green, dreaming summers, I always think of blistering heat and ice-cold water. Some afternoons, when I couldn't go to Blaine's, I sat in my shorts and halter in our steaming living room, damply reading, feeling the old wool upholstery of the comfy Morris chair rub against my thighs, while I sucked and chewed on ice cubes and balanced the glass, painfully cold, on my knee for as long as I could stand it. That was the kind of intensity I felt at Blaine's. Emerging from the shaded dressing room, I always blinked, temporarily blinded, in the dazzling light that reflected from the white bleachers, shining metal slides, and of course the glittering blue water. It was as though all the colors had been turned up just a bit too bright.

As the sun beat down on my head, shoulders and thighs, I had to decide how to get into the water. It was inviting, but very cold. So my friends and I edged gingerly into the shallow end, stepping daintily down the little children's steps, and then began rubbing our tummies cautiously with the cold water. We seldom got the chance to edge much farther, because by that time one of the boys saw us. Whooping and splashing, he leaped into the water, scooping up water with the palm of his hand in a practiced, skidding gesture, covering our exaggerated screams with shock waves. By the time the lifeguard blew his whistle and shook a finger at us, we were wet, initiated, ready to paddle down to the deep end and continue the Blaine's ritual. Some afternoons I was braver. Standing for only a few moments on the pool's edge, before anyone could push me in, I looked down and anticipated with a delicious shudder how the water would feel, closing over me in a total embrace. Then I jumped. For one brief moment as I went under I wondered if I would ever come up again. Then I surfaced, blowing, laughing, and waited for the others to join me.

Then, of course, we swam. We girls never did laps, and we seldom even swam in a straight line. Instead we darted back and forth, moving to parts of the pool where someone we hoped would notice us had last dived in. As we hung, treading water, chatting together in brief gasps, Tommy or Bob or Lon glided under water toward us, often in twos or threes, as though they needed support. We girls pretended not to notice them coming until they spouted to the top, with loud shouts, and pounced on us to dunk us. The lifeguards were supposed to stop any horseplay (a sign by the pool read: "No running. No bottles by the pool. NO HORSEPLAY."). But they usually looked the other way at such simple stuff as dunking. Being shoved under water was recognized as a sign that a boy had noticed you. He had at least taken the trouble to push you down. We certainly never complained, though I sometimes swallowed water and came up coughing. At other times the boys would ignore us and engage in their own elaborate games, diving for pennies or playing tag. We girls clung to the side, hanging on to the gutters, and watched.

When I grew older, I heard for the first time about something called battle of the sexes. It brought to mind an image that would doubtless seem ludicrously inappropriate to Millett or Mailer, but that's because neither one of them ever held on for dear life to the giant tops at Blaine's Pool.

Once there must have been two tops; one rusting anchor was still fastened to the bottom, a melancholy reminder of summers long gone. But by the time I was there, only one top was left intact, and we all wrestled and struggled to be among the few its surface could hold. The top was maybe six feet in diameter, with a steering wheel at the center that you turned to make the top revolve as you stood on its slanting, slippery surface. It spun on a slightly askew axis, so that as you turned the wheel faster, and the top whirled faster, it was harder and harder to hang on. The boys always had control of the steering wheel; at least, they felt they had a right to it, so that if we girls climbed on board when the top was empty, they soon spied us from wherever they were in the pool and came splashing noisily over to assume charge. Those of us girls who were sturdy, not easily scared off, or perhaps a bit foolhardy, stayed on the top. As the boys turned the wheel, we clung to whatever part of its metal rim we could grab. Faster and faster it spun, and before long, girls would begin to fall off, like bits of spray dashed away from a fierce centrifugal force. Even a boy or two might lose hold, pretending, if possible, that he had just decided to dive from the edge, or that he wanted to jump on one of the girls who had just fallen off, cannonballing on top of her.

Whoever stayed on top longest won. When competition got down to the last two swimmers, anything was acceptable, from prying someone's fingers off the wheel to tripping and pushing. The boys had fewer inhibitions about those tactics, and consequently one of them always won. I wish I could say I was often one of the last girls to leave the top, but I wasn't. I got dizzy quickly, and, stomach churning, ended up gulping mouthfuls of chlorine as I tumbled ignominiously into the water.

Climbing out, waterlogged, I felt heavy and washed out, so tired I forgot to hold in my stomach as I walked away. Stretching out on a wooden bleacher, I closed my eyes and listened to the shouting and splashing, which seemed dimmer and far away, even though the pool was just a few feet off. With dulled vision, I occasionally squinted at the swimmers hurrying along the pool deck to see who was still in action. But I was warm, drying, and strangely invisible. I can still feel how comforting the sun seemed then, how blissfully tired and somehow virtuous I felt, worn out by all my social exertions. As I shifted position, very carefully, I could feel the rough grain of the wood. The paint was worn off in many spots, and once when I moved too fast, I got a splinter in my hand. There I lay in the sun and baked, letting time pass over me.

When I finally got up, I could look down and see damp cool stains on the wood where I had been. Tired, but still anxious to extract the last bit of possible pleasure from the afternoon, I jumped in quickly. Soon we had to trudge to the dressing room; it was almost time for the mother to return.

Not everything connected with Blaine's Pool is illuminated in my memory with the blinding glare of sun and water. Though it was by day filled with open games, battles on the top, flirtations in the water, Blaine's Pool was reputed to be quite another sort of place at night. Its hidden location, surrounded by trees, naturally made it a favorite spot for "parking," or so the stories went. None of us girls had ever parked anywhere yet, so we didn't know. But sometimes, floating on my back in a quiet moment, I would look up at the overhanging trees and wonder. Occasionally a lifeguard left his post for a few minutes and walked over to the rattly stands placed just outside the pool enclosure for observers. Once I saw the guard talking to a pretty girl with red lipstick who stood, casually brushing back her hair, on the lowest step. After a bit he returned to his chair, and she left. I thought they were probably arranging to meet later that night, somewhere in the trees.

This suggestive air of illicit sex that hung over the pool, or so I thought, crystallized for me one late afternoon when we were still halfheartedly messing about in the almost empty pool. Most of the boys had gone home. Among the stragglers were an older girl with long black hair and lots of curves that owed nothing to elastic, and her boyfriend, who we knew was a football player on the high-school team. They were swimming lazily in the deep end, diving under water, tagging and laughing. As I bounced on the bottom of the shallow end, wondering if I could rub out the seat of the new swimsuit I now hated, Peggy O'Reilly came striding through the water toward me as fast as she could. "Susan!" she said breathlessly. "Guess what! I just saw Cindy and Steve! Do you know what they were doing?" No, I said, I didn't know. "Well," she announced with a sense of real importance, "they were *kissing under water.*" We were both silent. With one instinct, we turned to look at the deep end. Holding hands, Cindy and Steve were climbing out of the water. They walked toward the dressing rooms, and we watched them until they passed out of sight.

Soon we too left the pool. Dressing hurriedly in a tiny cubicle, I kept a close watch on the floor. A few of the booths had gaps in the floorboards, and a few weeks earlier they had caught some boys underneath the girls' dressing room, peering up. If you dressed in the open, walled section, where the sun could dry your hair, you had to look above the wall toward the trees. Sometimes a few boys shinnied up the trunks in order to be able to get a good view. It is only now as I remember these small terrors, our automatic precautions, that I realize with surprise we never dreamed of invading the boys' dressing room in return.

After we were all ready, we turned in our locker baskets and rolled our damp suits in our towels. Then we loitered around the pop stand, hung on the fence, or made patterns in the dust with our sneakers, talking about everyone we'd seen that day and what he had done and what we had said in return. The mother was later than she'd promised. I walked around the pool enclosure to the bleachers near the trees. The ground was littered with torn popcorn boxes, green Coke bottles, and candy wrappings. The grass there and under the trees was sparse and brown. It was hard to imagine anyone wanting to linger there, even at night. When I finally heard a horn honk, impatiently, I was glad to hurry over to the parking lot and squeeze comfortably into the back seat with my friends.

A few years after I began going regularly to Blaine's Pool, my mother joined the Country Club for one season. I may have learned something about sex at Blaine's, but I learned about social nuance at the Country Club. I'm still not sure how Mother got us in, though I think it must have been a sympathy vote. She was a widow, we were almost poor - the way an English instructor at a state college was poor in those days, three thousand a year in dollars and in freshman themes - and as a family, we had a noticeably deserving character. As I remember, they gave Mother a "single" rate, and for that both my sister and I were able to use the club's pool. I think I also remember that mother had to promise them that none of us played golf, so we wouldn't take advantage of our bargain by crowding the greens. We were, however, all allowed to swim.

Compared to Blaine's, the Country Club pool was small. One diving board, no spinning top. But its size only seemed to me to be a measure of its exclusiveness. Whoever had laid out plans for the Country Club was a entrepreneur with an eye for the one beautiful, rolling and wooded piece of land outside Ames. He must have known immediately that such an acreage had to be saved; he had a true aristocrat's instinct and converted it into a private preserve. Instead of the scraggly woods around Blaine's, the club had a real forest, shady oaks and maples that had escaped wholesale conversion into farmland. These trees clustered around a clear, grassy-edged creek, where white golf balls shone unexpectedly in the water. Dipping and swooping toward the creek, the hills were high enough so that at the bottom you couldn't even see the clubhouse. They were the only real hills for miles, and in the winter we children sneaked onto the golf course for forbidden toboggan parties. Those were the only times I ever saw the Country Club until the summer we joined.

Now that I have seen other private clubs, much larger and glossier, I realize that the Ames Country Club wasn't much: a nine-hole golf course, a ranch-style clubhouse built like a log cabin, a small pool, two picnic tables, and an outdoor water fountain. But its size merely insisted on its intimacy, that of a self-confident and rather comfortable small family. That whole summer I never really felt we belonged there. Mother, who was always anxious to please my sister and me, must have decided to join for our sake. But she didn't realize that we couldn't see any of our friends there. They were all down at Blaine's.

Instead we saw mothers. Nobody's mother ever went to Blaine's except maybe at empty hours, like Sunday morning or very late afternoon. But every day at the Country Club, two or three women would pull up in their Oldsmobiles and stroll down to the pool together. They wore bright scarves around tightly curled hair and very dark sunglasses. Propped discreetly on the grass next to the pool, they sunned and tanned. Many of them lived in the only part of town that had a signpost, a fancy development called Colonial Village, with expensive New England saltboxes on curving streets. They were mothers who didn't have to work, though they belonged to organizations, with mysterious names and initials, P.E.O., A.A.U.W., O.R.T., and Jayceettes. All afternoon these mothers basked and browned, watching the pool through dark glasses, staying carefully just out of range of splashes. At the end of the day their husbands puffed over the hill, pulling golf carts, wiping sweat from red faces. The women rose, slipped their baked feet into sandals, and went home.

Sometimes if my sister and I stayed late enough, close to suppertime, we could see the same mothers and fathers return to the club for a dinner-dance. Now the women had on gaily printed dresses with full skirts and bared shoulders, and the men's red faces looked even more burned above white shirts. Earrings sparkled, and polished black shoes gleamed in the dusk. We wheeled our bicycles away very slowly so we could see and hear as much of the party as possible before leaving. The pool closed early on those nights. Someone said it would be open later so the adults could swim in the dark under floodlights. From the bar, a musty pine-paneled room just inside the clubhouse, where we never could go, we could hear laughter, glasses clinking, loud voices, and music. Years later, when I read *The Great Gatsby* for the first time, I realized that I had always imagined parties like Gatsby's taking place at the Country Club: drinking, dancing, flashing color, romance.

The tinge of glamour that still invests the Country Club in my memory was probably also due to the presence there of some of the Central boys. Ames had two junior high schools, Welch for the college half of town, Central for the downtown half. Until they merged into one high school, the two sides never had much chance to meet each other, except perhaps at church youth groups, or the annual rival games. We Welch kids had always heard that the Central kids were "fast," familiar not only with parking but also with drinking beer. We learned to recognize a few Central boys from their appearance on the basketball or football teams; they seemed taller, older, and much more attractive than the boys we knew at Welch. Jay Gordon, for instance, always wore pale pastel shirts, pink or yellow or green, while the Welch boys invariably dressed in red checks from Penney's.

Jay's parents belonged to the Country Club, and so did Jack Bolton's. Jack was tall, already six feet, with an appealing shamble, and my heart leaped when he dribbled down the court in the midwinter Welch-Central game. Now in the summer he played golf with his father, and once in a while, with a shy smile, he would appear at the pool for a quick swim. A few girls from Central of course belonged too, and if they were together, Jay or Jack would stop to talk and joke with them. Sometimes they all teased and pushed their way to the water together, jumping in with loud splashes and laughter, just as we all did in a larger, noisier gang at Blaine's. Only here at the Country Club I wasn't one of them; I sat on my beach towel alone and felt awkward. In fact, I didn't enjoy swimming very much on the days when both the Central boys and girls were at the club. I was left out, a very diferent feeling from just being alone. One of the Central girls belonged to my church youth group, and sometimes she said hello, casually, as she passed by. That greeting was worse than anonymity, because it meant that she, and the others, knew I was there. I was acutely conscious that my little potbelly, easily lost in the crowd at Blaine's, seemed to stick out, downright protuberantly, at the Country Club.

If I became too depressed, I jumped up from my towel and headed toward a deserted part of the pool. Swimming under water, I pretended I was invisible. Or I did a vigorous sidestroke, as though I were practicing laps. Just being in motion made me feel better, and the cool water closing over my head calmed my feelings so I could emerge with some dignity, towel myself off, and go home. After a while, I simply stopped going to the Country Club. My sister found other things to do too. The next summer Mother didn't renew our membership.

Whatever impressions I soaked in with the chlorine or sun at those three swimming pools of my childhood must have stained me somewhere ineradicably. For ever since then, at bad times I have headed, like a lemming, to the water. When in pain, I can be found in a pool. Perhaps the noise of yelling children reminds me of happy afternoons at Blaine's, or perhaps I am obscurely pleased that I no longer need to be part of that boisterous group and that I can just swim, by myself, with my own thoughts. I don't know. Last summer, when a man I had much loved and I suddenly parted, I fled the house every afternoon at five for the new municipal pool in the city where I now live. This pool is much bigger than Blaine's; quite an impressive place, and at that hour the guards cordon off lengths for laps. I felt the tightness in my chest and stomach begin to ease the minute I stepped out of my car and saw that huge pool, almost empty, waiting for me. A few swimmers, whom I didn't know, already churned up and down the black lines: company, without the responsibility of conversation. They might comment on the weather, or the temperature of the water, but they wouldn't know or care about what I was feeling. As I undressed in the shower room, I could pat my snug, now familiar body, to reassure myself that it was still there, and I knew that swimming helped, as Big Mike always said, to "keep in shape."

Once in the pool, doing my laps, I felt a kind of anesthetic set in. Cold water slithered over me, a numb caress, promising relief. It seemed to wash off some of the unhappiness that clung to me all over like mosquito repellent. Even the chlorine helped: as I mechanically stroked, back and forth, I hoped it would disinfect my brain. Clinging to the pool edge between laps, breathing hard, I could look up at the empty sky and see blue peace mirroring back to the pool. Everything seemed far away, except the water, the cold tile I grasped, the blue of sky and water. No one knew who I was, and I didn't have the same feeling I used to have after an afternoon at Blaine's: exhausted, satisfied, with the hope of perhaps yet another hot afternoon before the summer ended. I was glad to be tired. I could tell I was still alive. Tomorrow I could go back to the swimming pool.

THE PHOTOGRAPHERS

CAROLYN BERRY is a midwestern photographer now living in Monterrey, California. She produces art books. She and her sister are the subject of the photo "Dress-Up," which her mother took in the 1940's.

CHARLES CORBEIL, SR. works at New Departure Corporation of General Motors in Sandusky, Ohio, and has made photography a very creative hobby.

ROBERT FOX (One of our authors) provides the photo of his farm in Pomeroy, Ohio, for his "Dog Holler" essay.

JIM GALBRAITH is a veteran photographer who with his wife Susan has put together an excellent book of photos and oral history entitled HARTLAND, CHANGE IN THE HEART OF AMERICA (Box 286 Hartland, Michigan 48029). He has allowed us to reproduce some of those photos here.

DENNIS HORAN lives in Huron, Ohio, where he works as an Instructional Media Specialist at Firelands College. He is also a photographer and carpenter.

JULIE KOBA and TOM KOBA are married to each other and direct T.R. Koba Associates Advertising; they both studied photography and film at Ohio University. Tom is the co-director/co-producer with Larry Smith of two literary docudrama video programs, JAMES WRIGHT'S OHIO and KENNETH PATCHEN: AN ART OF ENGAGEMENT.

EDITH LEHMAN lives in Oxford, Ohio. She didn't begin photography untill after she retired, and now has won several exhibitions.

ROBERT PFINGSTON is a poet, fiction writer, and photographer who teaches in Bloomington, Indiana. He has won numerous fellowships and his work has received many awards.

JOEL RUDINGER is a poet, folklorist, and photographer who teaches at Firelands College in Ohio.

BILL SCHNELL is a photographer from Willard, Ohio, who specializes in landscapes and portraits.

GARY AINLEY

JOHN AMELING

ACKNOWLEDGEMENTS

Bottom Dog Press, Inc. would like to acknowledge the following sources and express thanks for permission to reprint certain of the writings. All rights are protected by the authors and publishers.

Jim Barnes: "The Blacksmith Shop" from *Margins* Magazine, England.
Wendell Berry: "Higher Education and Home Defense" from *Home Economics,* Copyrighted © 1987 by Wendell Berry. Published by North Point Press.
Martha Bergland: "Salt Creek, Truly Toothacher, and Stringtown Lane" from *The New England Review & Breadloaf Quarterly.*
Conger Beasley, Jr.: "Blood for the Sun" from *Outlook* Magazine.
John Calderazzo: "Euology in a Churchyard," from *Ohio* Magazine.
Christian Davis: "How to Build a House," from *Country Journal* Magazine.
Michael Delp, "River Gods" and "The Legacy of Worms" from *The Michigan Sports Gazette,* "Steelhead Dreams" from *The Flyfisher.*
Annie Dillard, pp. 3-4, 6-12, 247-250 from *An American Childhood.* Copyright © Annie Dillard. Reprinted with permission from Harper & Row, Publishers, Inc.
Robert Fox: "Dog Holler" from the Columbus *Dispatch.*
Craig Hergert: "But Baby It's Cold Outside: Memories of Minnesotan Winters" from *Miscellany* Magazine.
Mark Masse: "The Chair-side History of a Master Craftsman" from Akron *Beacon Journal.*
Robert Richter: "Land Lessons" from *Western Outlook* Magazine.
Michael Rosen: "Under the Sign of Wonder Bread and Belmont Caskets" from *A Place of Sense,* ed. Michael Martone, University of Iowa Press, 1988.
Scott Russell Sanders. "Stone Towns and the Country Between" from *Stone Country.* Copyright © Indiana University Press, 1985.
David Shields: "Wells" is a biographical re-adaptation of a chapter from his novel *Heroes,* Simon & Shuster, 1984.
Susan Allen Toth: "Swimming Pools" from *Blooming: A Small-Town Girlhood,* Little, Brown and Company. Copyright © by Susan Allen Toth.